W9-BRI-230

Praise for W. Soliman and The Hunter Files

"A terrific mystery… I can't wait for the next Charlie Hunter novel!"
—Shirley Wells, author of the Dylan Scott Mystery series

"W. Soliman has created a tough, likeable hero with a charming and believable heroine.... I very much enjoyed this novel and I recommend it highly."
—*Writers Who Kill* on *Lethal Business*

"A solid novel with a compelling and suspenseful storyline, *Risky Business* is a must read for anyone who enjoys contemporary English mysteries."
—*Book Reviews & More by Kathy*

"Beautifully written, it is an attention-grabber, a relentless challenge to the mind and imagination and a deeply satisfying reading experience for those who love this genre."
—Judith, *Goodreads* reviewer, on *Risky Business*

"From the moment I started reading this series I was hooked!… Charlie Hunter is, all in all, a fascinating man."
—*BookBinge.com* on *Lethal Business*

Also available from W. Soliman and Carina Press

The Hunter Files

Unfinished Business
Risky Business
Lethal Business

Writing as Wendy Soliman

Of Dukes and Deceptions
A Scandalous Proposition
The Perfect Impostor

The Forsters

Compromising the Marquess
Beguiling the Barrister
Finessing the Contessa
Romancing the Runaway

LETHAL BUSINESS

W. SOLIMAN

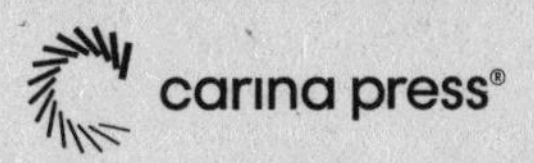

If you purchased this book without a cover you should be aware that this book is stolen property. It was reported as "unsold and destroyed" to the publisher, and neither the author nor the publisher has received any payment for this "stripped book."

PLEASE RECYCLE • THIS PRODUCT IS RECYCLABLE

Recycling programs for this product may not exist in your area.

ISBN-13: 978-0-373-00279-5

Lethal Business

Copyright © 2013 by Wendy Soliman

All rights reserved. Except for use in any review, the reproduction or utilization of this work in whole or in part in any form by any electronic, mechanical or other means, now known or hereinafter invented, including xerography, photocopying and recording, or in any information storage or retrieval system, is forbidden without the written permission of the publisher, Harlequin Enterprises Limited, 225 Duncan Mill Road, Don Mills, Ontario M3B 3K9, Canada.

This is a work of fiction. Names, characters, places and incidents are either the product of the author's imagination or are used fictitiously, and any resemblance to actual persons, living or dead, business establishments, events or locales is entirely coincidental.

This edition published by arrangement with Harlequin Books S.A.

® and TM are trademarks of the publisher. Trademarks indicated with ® are registered in the United States Patent and Trademark Office, the Canadian Intellectual Property Office and in other countries.

www.CarinaPress.com

Printed in U.S.A.

Dear Reader,

Even though I was raised on the Isle of Wight, headquarters of British yachting, horses were the only alternative form of transport that ever interested me. I saw too much of the *glamorous* world of boating to want anything to do with it.

Or so I thought.

When, years later, I was dragged into motorboating by a husband with a severe case of wanderlust, it confirmed my long-held belief that terra firma had much more going for it. I have always had a healthy respect for the power of the sea and really didn't take to the idea of bobbing about in a leaky tin can and being subjected to its mercurial whims. Still, every experience is grist to the writer's mill and my Hunter Files series wouldn't exist if I hadn't suffered for my art.

We really did attend a Day Skipper course similar to the one described in *Lethal Business*, and our dedication to night navigation was strongly influenced by the pub's hours of business. These things matter! As far as I'm aware, the people on the same course as us, unlike the ones Charlie got landed with, had no hidden agendas. Perhaps that's why it's called fictional licence.

The English Channel is one of the busiest shipping lanes in the world, but boats don't routinely explode in the middle of it. Blame my husband for that happening at the beginning of *Lethal Business*. He's the one who told me to think James Bond!

My live-aboard hero, Charlie Hunter, has taken early retirement from the police force. He gets a second chance at some of his old, unsolved cases, dragged back into a life he thought he'd left behind by a pretty girl with powers of persuasion that made it impossible to turn her down. In spite of my lukewarm enthusiasm for all things maritime, there's a certain camaraderie among the boating fraternity that holds an enduring appeal. I hope I've managed to express it in this series and that you enjoy reading about Charlie's cold cases. Do let me know what you think. I'd love to hear from you.

Wendy Soliman

WendySoliman.com

Acknowledgments

As always I am deeply indebted to my talented editor, Deborah Nemeth, without whom mixed metaphors and misplaced commas would abound in this novel. Thanks also to the entire team at Carina Press for their help in bringing this latest Charlie Hunter book to life.

LETHAL
BUSINESS

ONE

THE SEA LAPPED against the boat's hull as though it were almost too much effort. I leaned on the guardrail and breathed deeply, filling my lungs with moist, tangy air. The surreal post-dawn tranquillity seeped into my bones, heightening my appreciation for the simple things in life. I gazed at the sea, a dozen different shades of turquoise reflected in its torpid surface, thinking about all the stuff I'd learned—or rather hadn't—during my trip to France.

The shrill urgency of a Mayday call crackled loud and intrusive across the airwaves, abruptly shattering my mellow mood. I scurried back to the wheelhouse to establish the precise nature of the emergency, not unduly worried because I doubted there actually was one.

"Some idiot's probably run out of fuel," I muttered, glancing at the flat, calm sea.

As it transpired, I couldn't have been more wrong.

"Mayday, Mayday, Mayday. This is the motor vessel *Mistral*, a 62-foot Azimut, current position..."

The caller reeled off his compass location. I checked the coordinates against my GPS and identified the boat in question as the closer of the two vessels I had visual contact with about five miles off my starboard bow. Their location explained why I'd been able to pick up their transmission so clearly. An adrenaline rush flooded my veins.

"We're bound for Dover, but have an uncontainable fire in our engine room."

Fire! My core temperature dropped several degrees. Boats might be surrounded by water, but fire was still one of the most feared shipboard catastrophes. A lot of craft had automatic fire extinguishers in their engine rooms for precisely that reason. If the vessel in trouble was fitted out with the appropriate fire-fighting gear, they obviously weren't using it. I pondered on that and missed some of the vital details that were supposed to be included in an emergency broadcast—such as how many people were on board, and whether anyone had incurred life-threatening injuries.

But then again, perhaps I hadn't. As an ex-copper, I'm used to listening to panicked accounts from victims of accidents or violent crimes. I'd developed a sort of sixth sense over the years for separating vital information from all the garbled excess. I was pretty sure *Mistral* hadn't broadcast that information, which didn't altogether surprise me. It's all very well practising these things, but when it's for real it's a different story. Thankfully I'd never been in that situation so I wouldn't know. Still, faced with the prospect of abandoning ship and bobbing about in a flimsy life raft, at the mercy of whatever the elements decided to throw at you until help arrived, following correct procedures probably didn't seem all that vital.

I reached for the microphone attached to my shipboard radio, and depressed the transmit button.

"*Mistral*, this is the motor trawler *No Comment*," I said calmly. "I'm five miles off your port bow. How serious is your situation? Over."

"Critical, we can't contain the fire."

I didn't waste time asking about fire extinguishers. If they had them, presumably they'd be using them. Trailing the long microphone cord behind me, I grabbed my binoculars and went out to the Portuguese bridge to better assess the situation. The enclosed walkway around my wheelhouse enabled me to step outside and still be protected from the elements.

When I trained the glasses upon *Mistral*, I realised that what I'd mistaken for early-morning sea mist a few minutes before was, in fact, smoke. Light grey when I first saw it, it was now a thick, heavy black cloud of pollution billowing above the Azimut. The boat had clearly lost all power and was dead in the water. I did a quick mental calculation, wondering how best I could help them. Even at my top speed of eight knots—nine if the currents were being kind—it would still take me half an hour to cover the five miles separating us.

Then I remembered that there was another boat out there, just a few miles away from *Mistral*. I looked at it through the glasses and immediately felt reassured. It was a cigarette boat, so it could reach them in a matter of minutes. Such boats were first used to smuggle cigarettes into Canada, hence the name, and are now a familiar part of the offshore powerboat racing scene. With engines capable of producing speeds of up to eighty knots on calm seas—such as today's—this boat was the answer to *Mistral*'s prayers. No tankers or container ships were close enough to pick up *Mistral*'s distress call, but even if they had been, they'd have taken at least as long as me to reach her.

Back in the wheelhouse, I pushed the throttle controlling my single engine fully forward, setting a course directly for *Mistral*'s position. I didn't immediately speak to them again, keeping the airwaves clear for the cigarette to offer her services.

Nothing.

Perhaps they were asleep with the radio turned off. That would be foolish, given that they were in one of the busiest shipping lanes in the world, but it'd been known to happen. In England, anyone could buy a boat and put to sea without knowing the first thing about the rules of the sea, to say nothing of boat handling or safety procedures. Unbelievably, some people actually did that—mostly young males with money to burn and inadequacies to make up for.

The type who bought fast boats like cigarettes.

I checked that my throttle was set at maximum, trying not to mind that the rev counter was reading dangerously high, placing my precious engine in danger of overheating. I'd never get to *Mistral* in time if their situation was as serious as they'd implied, but couldn't live with myself if I didn't at least give it a go.

"*Mistral*, this is *No Comment*. There's a vessel just off your starboard beam. Do you have visual contact? Over."

"We see them but they're not responding."

"Try letting off a flare," I suggested. "They obviously have their radio off, but they might hear or see the flare."

"No time," said the panic-filled voice. "We're abandoning ship."

"Do you have an EPIRB?" Some boats carried an emergency positioning beacon that transmitted a signal to the nearest satellite, alerting the Coastguard when a vessel was in trouble, giving them its precise coordinates. Presumably, if they did, they would have activated it, but people have been known to forget the most basic things when in panic situations.

"Yes, but we can't get it to work."

"How many of you are on board?" There was no response, so I assumed they hadn't heard me and repeated the question. "*Mistral*, I say again, how many of you are on board? Over."

"Oh, er…ten."

"I'm heading your way, *Mistral*, but it'll take me thirty minutes to get there."

Before *Mistral* could respond, the reassuring tones of the Dover Coastguard cut into the broadcast. I'd been wondering why they hadn't done so earlier. At ten miles or so off the English coast, they must have picked up the Mayday. They'd obviously been waiting to see if I could get to the scene of the disaster before them but, presumably, had launched the lifeboat in the interim.

"*Mistral*, this is Dover Coastguard. We're launching the lifeboat." I nodded my approval, glad of their calmly competent approach. "ETA ten minutes. Can you isolate the fire and remain on board that long? Over."

"Negative. Our situation is critical. We're abandoning ship now."

"Understood. *No Comment*, request you maintain your course in case you're needed. Over."

"Dover, *No Comment*. Will do."

"*Mistral*, Dover Coastguard. Launch your life raft and we'll pick you up in nine and a half minutes."

"We copy that, Dover."

I decided to let off a flare myself, even though the rescue services would soon be on the scene. Technically only a vessel in trouble should use a flare, but I was obviously dealing with a bunch of idiots on the cigarette, so unorthodox action was called for. There was a slim possibility they might see it and finally wake up to the fact that they could actually do something to help.

I went out onto the Portuguese bridge again, to the locker where I kept the emergency equipment, and took another look through the binoculars. I could see the life raft, webbing strap attached to the guardrail, being thrown over the side. As it hit the water, the pressure being exerted on the strap was supposed to make the craft automatically inflate. Given the state of *Mistral*'s fire-fighting equipment and EPIRB, I wasn't holding my breath.

This time something went right for the poor devils, and as soon as the flimsy life raft hit the sea's surface, it unfurled as gracefully as a blossoming flower. A number of people, all wearing fluorescent life jackets, scrambled into it. There didn't appear to be any order about the evacuation. Blind panic had taken over. Hardly surprising since flames were now visible leaping from the boat's mid-section. I counted ten people, barely discernible through the thickening smoke, relieved they'd all made it into a raft that looked as though it was only intended for six.

I blinked in confusion as another figure hurled himself into it, and another two after him. None of these late arrivals wore life jackets. I scratch my head, concluding that the mayhem had caused me to miscount. It was difficult to see exactly what was going on. With my boat moving at maximum speed I couldn't hold the binoculars steady. The life raft was dangerously overloaded, as its low position in the water attested, but if they could just hang on they'd soon be rescued.

They had to be terrified, and I felt like a spare part just watching them, immobilised by my lack of speed. I fired up my wing engine—the small auxiliary I use when parking the boat—which afforded me another precious knot of speed. There was absolutely nothing more I could do to help. I tried calling them on the radio again, just to make sure they were hanging in there.

Boats are supposed to keep what's known as a grab bag for emergency situations. Such bags contain bottled water, high-energy snacks, blankets, basic first aid equipment, flares and, crucially, a hand-held radio and spare batteries. Either *Mistral* didn't have such a bag or, more likely, they'd forgotten about it in their anxiety to get clear of the stricken craft. Whatever the reason, my call went unanswered.

I pointed the glasses toward the cigarette again, more in hope than expectation of seeing any signs of life on board. To my utter astonishment I discerned two men, also with glasses pressed to their eyes. They were observing the plight of *Mistral* but clearly didn't intend to offer their help. Furious about their total disregard for human life, I set off my flare, wondering what I hoped it would achieve. They could see what was going down, but if they were the sort of callous individuals who were prepared to stand by and watch people drown rather than try to help them, I didn't see what difference my warning shot would make.

I mulled over the peculiarity of the cigarette crew's reaction, or lack of it, as I made slow progress toward the life raft's position. Something wasn't quite right about their determination to remain uninvolved. My copper's antennae were on high alert, but I couldn't figure out what their game was. They'd been travelling at just ten knots earlier, the same speed as *Mistral*. I was sure of that because I'd been watching them on my radar screen for quite a while. Were they shadowing her for some reason? It seemed like an odd thing to do, but why else would they elect to move so slowly when they had all that power at their disposal? They might not want to go flat out all the time—the fuel costs alone would be prohibitive—but why would speed freaks (which all cigarette owners by definition have to be) travel at a measly ten knots?

Unless my previous conclusion was correct. They'd been asleep, and the smell of smoke had woken them. That would explain why they'd now stopped altogether, apparently wondering what to do. It was against maritime law to ignore a vessel in distress, but if these were the type to put to sea without even turning their radio on, they probably weren't aware of that.

I adjusted my glasses, endeavouring to read the cigarette's name from its transom, determined to report their lack of cooperation to the authorities when I reached Dover. It was turned away from me, my angle wasn't right and I was swaying about, legs braced against the motion of the boat. The cigarette swung with the current, and for a fleeting moment its name came into my line of vision. I only caught a glimpse, but I was pretty sure it was called *Spectre.* As I continued to observe them, I noticed the men on board training their binoculars on the *No Comment.* Perhaps they thought I'd be undertaking a rescue, so I tried the radio again to put them straight.

No response.

My attention was diverted by an earsplitting explosion. I could only watch, helpless as *Mistral* erupted in a spectacular ball of flame. The fire ignited the fuel tanks, making it feel as if the oxygen had been sucked out of the air. Gil, my shaggy mongrel, whined, looking first at me and then toward the scene of the disaster, as though wondering why I wasn't doing something to help.

"I wish I could, mate," I told him, sighing with frustration.

Debris shot high into the sky like an uncoordinated pyrotechnic display. Flaming pieces of motor yacht fell back to sea, fizzling out as they floated for a while and then slowly sank. Fire streaked across the surface of the sea in crooked lines, the putrid smell of burning oil reaching me on the wind. *Mistral*'s bow pointed skywards, as though in supplication to a higher deity, but whatever prayers she offered up fell upon deaf ears. She broke apart and the sea rushed in to claim her. Slipping in graceful slow motion, she quickly gave up all resistance and disappeared below its surface.

I held my breath, waiting for the smoke to clear, aware that the overloaded life raft had been right in the middle of all that devastation. I didn't see how it could have survived such a violent explosion at close quarters and wondered why they hadn't evacuated earlier. Any captain with half a brain ought to have known they were doomed and taken the appropriate action much sooner.

I scanned the area through my binoculars. To my considerable surprise I located the life raft bobbing about in the centre of the debris, singed but still just about floating. Euphoric, I punched the air in celebration. They were going to survive!

Finally the cigarette's engines roared into life. Better late than bloody never. The lifeboat would have a wasted journey but they wouldn't mind about that. It was better for the survivors to be picked up immediately. They must have incurred burns at the very least, being that close to the explosion. Anyway, their ordeal was almost over because the helmsman of the cigarette was certainly making up for lost time. He'd thrown both throttles fully forward, and the powerful boat now leapt and crashed through the water as it cut a path directly toward the tiny life raft.

"Careful," I muttered. "You'll make it capsize if you don't slow down."

The occupants of the life raft waved to their would-be rescuers. The two men on board waved back and, still at full speed, hit the tiny rubber boat amidships.

Holy shit!

I briefly closed my eyes, appalled that their over-exuberance had made the disaster worse. The cigarette, with its sharp bow, sliced through the life raft like it didn't exist, puncturing the hull and sending its occupants screaming and panicking into the cold water.

Hell, that was more than just incompetent enthusiasm. The guys in the cigarette had had no intention of rescuing the poor sods.

I had just witnessed a crime.

TWO

AT A LOSS to know what I could do, I briefly considered launching my tender and speeding to the scene to see if I could pick up any survivors. But that wouldn't work. Leaving the *No Comment* drifting in the middle of such a busy shipping lane would be a worse folly than doing nothing.

By the time the lifeboat arrived on the scene, the cigarette was already several miles away. The lifeboat circled the area where *Mistral* had gone down, pulling bodies from the water. It was impossible for me to tell if any of them were still alive. Somehow, I doubted it. Almost all signs of the stricken craft itself had been swallowed up by a greedy sea, with barely a ripple to show that she'd ever existed. Just an oily patch of water and a few pieces of floating debris marked her grave.

I was still a mile away when the crew finished their grisly task and contacted me on the radio.

"*No Comment*, this is Dover lifeboat. Thanks for your offer of help but there's nothing you can do here."

"Dover lifeboat, *No Comment*. Copy that. Are there any survivors?"

"Negative," replied a grim-sounding voice. "They were pretty badly burned. Some of them were probably dead before they hit the water."

"Yeah, I'm not surprised."

"You'll need to file a report. Will you put into Dover straightaway?"

I'd been expecting the request. "Yes, but it'll take me a while to get there."

"Understood. We can arrange an escort for you, or transfer a crew member aboard to give you a hand, if you'd prefer."

I declined his offer, assuring the skipper I wasn't traumatised. That wasn't exactly the truth. I was pretty shaken up—hell, anyone would have been. I'd dealt with my fair share of tragedies during my time on the force but had learned to compartmentalise. Putting emotional reactions aside was the only way to get through all the crap that got thrown our way. That being the case, I was perfectly capable of putting into Dover without help.

I might have done some damage to my newly serviced engine by running it flat out for so long, and we were still several miles off Dover, but I needed the time it would take to make port to come to terms with what I'd seen.

With the autopilot driving the boat, I made several visits to the engine room over the next half hour. Each time, the sound that greeted my ears was satisfyingly reassuring. Two hundred and fifty horses had stretched themselves to the limit, trying to get me to that stricken craft, but were still thrumping away as if it was no big deal. I'd have to give the engine a thorough servicing when I got back to Brighton, but didn't think any permanent damage had been done.

Being alone at daybreak on a boat was the closest I've

ever come to all that communing-with-nature bullshit you heard so much about nowadays. I'd set off on the home leg from a trip to France when it was still dark so I'd get to watch the new day take shape. The tranquillity was enough to make even the most entrenched atheist question his beliefs—or lack thereof—and wonder if perhaps the God-squad was on to something after all. The horizon gradually taking shape was a welcome relief after hours of either staring into the inky blackness or dodging container ships operating on the assumption that tonnage rules apply. You got to watch the curling sea mist dissipate and the coastline take on definition as the new day slowly made its presence felt. Whatever the weather threw at you the previous day, it was nearly always at its most mellow at first light, as though it was drawing breath, thinking up fiendish new surprises to unleash once it lulled you into a false sense of security.

Mother Nature enjoys her little jokes.

Today had been no exception. There was just a gentle swell rocking the *No Comment* as she forged ahead at a stately six knots, heading for England's south coast. As the sky lightened, I could detect streaks of pink. *Red sky in the morning, sailor's warning.* I didn't think it applied today. It was early July and the weather had been good for a couple of weeks now. If the Met Office had got it right for once, that trend was set to continue.

Very few tankers or cargo ships were in evidence this morning, so even the radio was quiet.

Gil stuck close to me, looking worried. Presumably his instincts told him that some sort of disaster had occurred. He pushed his big head under my hand and wagged half-heartedly. I scratched his ears for a minute or two, then let him out onto the foredeck to resume his interrupted ablutions. He shook himself, trotted to the forepeak and lifted his leg against the windlass, peeing for what seemed like an eternity. I followed along behind him, hose in hand, and got rid of the offending stream before it stained my teak decks yellow.

Gil misses out on his usual quota of walks when we're at sea, so I've devised a programme of shipboard activities to keep him exercised. I threw his Frisbee down the deck and he chased after it, claws scrabbling on the slippery surface, but not slowing him down from his usual bat-out-of-hell speed. He brought it back and I threw it again. And then again. After that I grabbed the webbing strap reserved for his leisure pursuits, and we engaged in an energetic game of tug. When I'd had enough, I resorted to bribery to get him back inside the boat.

"Hungry, mate?"

Woof! And then *woof* again, presumably in case I'd failed to get the message.

I checked that the autopilot was holding us on course and no other vessels were close to us. Then I attended to Gil's culinary requirements, making myself a strong black coffee at the same time. He'd finished and was licking his bowl clean for the third time before the kettle even boiled.

Back in the wheelhouse I became aware of a Coastguard launch close to my starboard beam, escorting me into Dover even though I'd declined their offer. Feeling no requirement to communicate with them, I applied my mind to all I'd witnessed that morning, trying to make sense of it all. The *Spectre*'s crew had shadowed *Mistral*, watched her get into trouble and then deliberately run down the survivors. I thought I'd seen it all and that nothing could shock me anymore, but their callous actions left me stunned, disgusted and despairing of humanity.

As I entered the busy port, a Harbourmaster's launch also pulled alongside me, forming a mini flotilla with the Coastguard boat. Was I getting the VIP treatment because of what I'd witnessed or did they think I might cut and run too?

"Get a grip, Hunter," I told myself, suddenly overwhelmed with fatigue as I fired up the wing engine. I engaged the bow and stern thrusters, moving the boat sideways until she gently nudged against the floating pontoon I'd been directed to. One of the crew from the launch grabbed the lines I'd already prepared, making them off on stout bollards. I shut down the engines, made sure everything was secure, and leapt ashore, Gil at my heels. Only then did I spare a thought for my appearance. Sorely in need of a shower, I had a day's growth on my chin and was wearing jeans, deck shoes and a black Harley T-shirt sporting that legendary mantra, Born to Ride. Hardly appropriate attire in which to report a multiple accident at sea, but it was too late now to do anything about it.

Responsibility for taking details of the incident fell to the Coastguard Service. When I entered their offices, the policeman in me took over and, in a dispassionate voice, I related it just the way it had gone down. I emphasised how helpless I'd felt, speculating as to why the skipper of *Mistral* hadn't taken the decision to abandon ship earlier. The two officers interviewing me listened intently and recorded everything I said.

"Any theory on why he didn't?" the older officer asked.

"Inexperience? Unwillingness to lose the boat?" I shrugged. "Hell if I know."

"And you're convinced that the *Spectre* didn't have its radio on?"

"If they did, they weren't responding."

"Hmm," the young blond officer said, tapping away at a keyboard and peering at the resulting information displayed on his computer screen. "There's no trace of a cigarette named *Spectre* on the Small Ships Register. Are you sure that was its name?"

"No, I'm not." I leaned back in my chair and briefly closed my eyes, recalling a scene I'd prefer to forget. "Like I've already told you, I couldn't get a clear enough view to be absolutely certain."

"Not to worry, we can run a check on all the cigarettes registered in the U.K. A yellow-and-white hull, you said? Well, if they made for a local marina on this side of the Channel, we'll soon find them. Unless they have a very private berth somewhere, they won't be able to hide for long."

I nodded, relieved to have got it all off my chest. Now it was up to the authorities to decide what action to take. I'd done my civic duty and wanted to put the incident behind me.

"Why don't you tell us what you think the cigarette was trying to do?" the older officer suggested.

With a sigh, I sank lower in the upright chair I'd been given, trying to get comfortable. "I've already been through it twice."

"You told us they didn't have their radio on, but you haven't voiced an opinion why that might have been." The senior officer flashed a grim smile at my reaction. "You're an ex-copper. You must have a view."

"Well, they could have been Brits on their way back from a few days in France. They'd probably had a skinful the night before, set the autopilot and got their heads down to sleep it off on the way home."

"Bloody stupid thing to do, especially on that stretch of water. Still, it's been known to happen."

"And waking up to a full-on disaster at sea would be enough to frighten the shit out of anyone." I frowned, trying to put myself in the place of the wide boys on the cigarette. "Especially if they didn't know one end of a boat from another." I rubbed my stubbly chin. "Trouble is, like most cigarette owners, they thought speed was the answer to everything."

The older officer looked me squarely in the eye. "Is that what you really think?"

"No," I said, holding his gaze. "I think they deliberately ran the survivors down."

"Yes, that's how it looks," he agreed, sighing. "What a thing to do. Was *Spectre* flying a red duster?"

It was a good question, and one that hadn't occurred to me. I screwed up my eyes, trying to recall if I'd seen the red ensign flown by all British registered vessels.

"No, I don't think she was actually flying any flag at all."

"Hardly surprising," the blond officer remarked with a final flourish of his computer keys. They'd both told me their names twice, and I'd forgotten them twice. "But still, perhaps it wasn't a British boat."

"Possibly not. Perhaps the closest ports in France might have a record." Weariness seeped through my bones and I stifled a yawn. "Is there anything else I can help you with?"

"No, I think that's about it," said the senior officer. "Dreadful business," he added, shaking his head. "It's about time we did something to force boat owners to gain basic qualifications. If we did, then thirteen lives could have been saved today."

"Not if they acted deliberately," the younger man pointed out.

I sat up straighter, my tiredness forgotten. "Thirteen?"

"Yes, that's how many were recovered. Why?"

"Oh, nothing. It's just that the skipper told me there were only ten aboard."

The two officers shared a glance. "Strange. Still, he was probably in too much of a panic to count properly." He shrugged. "After all, it was a charter. Don't suppose he remembered exactly who *was* on board."

"I expect you're right," I said.

"Even the most experienced captains make basic mistakes in such circumstances."

"I hope I never find out for myself." I rubbed my face

in my hands, dead tired and now in even more desperate need of a hot shower.

"Are you sure you don't need to see anyone? Talk about what happened. It'll make you feel better."

He meant counselling but I shook my head emphatically. The police had started insisting upon that sort of thing during the latter half of my career, if we had to attend a particularly gruesome scene, but I avoided those navel-gazers like the plague. As far as I was concerned, all that introspective baloney created more problems than it actually solved.

"All right then," said the senior officer. "I think that's all we need. Thanks very much, Mr. Hunter, we'll let you get on your way now. We'll be passing this on to MAIB, obviously, and I dare say they'll have a few more questions for you."

I nodded. The Marine Accident Investigation Branch investigated all types of marine accidents. "You know where to find me." I shook hands with them both.

"Oh, you're not planning any more trips for a while, are you?" the older man asked, looking me squarely in the eye in a manner I found rather disconcerting. "We might need to talk to you again."

Someone walked back to the boat with me to let the lines go, and I was finally alone with my thoughts, which were still occupied with the dreadful spectacle I'd witnessed. I'd been invited to stay where I was until I'd had a chance to rest. It was tempting but in the end I declined. I'd rather head home, away from officialdom, out of the spotlight. The press had got wind of the disaster and last thing I needed was reporters sniffing round me, compelling me to relive the entire nightmare.

Besides, I didn't like the way the officers had asked—no, make that *told*—me to stick around, like they thought I knew more than I was saying.

THREE

Once we were tied up at my home marina in Brighton, I took Gil for an overdue run. I wouldn't get any peace until he got rid of some excess energy. Besides, a taste of normality might dispel some of the stuff whirling through my head, and stop me thinking about the discrepancy in the numbers aboard *Mistral*. It absolutely had nothing to do with me.

My boat needed a good wash, but I needed one a hell of a lot more. And I needed to sleep. As soon as my head hit the pillow, I went out faster than an ebb tide. My dreams were vivid, filled with visions of my dead mother rather than the disaster at sea. She'd been gone for well over twenty years—murdered by an as-yet-unknown assassin—but she was never far from my thoughts, especially in times of stress. My trip to France was supposed to shed more light on the reasons behind her senseless murder. Things hadn't gone to plan and I'd come back with little more information than I'd started with.

"Perhaps it really is time to give it all up, Mum," I said to her picture on the cabin wall opposite my bed immediately before I lost consciousness.

A sound in the cockpit, and Gil's excited yaps, woke me two hours later. Even without Gil's reaction I would have recognised the light step on the deck above my head. My heavy heart lightened but I stayed where I was, naked and ready for her. The door opened less than a minute later.

"I assume you intended to let me know you were back sooner or later?" Kara, my exclusive girlfriend, stood in the doorway, hands on hips, biting her lower lip to prevent herself from smiling.

"Ur, what?" I half sat up and rubbed my eyes. "I must be cracking up. I'm hearing nagging voices inside my head."

"You look terrible," she said, coming closer and peering at me.

"Thanks, darling. I love you too."

"Do you?" She looked highly sceptical. "You never said."

Nor did I intend to. Not until I figured out where it would lead.

Kara had contacted me a year ago, enlisting my help to find her missing sister. We found Jasmine, only for Kara to witness her murder. Bottom line, she'd finished up as guardian to Jasmine's two children, Sergei and Saskia. It was a heavy responsibility but she coped surprisingly well with having motherhood thrust upon her.

I'd inherited a bungalow and offered it to Kara as a temporary residence, not wanting to give up living on my boat. She was still there and I was still denying I was in love with her. Once I 'fessed up, I'd have to make choices I wasn't ready to think about.

As soon as she was within range I snaked out one

arm, snagged her round the waist and pulled her down on top of me.

"Hey!"

Her protest lacked teeth, so I kissed her before it could gain any. And because I wanted to kiss her. Kara has a very kissable mouth. To say nothing of the rest of her.

"What was that for?" she asked, sounding a bit breathless.

"I missed you."

"So I see." She stroked my erection through the sheet. "How did you get on?"

"I'll tell you later."

The sex, as always, was mind-blowing. The urgency behind it made it seem like I'd been away for a lot longer than a week. Satiated, at least temporarily, some of the accumulated tension left my body. I pulled her down beside me and she rested her head on my shoulder.

"Right, come on then. What did you find out?"

I let out a long breath. "Well, I found Graham Sullivan playing saxophone with a mediocre jazz group in a bar outside Calais."

She pulled a face. "Bit of a comedown, isn't it?"

"He's a total mess, but oddly enough he seemed pleased to see me." And tapped me up for a hand out, but Kara didn't need to know that.

"That's odd." Kara frowned. "I mean, if he had anything to do with the death of your mother, you're the last person he'd want to see."

"I don't think he did. I asked him outright about that telephone conversation he had with Marianne." I paused to assemble my thoughts. Kara, ever intuitive to my moods, waited me out in silence, drawing intricate patterns on my chest with her forefinger to pass the time. "I thought he'd claim not to remember but he confessed at once."

"So it couldn't have been anything sinister?"

"It was, but it had nothing to do with Mum. Graham had a brother who was a pharmacist—"

"Let me guess. He had access to pain-killing drugs and Marianne was an invalid."

"Sometimes you're too sharp for your own good."

My mother had been a renowned concert pianist. Marianne, her manager's wife, had been disabled following an adverse reaction to an over-the-counter painkiller. Her husband, Jarvis, had been planning to leave her for my mother just before Mum was murdered. My stepbrother had overheard an angry telephone conversation involving verbal threats and large sums of money shortly before Mum was killed. Hence my trip to France to track Graham down.

"Marianne was addicted to the black market drugs he'd been getting her. He'd been supplying some of the orchestra members as well, apparently."

"He told you that?"

"I think he was glad to come clean. It's been troubling what passes for his conscience."

"Hard drugs, you mean?"

"He says not. Just stuff to keep them awake. Or to help them sleep, or whatever."

"That's how people get addicted."

"Yeah, it is." I sighed. "But I only care about Mum's

murder and she wasn't into drugs so it's another dead end."

She shuddered. "I can't stand drug dealers. They're vermin."

"I agree, but it happens. When an orchestra's on tour, the schedule's frenetic."

"So some of the musicians needed a little chemical assistance to stand the pace?"

"That's my guess. I was too young to know anything about it, but I've heard a few things since."

I shifted position and resettled her head on my chest. "Graham's a bit of a pathetic creature now. He used what money he'd made to buy his place in France, but it's a shit heap and he's not a happy man."

"Nor does he deserve to be."

I kissed the end of her nose. "You're a hard woman, Kara Webb."

"I'm sorry, Charlie," she said, her big eyes soft with sympathy. "I know you thought you were on to something this time."

I exhaled slowly. "Perhaps it really is time to admit defeat."

She glanced at my mother's picture. "You can't put the entire world to rights single-handed."

"What!" I feigned surprise. "So I'm not James Bond then?" I shook my head. "Damn, people have been lying to me for years."

She punched my side and laughed at my puny attempted to lighten the mood.

"Ouch!" I leaned up on one elbow and told her all about the accident at sea.

"God, Charlie, that's terrible! Why didn't you say something at once?"

"I've been trying to forget about it."

"I'll bet you have, poor baby."

"Come on," I said with a dramatic sigh. "Let's go out and eat. I'm famished."

We took Gil with us and hit the nearest restaurant, sitting on the terrace overlooking the boats so that Gil didn't pollute the interior of the place with his hairy presence.

"You've got Harry this weekend?" she asked, referring to my nine-year-old son.

"Sure have."

"We've been invited to a birthday party on Saturday afternoon. Well, the kids have."

"Oh, you didn't say."

"The invite only just came through. One of Sally's."

Sally had been Jasmine's best friend when they'd been at school and was married to a mate of Kara's brother. Brett had also died under suspicious circumstances. Some families are just plain unlucky but Kara was bucking the trend and getting on with her life. Since becoming a mother, she'd picked up her friendship with Sally. Two women with young kids—it made sense.

Whenever I had Harry we tried to do something together with the kids. This party would save me the trouble of dreaming up entertainment for Saturday afternoon. Besides, it would be good for Harry. Since he was an only child, I sometimes worried about his lack of interaction with other kids. Not that he'd be an only child for much longer. My ex was expecting, but the age gap would be too great for there to be much connection between Harry and what he fervently hoped would be a younger brother.

Kara glanced at her watch. "School's out. I have to go."

"I'll see you on Saturday morning then. The kids might as well stay on board over the weekend."

"What about me?"

"Hmm, not so sure there'll be space for you."

"I'll share your space."

"Well, in that case…just so long as you promise not to behave."

"Oh, I think I can safely assure you of that."

Gil and I walked her to her car and she kissed us both goodbye. I watched her drive away and went back to the boat. I had a ton of maintenance jobs to catch up with, but they could wait until tomorrow. I poured myself a beer, put a Cecil Taylor jazz CD on the stereo and sat with Gil in the cockpit, eyes at half-mast as the music seeped beneath my skin. Only two things relaxed me more than listening to decent jazz. One was being in bed with Kara. The other was when I was the one making the jazz. A promising jazz pianist when my mother got killed, I'd given it up in a hopeless quest to find her killer. Since leaving the police I'd started to play again occasionally, lured back into it by that meddlesome witch Kara.

THE NEXT COUPLE of days passed in a flurry of activity. Ask any boat owner how he passed his day and he'd be hard pressed to tell you. But there was always something to be done and time had a habit of slipping away. By the time Harry descended upon the boat on Saturday morning like a mini-tornado, I was more or less under control with my jobs.

My ex, Emily, waddled down the pontoon behind our son.

"You should have let me pick him up," I said, giving her the obligatory peck on the cheek. "You look ready to explode."

She sighed. "It's this damned heat. It has no consideration for pregnant women."

"Not long to go now."

"No, thank God."

"Have you told him yet?" I nodded towards Harry in the cockpit, playing with Gil.

"No, I can't figure out a way."

Emily couldn't bring herself to tell him she was expecting a girl, and I sure as hell wasn't going to burst his bubble by breaking the news. It was nothing to do with me.

"He'll ignore the baby and guilt trip you and Phil into spoiling him," I predicted.

"You're probably right." She smiled fondly at our son and returned his wave. "If this one's only half as good as Harry was as a baby, then I'll not complain."

"You won't get that lucky twice."

She expelled a long breath. "Probably not."

Kara arrived at that moment, her two in tow. She and Emily were still cagy in one another's presence but at least I no longer feared an outbreak of physical violence.

"I got Becky a present from the three of them," she said when Emily took herself off.

"Who's Becky?"

Kara sighed. "Sally's daughter. The birthday party this afternoon." She waved a hand in front of my face. "Hello, earth to Charlie."

"Oh yeah, sorry. Thanks for doing that." We both knew it wouldn't have occurred to me.

After lunch we piled into Kara's VW Beetle. My sole forms of transportation were my beloved Harley or the local bus. I briefly wondered about buying a car and quickly dismissed the thought. I was *absolutely not* ready to make compromises to my lifestyle yet, not even for Kara. So we all squeezed into her wagon and I pretended not to notice the cramped conditions. Small cars weren't designed with men of six foot two in mind, or a son who seemed to have grown another inch every time I saw him. His arm came forward from the backseat and clouted the back of my head. Not his fault really. He hadn't quite figured out how to control his elongated limbs yet.

As soon as we got to Sally's the kids disappeared, dashing round the large, rather untidy garden like wild animals. There seemed to be dozens of them and I definitely didn't want to get in the middle of them. I wondered what happened now. Did we go off and come back later? I was about to ask when Sally's husband, Pete, appeared. We shook hands and Pete ushered us into a room at the back of the house—a child-free zone where blessed peace reigned.

"We'll be safe in here, at least for a while," he said, shuddering.

"Perhaps I should give Sally a hand?" Kara said.

"Don't worry, she's got caterers in. You're probably better off out of it."

"Oh well, if you're sure."

Drinks were offered and accepted and the three of us settled down to enjoy them.

"You seem to have adapted well to motherhood, Kara," Pete remarked.

"Needs must," she said, smiling. "It can be a bit of a tie, but Mum's always on hand when I need her. I've kind of made the adjustment now and can't really remember what it was like before. Besides, it's not the kids' fault and, I have to say, I do love them."

"Yeah, they tend to get under your skin."

Kara cleared her throat. "How's Gordon?"

"Ah, funny you should say that..." Pete went on to say something about Gordon—whoever he was—disappearing. It all sounded rather contrived and my suspicions were on high alert.

"Gordon is Pete's younger brother. He, Peter and Brett were inseparable as boys," Kara explained. "Always either up to mischief or out sailing."

"And now Gordon's gone on the missing list," Pete said with a heavy sigh.

"What happened?" Kara asked.

Why did I get the feeling that she already knew?

"He took Brett's loss badly." Pete slugged back his whiskey and reached for a refill. "Well, we all did, but it was especially hard for him. Once Sally and I married, I dropped out of the scene and Brett and Gordon became inseparable. They even went into the delivery skipper business together. They both loved the solitude and being their own boss."

I recalled how I felt that morning, alone on the *No Comment* as the sun came up, and nodded. Much as I didn't want to get involved, I already had questions forming. "Was he doing a delivery?"

"No, about six months ago he started freelancing for a company in Southampton that does boat-handling courses. Day Skipper right up to Yacht Master, that sort of thing. Brett referred him to them, I think."

Kara piped up. "I think Brett did a few jobs for them."

"That's very different to what he had been doing," I said, accepting a refill from Pete. Kara, as a responsible driver, declined. "If he liked solitude so much he'd get precious little of it with punters all over the place twenty-four/seven."

"Yes, but the money's good and with the economy the way it is, deliveries are drying up. He still does them when they come his way but had to find some other way to support himself."

"Okay, so he's got a new job training would-be sailors. How has he gone missing?"

"I'm not sure." Pete hesitated. "The company also specialises in cruises to the French coast. You know, like those Red Letter Day things—ballooning, motor racing and stuff. Two or three couples can have a few days' break on a luxury motor cruiser, their every whim catered for. In spite of the tough economic times, those with money still have it, according to Gordon anyway, and are always on the lookout for diverse ways to part with it. Apparently most of the punters aren't with their wives but are trying to make an impression on—"

"Yeah, I get the picture." But I still didn't see where I fit in. "So where did he go?"

"That's just it, you see. I haven't heard from him for two weeks."

"Two weeks?" I eyed Pete with open astonishment. "He's an adult male living his own life. Two weeks isn't so long."

"Perhaps not to most people, but Gordon's been under a lot of strain since Brett died. He fell apart for a while and we had him here with us. Once he got better and went back to work I made him promise to keep in touch." Pete lifted his shoulders. "Oh, I know what you're thinking, but you don't know him. He might be an adult in the strict sense of the word but he's also sensitive, a bit naïve *and* he's my baby brother. With both our parents dead, I feel responsible for him. We never go for more than a day or two without talking to each other."

Sally came into the room. "The magician's working his magic," she said, giggling at her clumsy use of words. "Gin, at once!"

Pete was already on his feet, pouring a large one for her. She sat on the arm of his chair and took a healthy slug, sighing with obvious pleasure as it hit her bloodstream.

"Ah, that's better!"

"Make the most of it," Pete said, chuckling. "The

peace won't last for long. One of the little monsters is bound to figure out how the magician does it and then all hell will break loose."

She rolled her eyes. "So true."

"Okay, what do you think happened to him?" I asked.

"Gordon, I assume you're talking about?"

I levelled my gaze on Sally's face and said nothing. She knew damned well who we were talking about. I was the only one in the dark here.

"I don't have a clue." She spread her hands and frowned at the back of them. "When I couldn't get him on the phone, I rang his work but they told me he'd got another job on."

"There you are then." I leaned back and stretched my arms above my head. "Perhaps he's gone back to delivering boats."

"No." Pete said the one word emphatically. "Well yes, actually it's possible I suppose, but he wouldn't have gone anywhere without telling me first."

Sally smiled at me and ran a hand across the back of her husband's neck. "We're both really worried," she said softly.

"So what have you done to try and find him?" Apart from teaming up with Kara to bug me about it.

"I went to his flat in Cowes the other day but it told me precisely nothing." Pete flashed a humourless smile. "My brother is fanatical about neatness. Anal retentive, some might say. Everything in his place was exactly as it should be, nothing missing that I could see, and nothing to indicate where he's taken off to. And yet he's disappeared into thin air. His neighbours haven't seen hide or hair of him for two weeks either."

"What about his work colleagues? Do they know where he went?"

"No, I spoke to his boss on the phone but he wasn't very forthcoming. Said Gordon had left him in the lurch and sounded annoyed about it." He expelled a long breath. "That's not like Gordon at all. If he says he'll do something then he does it. I thought about talking to his colleagues to see if they knew where he's got to, but that was a non-starter. All the people at Ultimate Marine are self-employed so Gordon didn't get to work with the same people on a regular basis."

"He didn't give you names of anyone there he'd struck up a friendship with?"

"No, unfortunately not, but then boating can be a solitary existence."

"Then I'm not sure what can be done." I felt for him, but it wasn't my problem. "I'm sorry, I know you're worried but, like you say, your brother's an adult. If he wants to disappear, and if there's no sign of anything suspicious, I don't see what you expect me to do."

"I thought of you as soon as I heard what happened," Sally said.

"Sorry, you've lost me."

"About *Mistral*."

My heart quickened. "What about it?"

"Well, you witnessed the accident, didn't you?"

I glanced at Kara. She mouthed *sorry* at me.

"How did you know that?" I asked, aware that the

answer was sitting next to me, not looking particularly sorry at all.

"The accident was reported in the paper," Sally pointed out. "I immediately thought the worst. Then Kara and I were talking and she mentioned that you witnessed the accident. It kind of seemed like…oh, I don't know—like you were supposed to help us, I suppose."

"I don't see how I can."

"It can't have been easy," she said sympathetically. "I don't suppose you can get the scene out of your head. I know I wouldn't be able to."

"Wait a minute," I said, frowning. "Are you saying that *Mistral* belonged to the company your brother worked for?"

"Yes." Sally raised both brows. "Didn't Pete point that out? It's one they used for their luxury cruises to France."

FOUR

"Gordon's boss says he definitely wasn't on board," Pete said. "But I can't get it out of my head that he must have been."

"Well, the boss must have known what crew members were working that trip. What reason would he have to lie about it?"

"If he was alive and well somewhere, he'd have found a way to get in touch with us, no matter what sort of trouble he's in." Pete set his jaw in a stubborn line. "He must have been on that boat."

"You sound as though you wish he had been."

"No, of course not." Pete ran a hand through his hair, looking harried. "But if he was, I'd much rather know."

"Identification of the bodies recovered from *Mistral* is ongoing, according to the papers," I said.

"That's what the authorities told me when I asked about Gordon."

"The owners of the boat would have supplied a roster of the names of the passengers and crew," I said. "Was Gordon's name on it?"

"No," Sally conceded. "But that could have been a mix-up. If he took the run at the last minute, they might have forgotten to change the crew names. They're not always terribly efficient about that sort of thing."

She was clutching at straws and appeared to know it. I ignored the niggling voice that kept reminding me about the extra people I'd seen leaving the boat. I also ignored the fact that the papers had reported the loss of just ten lives. If the Coastguard hadn't told me it was thirteen, I'd have assumed that I'd miscounted. As it was, I no longer had a clue what was going on.

"If Gordon had been amongst them, you would have been notified, so that has to be good news."

"I *have* to know for sure." Pete turned to me, his expression resolute. "Will you help me?"

"Have you been to the police?" I asked, ducking the question. I was drinking the man's single malt. It would be rude to turn him down outright.

"Yeah, and they don't want to know."

I nodded. "They wouldn't. Gordon's an adult and there's no indication that anything's happened to him."

Kara flashed an innocent smile. "Perhaps you could go to Ultimate Marine and enrol on one of their courses, Charlie?"

I sat bolt upright and glowered at her. "You've got to be joking!"

She smiled contritely. "It's just a suggestion."

"And not a particularly intelligent one." I pretended not to see her flinch at my harsh words. She only had herself to blame. She'd set me up and I wasn't happy about it.

"Well," Sally said, clearly sensing the annoyance I wasn't particularly trying to hide. "It was just that—"

Loud whooping noises filtered through from the garden.

"Oh, Lord!" Sally jumped up and downed her drink in one. "Sounds as though the magician's losing them. I'd better go and play referee before they brain one another."

Saskia appeared in the doorway, her face smeared with chocolate, red hair as rich as Kara's falling out of its braid, also covered with a healthy layer of chocolate.

"Aunty Kara, Harry won't play with me." She stamped her foot, close to tears. We'd had this problem with the kids recently. The boys wanted to play boys games. Trouble was, Saskia wanted to play them too. Harry and Sergei were at an age where girls were the antithesis of cool and only condescended to include Saskia when there were no other kids to be had. I felt sorry for the little squirt and did what I could to cheer her up.

"Tell you what," I said, stooping to pick her up and sitting her on my shoulders. "How about we play a game instead?"

"Yes! Gee up, horsey."

Tiny fingers sank their way into my hair and her little heels bashed against my shoulders. Too late to do anything about it, it occurred to me that her fingers were probably covered in chocolate too. I guess I was getting sucked into this family man shit whether I wanted to or not.

I made vague promises to Pete that I'd look into Ultimate Marine's background, just to see if anything jumped out at me.

The kids, on chocolate overload, were boisterous during the ride home. Kara, driving and playing referee, had her work cut out so perhaps she didn't notice how quiet I was. There again, perhaps she chose to ignore it. I took Gil out when we got back to the boat whilst she cleaned the kids up. She joined me in the cockpit when she'd finally got them to bed.

"You're cross with me," she said simply.

"A bit more than that." I shot her a sideways glance. "The last thing I need is to keep thinking about that accident."

"I know." She touched my hand but I removed it from her reach. "I'm sorry, but Gordon and Brett were such good friends, and my feelings about Brett are still so raw that I just thought—"

"You still should have told me first."

"And what would you have said if I did?"

She had me there.

"Exactly!" she said when I didn't respond. "You didn't want to help me to look for Jas, but you did it because you hated thinking of a poor helpless female taking up the search alone. But Pete..." She reached up and touched the side of my face. "I'm sorry, Charlie."

When a fat tear slid down her cheek, I knew she meant it. We'd never had a serious argument before and, as my anger dissipated, I realised just how much I disliked being at odds with her. I slid my arm round her shoulders and pulled her towards me. "Just don't do it again."

"Promise."

"How are you gonna make it up to me?"

"Oh," she said, smiling angelically through her tears. "I'm sure I'll think of a way."

"Am I allowed to throw a few suggestions into the pot?"

"Absolutely not!"

"Damn."

We put the incident behind us and didn't refer to it for the rest of the weekend. Kara dedicated herself to making amends, and by Sunday evening she was well and truly forgiven.

"Perhaps I should lose my rag with you more often, if that's how you make amends."

"Don't push your luck, Hunter."

I winked at her. "Can't blame a guy for trying."

"You're insatiable."

"Not true," I said, flat on my back in our cabin, stark naked and literally shagged out. "I don't think I could possibly rise to the occasion again for…hmm well, at least another half hour."

"That long, huh."

Just as I'd known would be the case, she set out to prove me wrong. Needless to say, I agreed to help her look for her brother's friend. I would have done so, even before she used her feminine wiles to persuade me, but she didn't need to know that.

ALONE AGAIN ON Monday I phoned one of my old colleagues, Detective Sergeant Jimmy Taylor, catching him at the nick. His star was very much in the ascendancy since he caught the murderer of a local solicitor—with a little help from yours truly—so he owed me big time.

We did the small talk thing and then I got down to business.

"Do me a favour, mate, and see what you can dig up on the background of a company called Ultimate Marine based in Hythe Marina."

"Why, what have they done?"

"Nothing as far as I know. It's just that I might have to start working for a living again sometime soon and I hear they're recruiting. I want to make sure they're kosher before I even consider applying."

"You could always come back. Good DI's are in short supply."

"What, and lock horns again with the DCI Slater." I shuddered. "I think I'll let you keep her all to yourself, thanks all the same."

"Locking horns was all she ever wanted to do with you, and she's been acting like a woman scorned ever since," Jimmy said in a peeved tone.

And I'd pissed her off even more when, instead of pointing her in the direction of the solicitor's killer, I gave the lead to Jimmy.

"I thought she was being moved sideways to another division."

"We live in hope, but for once the rumour mill seems to have got it wrong." He sighed down the line. "So far we're still stuck with her."

"Get back to me as soon as you can, mate," I said, cutting the connection.

I did an internet search on Ultimate Marine and was presented with a professional-looking website. Several instructors, all male, were lined up in front of a Ferretti 70 that, judging by the angular shape of its hull, was at least ten years old. According to the Coastguard,

Mistral had also been an older boat. Ultimate Marine clearly picked up its fleet cheaply and tarted it up. Give the interiors a makeover, lots of flashy furnishings and comfortable beds, keep the punters well clear of the galley and engine room, and they'd never know any better.

It would explain why the safety equipment wasn't up to scratch on *Mistral*, although if they were licensed to carry passengers then it ought to have been regulated and inspected. They should, at the very least, have had automatic fire extinguishers in the engine room. I didn't imagine there was much the authorities could do to prove negligence because she was at the bottom of the Channel now, unlikely ever to be recovered. But they could sure as hell swarm all over the rest of their fleet to make sure that no corners were being cut. I wondered how that would go down with the owners. The negative publicity about *Mistral* would hurt them. If they were harassed by the bureaucrats as well, it could put them out of business.

I focused my attention on the picture of the instructors, all identically dressed in white polo shirts bearing Ultimate's logo of a motor cruiser head to head with a sailboat and the company's name in bold two-colour type beneath it. Navy cargo pants and deck shoes completed the rig-out. I wondered if any of them was Gordon.

I hadn't decided on my next move when Jimmy called me back.

"That was quick," I said. "Quiet day?"

"Yeah, all the old Brighton lags threw in the towel when they no longer had to pit their wits against yours.

They don't stand a chance now the real brains are in charge."

I chuckled. "Tell me what you've got for me."

"Ultimate Marine hasn't been in business long, less than two years, but they're doing okay according to their first year's returns. They're making a modest profit, thanks to their have-it-away days to France."

"Is that what they're calling it this week?"

Jimmy laughed. "Why else would Joe Average shell out all that dosh for a few days in rainy France when he could hop on a budget airline and go somewhere warm and vibrant, like Barcelona?" I could just imagine Jimmy, feet up on the desk, twiddling an unlit cigarette between his lips. The smoking ban was hell for addicts like him. "The only conclusion is that he wants to impress his bit on the side and get his leg over."

"Who owns the company? I've been looking at their website but there's no mention of the power behind the throne."

"Haven't been able to find out," he said, which didn't surprise me. If people didn't want to boast about their business empire by plastering their name all over the web then there was usually a good reason for that. Besides, a fledgling business at the luxury end of the market making a profit in its first year of trading made me suspicious. And, in spite of myself, interested.

"Sorry, Jimmy, the line went dead. Say that again."

"I said I'll keep digging if you like but my guess is that the owner's hiding behind an offshore corporation for reasons best known to himself. But whatever they are, they can't be kosher. I'd steer well clear of their offer of employment if I were you."

"What...oh yeah, thanks." I'd forgotten that I'd got him into this by pretending that Ultimate had offered me work. "Still, see what else you can dig up for me when you have time. No urgency."

"Yes sir, right away, sir!"

That evening I enjoyed a few beers, took Gil for his late night perambulation and then turned in, thinking about the anomalies that were stacking up.

Ultimate Marine's owners didn't want to be identified.

They'd made a reasonable profit in their first year.

They purchased old boats and probably didn't maintain them to the required standards, so perhaps someone in authority had been given a backhander to look the other way.

Mistral almost certainly had more people on board than the skipper had admitted to, which would explain why he left it so long to abandon ship. He'd hoped to get the fire under control and avoid that necessity.

And, crucially, Gordon Reed, self-employed occasional worker at Ultimate, had gone missing.

But it was all circumstantial, and most definitely someone else's problem.

KARA SPENT THE night on board on Wednesday. We ate out, walked Gil and, inevitably, finished up making love. Afterwards, she brought the conversation round to Gordon Reed.

"Did you find out anything interesting?"

I told her what little I knew about Ultimate Marine.

"Hmm, that doesn't help much." She wrinkled her brow. "What would you do next if you were looking for Gordon?"

"Which I'm not," I told her, scowling. "But if I was, the first thing I'd ask myself is why Ultimate Marine is so keen to hide the names of its owners? Surely whoever's behind it would want to blow his own trumpet about his boating experience and try to encourage people to sign up for their courses."

"Perhaps the owner is just a front man who doesn't have experience."

"Possibly." But I doubted it. "Do you know who Pete spoke to when he asked them about Gordon?"

"His call got put through to the manager. Someone called Wayne Richards. He told me that he had an East End accent and was businesslike but brusque, like he was busy and didn't really have time to talk about Gordon." She worried away at her lower lip with her forefinger. "He must have been on *Mistral*, Charlie. There's simply no other explanation for his disappearance."

"There is absolutely no reason on this earth why Ultimate Marine wouldn't give his name to the MAIB if he had been on board," I lied, easily able to think of any number.

"The Marine Accident Investigation Branch? They're the people you spoke to?"

I frowned at her. She didn't actually know that the MAIB had spoken to me on the phone but she would certainly be aware of their involvement. The love of my life had switched to the role of dumb female, presumably in the hope of bringing out my protective instincts. "Anyway, Pete hadn't heard from Gordon for over a week before *Mistral* went down, and they were adamant that no more than two days ever went by before he got in touch."

"True." She rested her hand on her clenched fist and frowned. "I don't like this one little bit."

Nor did I.

She glared at me, her eyes alight with suspicion. "Is there something you're not telling me?" Damn, this woman was getting to know me too well. "Have you thought of something else?"

"No, you know everything that I do."

"And I can't persuade you to sign up for a course at Ultimate Marine?"

I shook my head. "Kara, we've been here before. I'm not getting involved."

She pouted. "Perhaps I'll go and sign up myself then."

"Do you think that's a good idea?" I asked mildly.

"No, Charlie, since you ask, I think it's a lousy idea. I'm hopeless at pretending to be dumb, and they'll realise immediately that I know how to sail. You however are a different kettle of fish. You had lots of occasions to pretend to be something you're not whilst chasing down villains."

"Have you forgotten that you have two children to take care of?"

"As if I could."

"Well then." I let the silence hang for a moment before asking a question. "Pete went to Gordon's flat."

She nodded. "He must have found something that lent a clue as to where he's gone. People don't just disappear. Letters, notes to himself, things like that?"

"He said not. You heard him."

"If he'd taken a new job, presumably there would have been something in writing, or at the very least in his email."

"At the time he still thought he'd turned up again, so it would have been an invasion of his privacy to go snooping through his things."

"Well, why doesn't he go back and look a bit more thoroughly?"

She turned to me, her eyes alight with renewed purpose. "That's something we *could* do ourselves." I was shaking my head before she'd even finished posing the question. "Please! You'll know better than Pete what to look for, and you'd do it with greater detachment too, because you don't have any emotions involved."

It was a reasonable request and I knew she'd give me a hard time unless I agreed. I was trying to think of an irrefutable reason why I couldn't go when someone pounded on the hull. Gil barked his head off.

"What the hell?" I leapt out of bed and pulled on a pair of jeans over my nakedness, worried about the security of my floating home. "Stay here," I said to Kara.

I slid open the door to the cockpit and stepped onto the aft deck. Gil actually pushed past me, hackles raised, a rumbling growl reverberating in his throat. When I realised who'd come calling at such a late hour, I decided he was a better judge of character than I'd given him credit for. I made a big show of holding him back by his harness, even though I was pretty sure he wouldn't actually attack.

Detective Chief Inspector Jillian Slater stood on the pontoon. Jimmy Taylor was right behind her, looking as though he'd much rather be somewhere else.

"Not interrupting anything, are we?" Slater asked with a malicious glance at Kara, who, predictably, had ignored my instructions and followed me outside.

FIVE

TALK ABOUT *DÉJÀ-VU.* Slater had tried this stunt once before. She liked turning up for no apparent reason, hoping to embarrass me. It didn't get her far last time, and wouldn't do her much good on this occasion. Not that that would stop her. Slater enjoyed her petty attempts at revenge.

"Evening, Jimmy," I said, ignoring Slater altogether. "Kind of late for a social call, isn't it?"

"Hi, Charlie, we're…er, just—"

"This is official," Slater said, cutting across Jimmy.

Her air of smug satisfaction told me she thought she knew something I didn't, and wanted to cause me maximum grief. A few months back I'd solved the solicitor's murder, sorted out a drug smuggling operation, and proved that she'd convicted the wrong man of murdering a bookie. I'd made her look bad—well, even worse than usual—so my card had been marked.

"Something I can do for you, Chief Inspector?" I thrust my hands into my pockets and leaned against the door frame.

"We need to talk." Slater glowered at Kara. She was wearing an old towelling robe of mine that swamped her. Her messed-up hair and flushed face made it pretty obvious what Slater had interrupted. She looked rather pleased with herself about that but then it didn't take a lot to make Slater happy.

"I'm always at your disposal, you know that." Gil followed me onto the dock, growling at Slater. "Your timing couldn't have been better. We'd just finished what we were doing."

Jimmy turned a laugh into a cough and winked at Kara. Slater looked like she'd swallowed a lemon.

"Right then, Detective," I said, aware of her eyes fastened on my bare chest like she'd never seen a half-naked man before. "What's so important that it's brought Brighton's finest calling at such an unsocial hour?"

"Sorry to interrupt your cosy little evening," she said, looking anything but sorry. "I need to talk to you about a serious misuse of resources."

I didn't need to feign my incomprehension. "You've lost me."

"Well, that's not much of a challenge."

I sucked in a long breath, already bored with the exchange. "Do you want to waste time trading insults, or tell me what this is all about?"

"It's about you dropping Jimmy here right in it."

"Don't have a clue what you're talking about."

She rolled her eyes. "How often have I heard that one?" She laughed but no one else appeared to get the joke. "Ultimate Marine," she said, resorting to a smile that would have made a shark back off.

"What about it?" But I already knew where this was going with this. She'd caught Jimmy researching the outfit and discovered that he was doing me a favour. Now she was causing trouble for Jimmy, knowing we were good mates. She'd be wondering about my interest in Ultimate Marine and whether there was something in it for her. The degree of her vindictiveness surprised me. Her eagerness to follow up anything, however tenuous, if she thought it would enhance her career, didn't. Her continued interest in my affairs, even though I was no longer a copper, was something I didn't even want to think about.

"You asked Jimmy to look into their background. And why was that?"

"Curiosity."

She raised her eyes to heaven. "Oh, come on, Charlie, you can do better than that."

I took my time responding. "Am I being accused of something?"

"I haven't decided about that yet, but if I think of something that might stick, then you'll be the first to know."

I actually smiled at that one. "I won't be able to sleep," I said, hoping I sounded unconcerned. She couldn't do much to me, other than be a constant thorn in my side. But she could sure as hell make life difficult for Jimmy, and we both knew it.

"Come on, Ultimate Marine, what's your interest?"

"Academic."

"I don't believe you."

I shrugged. "Can't help what you believe."

"You went to the trouble of asking Taylor to look into them, after you've failed to rescue one of their boats in distress." She paused, presumably for effect, plucking at her lower lip as she pretended to mull it over. "That makes me wonder just how hard you actually tried to save it. So, I ask myself, what's he looking for? Is there more to this than meets the eye, or is he simply trying to cover his own back."

She was deliberately goading me, hoping I'd lose my rag. When I thought about how helpless I'd felt when all those people drowned unnecessarily, she damned nearly got her wish. How had she found out about my involvement in *Mistral*'s accident? It would be easy enough for someone in her position to get a look at the reports, but why would she even think to do so? I didn't flatter myself that she was quite that desperate to keep in touch.

"Investigating maritime accidents now, are you, Jillian?" I asked caustically. "Well, perhaps you'll have better luck building a career in that sphere, but I'm not holding my breath." Jimmy sounded as though he was choking. "Anything else I can help you with this evening?" I stood my ground, levelling my eyes on Slater's face without blinking.

She turned away first. "You're up to something, Charlie," she said. "And I'll be watching you closely. You can't stop meddling in things that don't concern you. Your type never can." Without another word she turned on her heel and headed off down the pontoon. "Are you coming, Sergeant?" she asked, not looking back to see if he actually was.

"Sorry, mate," I said to Jimmy in an undertone. "Didn't mean to drop you in it."

"Not your fault," he whispered back. "She heard me on the phone to you. I didn't even know she was in the squad room. She's got ears like a bloody bat and started digging to see if she could find out what we were talking about." Jimmy grinned. "Don't worry about Slater," he added, "she's just blowing hot air, like always."

"What was that all about?" Kara asked once they'd gone.

"Your guess is as good as mine." I poured us both a drink, deep in thought. Slater had inadvertently bolstered Kara's campaign and ignited my interest in Gordon Reed's disappearance. "About Gordon's flat," I said. "I've had a change of heart. If you like, we could go to Cowes together on the *No Comment* tomorrow."

"That would be great, but why have you—"

"You were planning to stay with me tonight, which means we can get away early. You'll be back in time to collect the kids from school."

"Why the change of heart?" she asked. I merely shrugged, causing her to cast a long, considering look in my direction. "It's Slater, isn't it? She's sticking her nose in and you can't stand her telling you not to do something."

As always, Kara had pretty much got me pegged. "If you don't want to go..." I left the words hanging.

"Oh, no, I do. Thanks."

"I need to give the engine a test after the repairs I had done to the filtration system yesterday." It had overheated when I thrashed it for so long and a mechanic had to sort it for me. "Cowes is as good a place to go as any."

"I'm sorry about Slater giving your grief but glad she's made you want to help Pete.

"Perhaps I'll notice something Pete didn't. It's a long

shot, but you never know. At least then you can tell your friends I tried."

"Yes, it'll make them feel better, just knowing that you're taking a look."

"Can you get a key?"

"I'm sure I can." She furled her brow. "What is it? You looked preoccupied."

"I'm wondering how Slater got wind of *Mistral*'s accident, that's all."

"It was in the paper."

"Yes, but my name wasn't mentioned. She's not the world's greatest sleuth, so something obvious must have alerted her to my involvement. Jimmy wouldn't have researched the outfit when she was around because she'd want to know why." My bruised fingers absently tapped out the tone clusters and intricate polyrhythms of a Cecil Taylor number on the galley surface. "I don't know, but something just doesn't feel right. If whatever it is has got Slater on my case, then I'd prefer to remain one step ahead of her."

THE BENEFIT OF having another person on board who knew her way around a boat was that whilst I walked Gil and did the engine room checks, Kara attended to everything else without needing to be told. Like feeding me breakfast and making sure that anything fragile was put somewhere safe. I started the engine and Kara handled the lines and fenders with smooth efficiency. The weather was fine and the *No Comment* behaved perfectly all the way to Cowes. To my relief, the engine seemed back to normal. We arrived late morning and, although it was high season, managed to get an inside berth because I'd radioed to say we'd only be staying for a few hours.

"Come on," I said when we'd finished making the boat secure. "Let's give Gil a run and visit Gordon's flat at the same time."

"Just give me a moment to tidy myself up a bit first."

She looked fine to me but, knowing how women can be about these things, I settled in for a long wait. She surprised me by re-emerging just ten minutes later wearing light cotton trousers and a strappy top. She fished the keys to the flat out of her bag. I've no idea how she got hold of them so quickly and didn't bother to ask. We'd been together all night and no one had delivered anything to the boat. Presumably she'd had them all the time, anticipating that I'd eventually weaken. It wouldn't surprise me.

I locked the boat and we made our way up the walkway to the pedestrianized high street, Gil pulling on his leash, eager to investigate. Our walk took us behind the Royal Yacht Squadron. We veered off there, leaving the sea on our right as we meandered through a park situated next to a school. Gil took that to mean playtime and barked like crazy until I produced his Frisbee and threw it for him.

When the heat of the day finally got to him, he collapsed on the grass, panting, tongue hanging stupidly from the side of his mouth. I hid his toy and we emerged from the park on the opposite side. Another short walk and we finally reached the back street of terraced houses in which Gordon's flat was situated.

Kara had taken the scenic route. We could have come directly up the hill from the marina.

"I thought Gil would enjoy the park," she said, answering a question I hadn't asked.

"Right."

But I wasn't buying it. These were obvious delaying tactics. I put it down to the similarities between Gordon and her late brother, Brett. They'd been mates, both delivery skippers, both living in Cowes. It would be enough to upset anyone.

"Come on then." I took the keys from her hand. "Let's get this done with."

The flat was on the ground floor of a three-storey house. I opened the outer door and then the one to the flat itself. There were two locks involved—a Mortis and a Yale. The Mortis was stuck and required a bit of manipulation.

"If Gordon's as neat as Pete implied, then it shouldn't take us too long to…Ohmygod!" She stopped dead in her tracks, a hand covering her mouth.

"What is it?"

She didn't need to answer because as soon as I stepped round her, I could see for myself. The place had been trashed.

She shook her head. "It must have been burgled."

"Yeah, most likely."

But I already knew it wasn't that simple. In policeman mode, I examined the door to the flat and then each window in turn. There was no sign of a break-in, just telltale scratches on the locks indicating that someone who knew what he was doing had picked them.

A modest flat such as this was unlikely to excite the interest of a professional, so whoever broke in had to have been looking for something specific. My guess was that they'd searched methodically, only throwing things around when they were through to make it look like a burglary. Even if I hadn't recognised the cover-up signs, the flat-screen TV and stereo system still being in place disproved the burglary theory.

The who and why questions would have to wait. Kara was trembling, and right now she was my first priority. I righted the sofa and guided her towards it.

"Sit down and try to keep calm. Breathe deeply, get some air into your lungs, and you'll start to feel better." I rubbed her back gently with the palm of my hand. "We'll sort this mess out in a minute."

"Shouldn't we leave it as it is and call the police?"

"And tell them what?"

"Well, that Gordon's missing, someone's trashed his place, and—"

"Is there anything missing, or more to the point not missing, that strikes you straight away?"

She looked round and quickly caught on. "The television, they didn't take it." A vein pulsed in her temple. "But surely that's all the more reason to call the police. They might take Gordon's disappearance seriously now."

"I doubt it."

She turned huge eyes, full of worry, in my direction. "I don't understand."

Nor did I, but there was obviously more to Gordon Reed's disappearance than I'd previously thought.

"I suppose, if nothing's missing and you're convinced the police still won't look for Gordon, there isn't much point in calling them," Kara said with transparent reluctance. "I mean, what can they do about it, other than give it a crime number so that Gordon can claim on his insurance?"

"Well, what can I say? They're overworked." I instinctively defended my ex-colleagues, even though I knew she was right. A break-in, where nothing appeared to have been taken, wouldn't feature high on their list of priorities.

She shot me a look and stood up. "Come on, let's get this place straightened up. If Gordon comes back and sees it like this, he'll freak out."

Tidying up gave us the time to examine his papers as we put them back in order. We were methodical but didn't come across anything that indicated where Gordon might have got to, or why.

"Does he have a computer?" I asked.

"Yes, a laptop, but he always carries it with him."

"I know this sounds like a stupid question, but if he's so addicted to cyberspace I assume Pete and Sally have tried emailing him."

She rolled her eyes. "Well gee, Charlie, that would never have occurred to them." I said nothing and had to wait a long time for her apologetic smile. "Sorry. Yes, of course they have but they've not heard back."

I switched on the kettle, made us both coffee and carried it through to the neatened lounge. I passed a mug to Kara and sat beside her.

"There's something not right about all this," she said.

"Surely you can see that now?" I schooled my features into an impassive expression. "Come on, Charlie, stop looking all deep and mysterious and talk to me. What's happening here?"

"I honestly don't know." I shook my head, still fighting against being drawn into this mess. It was now patently obvious that Gordon had got involved in something he couldn't handle. Kara probably thought she owed it to Pete and Sally, or to Brett's memory, to try and figure out what it was. I tried to figure out some way to give them closure as I sipped at my coffee. Nothing blindingly obvious sprang to mind, and in the end I gave up.

"Come on." I drained my mug, reached for her hand and pulled her to her feet. "There's nothing else we can do here. Let's get back to Brighton."

She was quiet on the journey back. She hadn't mentioned again her crazy idea of me enrolling on one of Ultimate Marine's courses. That didn't mean she'd dropped the idea. I was willing to bet she was more determined than ever, having seen the state of Gordon's flat, to get me involved. I was the tiniest little bit curious about the whole shebang myself. Old habits die hard.

"Well," she said when Brighton Marina came into view. "There's only one thing for it, I suppose. I'll have to enrol on a course at Ultimate Marine. I'll do my best to pretend I don't know one end of a boat from another and see if I can get anything out of the people who work there."

"Kara," I said wearily, "if that's your way of trying to guilt trip me into signing up for a course, it ain't gonna work."

"No, Charlie, that wasn't it, really it wasn't. You've done more than enough already. Besides, I've already dropped you in it with your old colleagues by asking you to look into Ultimate's background. You've done enough."

"Don't worry about Slater. She's just firing blanks, like always. There's nothing she can do, other than drop by unannounced every so often in the misguided hope of embarrassing me."

"Well, perhaps, but still…like I just said, I'm not asking you to do anything else. It was stupid of me even to try."

"And you rushing off half-cocked to try and help your friends isn't?"

"That's up to me."

"No, Kara. We're in a relationship, and people committed to relationships don't make unilateral decisions."

Something in my tone obviously got through to her. "I know you're only thinking of me but, really, there's no danger."

"Grow up!" I was getting irritated now. This Gordon guy wasn't even related to her and yet she wanted to risk everything in some misguided attempt to find him. Women! Sometimes I had no idea what made them tick. No, make that all the time. "Apart from anything else, you've got two kids to consider."

"Like I could forget that."

I shot her a look. It was the first time I'd heard her say anything negative about having motherhood thrust upon her. It also made up my mind for me. If either of us got involved, it wasn't going to be Kara.

"All right," I said. "You win. I'll think about going."

"You will?" She flashed me a radiant smile. "I don't know what to say."

That was a first. "We're here," I said.

"So we are."

My attention was now taken up with easing the boat into the marina whilst Kara scurried off to deal with fenders and lines. She threw one to a figure standing on the dock but I didn't immediately look to see who it was.

"Good afternoon, Charlie," said a well-modulated voice as I stepped onto the dock with Gil. "Good day out?"

Gil went crazy, jumping all over my old boss. Chief Superintendent Gerry Monk laughed and scratched his ears. They were old friends. Monk was one of those people who pulled all sorts of strings behind all sorts of governmental departments. His being here now made me want to go as crazy as Gil, but for very different reasons. He'd got Kara and me involved in all sorts of shit when her sister went missing. I really wasn't up for any more of that.

Kara, on the other hand, appeared delighted to see him. "Mr. Monk," she said, stepping onto the pontoon as well and smiling at him. "What a lovely surprise."

"Kara, you're looking well, my dear."

"Thank you, and you."

I had yet to say a word. Monk wouldn't have missed my deafening silence, or my ferocious scowl. He and

Kara chatted a bit more but I kept out of it, waiting. Whatever Monk wanted, it wouldn't be good news. I wished Kara wasn't here. I was all for a quiet life, but the same couldn't be said for my impulsive partner.

"I wondered if I could have a few minutes of your time, Charlie," he said.

I felt a juvenile pleasure when he broke the silence between us first. Even so, whatever he wanted to talk about, I was pretty sure I wouldn't want to hear it. A man with his responsibilities wouldn't be here by chance in the middle of a working day. He wanted to speak to me about something specific and wouldn't go away until he did.

"Come aboard," I said, sighing.

Gil thought it was time for his constitutional but followed us back on board without making a fuss. So too did Kara, who would be far less easy to appease.

"Don't you have to go and collect the kids?" I asked, not wanting her involved in whatever Monk had to say and siding with him, which she inevitably would.

She glanced at her watch. "Damn, yes, I do." She reached for her phone. "I wonder if I could get Mum to—" She caught sight of my set expression and her words trailed off.

"How are your nephew and niece?" Monk asked.

Like he gives a damn.

"Adjusting well, thanks, Mr. Monk."

"And you? How have you taken to motherhood?"

Her smiled appeared a little strained. "I suppose I'm making the adjustment too. Not that I'm complaining.

They're lovely kids, not difficult to love, and it's hardly their fault that they find themselves in this position."

I said nothing, my gaze resting on Monk. If anyone was to blame it was him, the master of manipulation, and something told me he was up to his old tricks again.

Kara sighed. "Anyway, talking of which—"

"It was a pleasure seeing you again," Monk said, shaking her hand.

"And you." Still she lingered, clearly dying of curiosity. I placed my hand in the small of her back, encouraging her towards the door.

"I'll call you later," I said, kissing her before she stepped onto the pontoon.

She flashed me a warning glare. "Make sure you do."

Left alone with Monk, I felt no need to keep my temper under wraps.

"Lovely girl that," Monk remarked. "You're a lucky man, Charlie."

"To what do I owe the *pleasure*?" I asked, in no mood to discuss my private life with him.

"Good day out?"

Why did I get the impression that he knew precisely where we'd been? And why? "And that would concern you because…?" I poured us both a healthy slug of single malt. It was still only late afternoon but I had a feeling that at least one of us was going to need it.

"Well, as you know," he said, taking a sip of his drink and elegantly crossing his legs, "I'm employed in an advisory capacity wherever I'm needed."

"And which department is the fortunate recipient of your services this week?"

Monk's enigmatic expression was impossible to interpret. "I'm here about Gordon Reed," he said matter-of-factly.

SIX

"WHY AM I not surprised?" I asked rhetorically, knocking back my drink and helping myself to a refill.

"People connected to Kara seem to have a habit of going missing."

I glowered at him. "Don't drag her into this."

"Ah, I see." Monk stroked his chin and lowered his eyes but I still caught a flash of amusement in them. "I didn't realise it was quite that serious."

"What's your interest in Reed?"

"I can't tell you much about what I do nowadays," he said. "I'm attached to the Anti-Terrorist Squad, involved on the periphery of a delicate operation that's reaching a critical point."

"What's that got to do with Reed? From what I know of him, he's hardly terrorist material."

"No, he isn't. Quite the reverse, in fact. He's very patriotic and until recently he was putting that trait to good use on behalf of Her Majesty's government."

"Go on," I said, aware that he wouldn't leave until he'd told me as much as he thought I needed to know to get whatever it was he wanted from me.

"In spite of what the media would have you believe, our borders have become much more secure recently. It's not nearly so easy to get into the U.K. and claim asylum as it once was. The tunnel, ferry terminals and airports are all on the lookout for people who don't have a valid reason to be here. They have orders to turn them straight back again instead of giving them leave to plead their cases."

I harrumphed. "You could have fooled me."

"Yes, well, I can see that you might have a problem believing me, but it's true. France and our other European neighbours used to pass the problem on to us, but we cooperate with one another now. We put up more of a united front against the influx, so organisations with a vested interest in getting certain individuals into the country have had to become more inventive."

"Ultimate Marine," I said, almost to myself, but not so quietly that Monk didn't hear me.

"Glad to see you haven't lost your edge, Charlie."

"They're using their trips to France as cover to bring in illegals?"

"As perceptive as ever," he said, a satisfied half smile playing about his lips, like he thought I was already game for whatever plans he had for me. If he could have felt the anger currently churning in my gut, he might have had second thoughts.

"It explains why Slater paid me a visit. Presumably you had Ultimate's file flagged, and when Jimmy looked it up for me, it set warning bells off."

"Yes. Slater was asked why it was of interest to anyone in her department. We don't want to frighten them off, you see, by having anyone else bumbling about in their affairs. Slater was told to back off, but not why someone in a high place was ordering her to. I knew she wouldn't let it drop and wasn't surprised when she led us to you."

"Especially because you've been having me watched."

I could tell from the miniscule elevation of Monk's brows that I'd said something that surprised him. "What makes you say that?"

"You haven't been watching me?"

"Good lord, no."

"But you were watching Reed's flat in Cowes." How else would he know where we'd been today? "Shame you didn't catch whoever trashed it."

"Isn't it just." He sighed. "I so dislike sloppy workmanship, as you well know, but we didn't know Reed had gone missing at first. By the time we did, and had the brilliant idea of checking his home, someone had beaten us to it."

Which had to have been after Pete went there looking for him and before Monk got interested.

"Ultimate Marine is owned by an individual named Wayne Richards," Monk said.

"I thought he was just the manager."

"That's what he wants everyone to think, but it's not the case. He hides his ownership of the company in the usual way but likes to be hands-on. That way, he's in control." Monk shifted his position and held out his glass for a refill, the cheeky bastard. I obliged anyway. It was hard to deny Monk anything, which was one of the reasons why I wasn't particularly pleased to see him. "Thank you, Charlie. Anyway, it's hardly surprising, about Richards wanting to be hands-on, I mean, given the lucrative nature of his current trade."

This was where I was supposed to ask what that trade was so, naturally, I didn't oblige. Besides, it didn't take a genius to join up the dots between terrorists, tightened borders and away-days to France.

"Richards is an East Ender, parents both deceased," Monk told me, even though I hadn't asked. "He grew up on the streets and was in and out of trouble as a juvenile. Quite a brain on him, in spite of his lack of education, and he's not been collared for anything as an adult. That makes him feel invincible, of course, which is a weakness. He'll do absolutely anything for money and doesn't care who gets hurt in the crossfire."

"Sounds charming," I said offhandedly.

"Well, I wouldn't go that far but he *is* charismatic, and if he takes a liking to someone he's generous to a fault. He's been connected with all sorts of dodgy scams over the years, but boats have always been his thing." Monk's expression was speculative, as though trying to piece together Richards' character on the hoof. I knew better. He probably had everything there was to know about the man already engraved on his brain, right down to the side he dressed. He was always several steps ahead of the game. "I guess that when he was approached about bringing in illegals, he had the bright idea of starting Ultimate Marine, combining his love of boating with making pots of money."

"Who approached him?"

"A radical Islamic group already established in this country."

"And Gordon Reed was helping you to find out what Richards was doing?" I said, glowering.

"Oh, we knew what he was doing. We just didn't have enough proof. Gordon offered to do a little digging on our behalf." Monk's penetrative gaze rested on me. "But you know what he was doing too, don't you, Charlie? You'd figured out that something was off long before you got dragged into Gordon Reed's disappearance." When I didn't respond he pushed the issue. "How many people did you report that you saw leaving *Mistral*? Thirteen, was it, and three of them at least without life jackets?"

Ah, so Monk had made sure the papers hadn't reported the extra bodies. It explained a lot. "Are you suggesting that one of those additional people might have been Reed?"

"I doubt it. He went missing in France a good two weeks before *Mistral* went down. There's no reason to suppose he was on board."

Annoyingly I could follow his reasoning. "If Richards got wind of what Gordon was up to and had him done away with, he could easily have given his name as having been one of the crew on board *Mistral*. That way his disappearance would never be looked into."

"Precisely."

"What do you think actually happened to Gordon, and why haven't you told his relatives?" I asked Monk. "Do you know where he is now?"

"No, unfortunately not. The last I heard from him he was about to take a boat to France. He got a message to me saying that when he got back he hoped to have more information on Richards' activities."

"But he never came back?"

"No, but I don't believe that necessarily means he's met with an untimely end."

Well, that made one of us. "What have you done to trace him?"

"As much as we can, obviously, but our activities are limited. If we go in mob-handed, we'll reveal our presence, they'll close down the operation, and all the work we've put in to get close to the hub of things will have been for nothing."

"I should have thought that saving Gordon was more important than your operation. Illegal immigrants come into this country all the time. What difference will a few more make?"

Monk shot me a look that said don't-be-so-naïve. "If these were just ordinary immigrants then I'd agree with you."

Had Monk just deliberately let slip that these were fanatical young men, brainwashed into believing that whatever they did would be for the greater good of Allah? Impressionable youths with nothing to lose. Prime targets for those with wider agendas.

Monk was talking the lethal business of suicide bombers.

"Can't you just close Richards' operation down?" I asked.

Monk didn't dignify my inane question with a response.

"If he goes then someone else will take his place," I said for him.

"This is an election year, and immigration is an election-winning issue. Even middle England has roused itself from its customary stupor and is getting all hot under the collar about it. Joe Public is starting to see major cities where the white population is in the minority, certain parts of other cities becoming no-go areas if your face is the wrong colour and…" He waved one elegant hand in the air. "We Heell, I'm sure I don't need to spell it out. Suffice it to say that the government wants this ring exposed in a blaze of favourable publicity, proving that they're getting tough on the issue. That's where I come in."

"And Gordon Reed was doing your dirty work for you."

"He came to us," Monk said softly, "and we explained the dangers to him very precisely."

"Not precisely enough, if the state of his flat's anything to go by."

Monk looked briefly defeated. "I had hoped that he'd just gone to ground for a while."

"It could well mean that, I suppose." I took a moment to think it through. "If they had him, surely they'd extract any knowledge he possessed and wouldn't need to search his flat."

"Yes, there is that."

But we both knew things were seldom that simple.

"So, what's your next move in the battle to keep this green and pleasant land safe?"

"Fancy a busman's holiday, Charlie?" Monk asked languidly.

I put my glass down on the galley surface. I'd been holding it so tightly that I was surprised it hadn't cracked.

"I'll admire your nerve," I said, adopting the quiet

tone I used on the rare occasions when I was almost too angry to speak. "You recruited Kara's brother into an investigation that cost him his life." I waved an arm in the direction of the pontoon. "You saw for yourself just how tightly wound she still is. And yet you now tell me you were using her brother's best friend for your own purposes too." I expelled an angry breath. It came out as a low hiss. "Is there anything you won't stoop to?"

"Just so we're clear," he said, an edge to his voice. "We don't usually involve civilians in our business. We pointed out the dangers to Brett Webb when our paths crossed—"

"Your paths just happened to cross?" I elevated a single brow.

"Well, no, we did approach him, but he was well aware what he was getting himself into."

Somehow I doubted it, but there seemed little point in debating the issue. "And Gordon Reed?"

"He was keen to do it, Charlie."

I couldn't look at him. "I'll just bet he was! Boys don't grow up. We all harbour images of saving the world—until the bullets start flying and reality sets in."

"You don't have a very high opinion of me." He'd got that dead right. But strangely enough, I respected him too. We lived in a dirty world and someone had to be the gatekeeper. "I can quite understand why." He fixed me with a penetrating gaze. "Sometimes I don't like the things I have to do for queen and country myself, but there it is."

"Even so, I'm still not sure what you want from me."

"You're already involved in this thing, whether you

like it or not. You witnessed that explosion, which must have been traumatic in itself. Then this thing with Gordon Reed. There's a connection, and if you believe in karma, you've been dragged into it for a reason."

I rolled my eyes. "It's me you're talking to."

"I know you, Charlie. You wouldn't even have gone to Cowes to look over his flat if you weren't intrigued."

"I am *not* getting involved in anything that will threaten what security Kara's managed to create for herself and the kids."

"I've no intention of involving Kara."

"Involve me and she's in too."

"Yes, I can see that." He paused, rubbing one hand across his chin. "Does she have to know?"

"I haven't agreed to do anything, so there's nothing for her to know."

"Did I mention that Her Majesty pays well nowadays?"

I pretended not to be interested, but the figure he mentioned caused me to raise my eyes. They clearly were desperate, so whatever he wanted me to do couldn't possibly be risk-free—not at that price.

"Sign up for one of Ultimate's courses and just nose around a bit," he said, flapping one hand like it was no big deal. "See if you can find out when the next lot of immigrants will be coming in so we can set up a sting operation."

"Just like that?"

"You're a first-rate boater *and* trained in detective work."

I drilled him with a look. "Let me see if I've got

this right. You figure that if I go on a course, ask them in casual conversation when they plan to smuggle in their next load of illegals, they'll just tell me." I paced the length of the salon and punched my fist against the closed glass door to the cockpit so hard that it to rattled in its runners. Gil looked up and whined. "What a brilliant master plan," I added sarcastically, wondering if I'd done any damage to my knuckles.

"You're a clever sod. You'll pick up something and read between the lines. We need someone who knows about boats so he can concentrate on what he's there for, which is not learning how to tie a bowline. Unfortunately none of the limited number of people involved in this operation from my end qualify."

I could see signs of strain and frustration etched round his eyes. There was clearly more riding on this than he was letting on. Monk was under orders to deliver and living with such relentless pressure couldn't be a bundle of laughs.

"But you do, Charlie," he added softly. "So does Kara."

"Christ, you really are desperate, aren't you?"

"There's more riding on this than you could possibly know."

"All right," I said through tightly clenched teeth. "I'll do it."

"You will?" Monk looked momentarily surprised.

"You haven't left me with a lot of choice."

He stood and straightened the razor sharp creases in his trousers. "Thank you." He placed his empty glass on the galley surface. "I'll be in touch tomorrow about the details."

I sat there for a while after he'd gone, listening to the water gently lapping against the pontoon, thinking it through. There was no doubt in my mind, or in Monk's either I suspected, that Gordon Reed was already dead. The people he'd involved himself with couldn't afford any loose ends. There was something else though—something obvious about all this that I was missing—but hell if I could think what it might be. Trouble was, that made me more curious than ever.

It's a bitch having an inquisitive mind.

I turned in early and lay on my bed, staring at my mother's picture. I wondered what path my life would have taken if she'd lived—if I hadn't been walking beside her when someone blew her brains out, splattering them all over me in the process. The Mozart sonata she'd played in concert on that final night of her life drifted unbidden into my mind. I tried to tune it out but it obviously wasn't going anywhere—a sure sign I was stressed.

"What have I got myself into, Mum?" I asked aloud, taking my frustration out on my pillows as I thumped them into a comfortable nest.

SEVEN

WHEN KARA APPEARED at the boat in the morning, I wasn't surprised to see her.

"Good morning," I said, kissing her. "This is a pleasant surprise."

"I was worried about you."

I'm not a great one for smiling but that one was so transparent that it was worthy of a full-on grin.

"What?" she said.

"Nothing." I switched the kettle on. "Coffee?"

"Please." Kara doesn't do subtle and got straight down to business. "What did Monk want?"

She wandered round the salon, restlessly picking things up and putting them down again, not meeting my eye as I told her.

"So, not content with using my brother, he pulled Gordon into his scheming as well." She scowled. "This keeps getting better and better."

"He's one of the good guys," I pointed out.

She quirked a brow. "Is he?"

I stifled a smile. The girl was catching on.

"What?" she asked, eyeing me with deep suspicion.

I resisted the impulse to tell her I'd told her so. "Nothing."

"Charlie, is something wrong?"

"What, apart from Gordon being missing and Monk's fingerprints all over his disappearance?" I shrugged. "Isn't that enough to be going on with?"

I'd spent the night trying to arrange my thoughts into some sort of coherent order but was still unable to decide why Richards would want to destroy his own operation by having the cigarette boat deliberately run *Mistral*'s survivors down.

"More than enough," Kara said with feeling.

I barely heard her since the truth hit me like a runaway truck. It was so obvious that it should have dawned on me long before now. Richards wasn't the culprit. Someone else had figured out what was going on and had put a stop to it. I was willing to bet that Monk knew it, which was why he wanted me to sniff round Ultimate and try and find out who did it.

"What are you going to do?" Kara asked.

"Well," I said, reaching for her and pulling her into my arms. "Since you're here—"

"Charlie!"

"Yes." I glanced up from nuzzling her neck. "What's wrong?"

"I didn't come here for that."

"You didn't." I cocked my head to one side. "Where do you usually go?"

"Oh, I can't tell you that. It would dent your manly pride."

"Well, you know what they say about pride coming before a fall."

To demonstrate my point, I fell down the cabin steps

and into bed, where I told her I'd decided to go on the course.

"Oh, Charlie, thank you!" She flung her arms round my neck. "I know you're only doing it for me, and I really appreciate it."

"Just so we're clear, Miss Marple," I added, "that's as far as I'm prepared to involve myself. I'll pass on any information I obtain to Monk and then it's over to him."

"No one could ask more of you than that."

I had a feeling she was wrong about that.

My phone rang. I wasn't surprised to see Monk's name flash up on the screen. He probably wanted to make sure I hadn't had a change of heart. "I do have a condition, though," I told him.

"Name it."

"Keep Slater off my back. The moment she hears I've signed up with Ultimate Marine, and somehow I get the feeling she will find out, she'll be all over me. She knows people in important places are interested in their operation and is too ambitious to steer clear."

"I can't make that promise, Charlie."

That surprised me. Monk had the power to make anything happen, if he felt so inclined.

"Can't or won't?"

"If I show my face it will only increase her determination to get involved." It was the closest I'd ever heard him get to an apology. "We'll keep a distant eye on her, intervene if we have to, but it's probably better to leave her floundering in the dark."

I rolled my eyes. "Wonderful!"

"Perhaps she won't realise you're doing the course,"

Kara said when I hung up and relayed Monk's words to her. "It only goes on for four days and she must have more important things to worry about."

"Perhaps." But I didn't share her optimism.

"When is the next course due to start?" she asked.

"According to Monk, Ultimate have received a bit of adverse publicity since the accident with *Mistral.* Questions in the local press about the level of safety equipment on board, the proficiency of their crew, and so forth haven't made them flavour of the month."

"The usual witch hunt the press likes to drum up to sell papers."

"Right, and because of that they've had a couple of cancellations on the course starting next week."

"That's a bit of luck."

"My sentiments exactly," I said drolly.

"It will get it over and done with." She grinned. "Wish I could come with you."

"Don't even think about it!"

"Obviously you can't go under your real name."

"Monk has suggested Charlie Harris. He calls it a precaution, even though he doesn't think people on boat handling courses will be viewed with suspicion." I shrugged. "Wish I shared his optimism."

Later that morning the marina office called to say a package had been delivered by courier. I went over to collect it straight away. Kara and Gil tagged along. It contained a Visa card and driving licence in the name of Charles Harris, showing an address in Hove. There was also a substantial wad of bank notes. I raised my brows when I saw exactly how much.

"Out-of-pocket expenses," I told Kara. "And the address on the licence will check out if anyone looks into it."

"Monk must have been pretty sure you'd do this, to have got all this together so soon."

"So it seems."

"You can still change your mind."

No, I couldn't. "Not a word to Sally or Pete," I said, making sure she knew that I meant it. "The less they know, or even suspect, the better."

"I won't say anything."

We strolled back to the boat. "There'll be others on the course, I assume," Kara said. "Did Monk say what to tell them about yourself?"

"There's just one married couple booked in at present, so that still leaves one place that might or might not be filled before next Monday. I'm an entrepreneur, into this and that. I've done a little bit of boating in the past."

"That will cover the fact that you clearly know what you're doing, I suppose."

"Yes, I'm thinking of buying a boat of my own and getting into charters, so I need a qualification." I furled my brow as I thought about that. "Is it my imagination or am I being set up to get further involved?"

I posed that question to Monk when he stopped by again later in the day.

"Not at all, Charlie." His innocent protestations would have satisfied anyone who didn't know him as well as I did. "But a good cover story is always a wise precaution. Anyway, you've got a girlfriend who's madly into boats and she's pushing you into the charter game with stories about how lucrative it can be. Since you're always on the lookout for a way to combine business with pleasure, you've decided to dip a toe in the water and allow yourself to be convinced that it's a good idea."

"It seems to me that I'm being convinced to do a lot of things that definitely aren't good ideas." I scowled at Monk. "Anyway, being on the dodgy side of legal is hardly going to make a pro like Richards open up to me. That's even supposing I come into contact with him, which is unlikely."

"Well, if you do, perhaps mentioning that you're an old associate of Danny Baxter's might ease your path?"

"Who's Danny Baxter?"

"He was the skipper on *Mistral*."

"Oh." The sound of Baxter's panicked voice coming through the radio into *No Comment*'s wheelhouse flooded my brain. I was briefly back in a hellish situation that prevented me from thinking of more constructive objections to a scheme that was becoming more harebrained by the minute.

"He'd done more trips for Richards than any of his other freelancers and was up to his neck in the operation. Richards'll be up against it without him."

"Yeah, but I didn't know him, and that will become obvious the moment anyone asks me about him."

"We had him under observation."

"Not closely enough."

Monk conceded the point by inclining his head. "He was into all sorts of things before he started working virtually full time for Richards. He's always been involved with boats and was collared ten years ago in Southampton flogging knocked-off designer gear he'd brought in from the Continent on a private yacht. I can give you the full SP on the life and times of Danny Baxter. Best of all, since he had no family and was a bit of a loner, there's no one Richards can check you out with. Just drop into conversation that you knew him and he recommended Ultimate Marine when you said you were thinking of doing a Day Skipper course. See if it leads to anything."

I raised a brow. "What, mention Danny, just like that and a canny bastard like Richards won't smell the setup?" My scepticism must have been apparent, even to someone as thick-skinned as Monk.

"Oh, you did much riskier things when you were in the job and managed to pull them off convincingly."

"That was then."

"Come on, Charlie," Kara said, refilling my coffee mug and offering me an upbeat smile, "think positive."

"I am. That's what worries me."

"You might even learn something on this course that will come in useful. About boat handling, I mean," she added sweetly.

"You think I lack the ability to handle my boat?"

"I don't think there's anything lacking about your abilities," she said with a wicked grin, "but there's always room for improvement."

"Well, you know what they say, sweetheart, practice makes perfect."

"Precisely my point."

"Ahem." Monk seemed embarrassed to be caught

in the crossfire. "I suggest you get a lift to Hythe Marina early Monday morning. It wouldn't do to go on the Harley. It could be traced back to you if anyone saw it. Not that I anticipate anything like that happening, but it pays to cover all the bases."

"I'll drive you, Charlie," Kara said.

Monk nodded. "You can be the boat-crazy girlfriend, if you like," he said with a twinkle. "Just to add credence to Charlie's cover story."

"Oh, there's just one thing," I said, looking at Gil, who was getting impatient with all this talk when I ought to be concentrating on more important matters, like his constitutional.

"He can stay with us whilst you're gone," Kara said. "The kids will love that."

My eyes swivelled suspiciously between Monk and Kara. "You two seem to have it all figured out between you."

"Just trying to help," Kara said with an angelic smile.

THE DAY BEFORE the course was due to start I got a call from my stepbrother, Paul Flint. Although we'd never got on particularly well, we'd reached the stage where we not only talked to each other without being forcibly locked in the same room, but we also understood one another a lot better. Paul's mother had married my father a year to the day after my own mother's murder, which kind of explains why I hadn't taken to Paul first time round. Not that it was his fault, but I hadn't seen it that way at the time.

"What can I do for you?" I asked briskly.

"It's short notice, I know, but I wondered if you were free for dinner tonight. There's an idea I want to run past you."

"Well, I—"

"My treat, and bring Kara. She can play referee if our fragile truce shows signs of strain."

I chuckled. "She's certainly capable of doing that."

"Right then."

He named a time and restaurant, hanging up before I could think of a good reason to turn him down. When I rang Kara, her enthusiasm dispelled my doubts. She presented herself at the boat that evening in a strappy black dress that hugged her figure and got me thinking all sorts of inappropriate thoughts. I whistled and she gave me a twirl.

"You don't look too shabby yourself," she remarked, running her eyes up and down my body.

"Probably not up to Paul's sartorial standards."

She laughed. "Thank goodness for small mercies."

We took a cab to Paul's restaurant of choice. He was ahead of us, sitting at the bar nursing a cocktail. He was dressed flamboyantly in a shiny mauve suit with a lighter open necked shirt beneath it. I'd never seen him wear the same thing twice and all his gear was top of the range. He kissed Kara, with whom he got on really well, and shook my hand.

Over a decent meal we made small talk. "Anyway," he added, pausing to sip his wine. "The reason I got you here is to talk about the old man. It's his seventy-fifth in a couple of weeks."

I probably looked as guilty as I felt. I'd forgotten

all about my father's upcoming birthday. "You have something in mind?" I asked. "I doubt whether he'd want a fuss."

"Ah well now, little brother," Paul said. "That rather depends upon your definition of a fuss."

I eyed him with suspicion. "Come on then, you obviously have a master plan."

He winked at Kara, causing me to wonder what he was up to and whether Kara was in on it. "Funny you should say that."

"Am I being set up for something? Something else, that is," I added, sliding a sideways glance at Kara.

"Nothing would please the old man more than to see you and me in the same room together *not* trying to kill each other."

I nodded. "The idea is novel enough to tempt even him, I'll give you that. But his birthday's coming soon and I'm not sure I can get to Yorkshire."

"There's nothing to stop the two of them coming down here."

"Won't happen," I said, thinking of my ailing father and the way he'd been a few months ago when I last saw him. "They're entrenched in Yorkshire."

Paul had a plan, that much was obvious, but rather than come straight out and say what it was, he posed another question. "What present do you think would give him the most pleasure?"

I shook my head. "You've got me there."

"How about you and I giving him a little recital?"

I groaned.

"You told me once that your father hates you having stopped playing jazz piano," Kara said. "Do you play too, Paul?"

"Paul plays decent acoustic guitar, but we'd hardly ever jammed together."

"Then I think that's a great idea," Kara said. "I don't know your father, Charlie, but if he cared so much about you abandoning your career, I'm sure it would make him happy."

Kara and Paul started making plans for this birthday party, like it was a done deal.

"I hate to put a damper on things," I said when I could get a word in, "but I don't have anywhere to practise."

"Oh, don't worry about that, little brother. I recently inherited a baby grand piano. It now sits proudly in my front room, awaiting your magic touch."

I snorted, sitting back as the waiter removed the plate from in front of me. "Okay," I said sighing, aware I was beaten. "What are we going to play and when shall we practise?"

"The night is young," he said, signalling for the bill.

"No, not now." I needed time to get used to the idea. "Make it towards the end of next week." I'd be back from the Day Skipper course by then. "Liaise with Kara, if you haven't already," I said caustically.

"Charlie," she said, running a hand across my thigh. "Whatever are you suggesting?"

In a cab on the way back to the boat I asked her outright if she'd been in cahoots with Paul.

"Guilty as charged," she said, smiling seraphically. "Paul called me the other day to ask me what I thought.

We both agreed it was a good idea but that you'd probably need a little coercion."

Actually I didn't, not really. Slowly I was learning to play the piano just for pleasure, expecting nothing more from it and not caring too much if I was no longer the whiz I'd once been. If doing so gave my father pleasure, then who was I to complain?

BEFORE I KNEW it I was sitting in the passenger seat of Kara's VW on my way to enrol on the Day Skipper course. When we neared Hythe Marina I emerged from my reverie. "Stop the car here."

She pulled over. "Why? I can take you to the door."

"No, I'll walk the last bit. I don't want you or this distinctive yellow bubble of yours to be seen by anyone at Ultimate."

"Oh, okay." She put the car in neutral and turned to give me a hug. "Take care. Don't do anything rash."

I shot her a look. "Like delving into smuggling rings?"

She didn't smile. "Just be careful, Charlie."

"Always. And you can make yourself useful by checking on my boat if you're passing." She knew as much about boats as I did, wouldn't panic if the shore power flipped and would know what to do if the lines acquired creaks. "Take care of this old mutt too," I said, ruffling Gil's head as I extracted my bag from the floor beneath him.

"We'll be fine. Call me when you can, and we'll be here to pick you up in four days' time."

I bent to kiss her lips, making it quick in case anyone

connected with the course saw us. "Be good," I said, walking briskly away.

"Charlie." Her voice stopped me and I turned back, raising a questioning brow. "Thank you. I guess I've bullied you into this, but I want you to know I'm really grateful."

"How grateful?" I'm always at my most flippant when in danger of getting emotional.

"Ah, well." She tilted her head and offered me a smile. "I guess you'll just have to wait until you get back to find out."

"I'll hold you to that."

Her smiled widened. "I'm counting on it."

I waited for her to execute a neat three-point turn and head back the way we'd just come, waving until she was out of sight. Then, with a deep sigh, I picked up my bag and trudged to the marina.

I had no idea why I felt so uneasy about this whole escapade. What I did know was that feeling I used to get in the job when some minutely planned operation was about to go tits up had lodged itself in my brain and refused to budge.

EIGHT

As I WALKED into Ultimate Marine's small office, a man and woman pacing about inside it, presumably the married couple taking the course, turned expectant faces toward me.

"Are you on the Day Skipper course too?" The woman's gaze, at first fastened on my face, drifted the entire length of my body as she blatantly sized me up.

"For my sins."

She giggled like a schoolgirl. "And I'll bet they're many and various."

There was absolutely nothing I could say to that, so I said nothing.

"I'm Julie Price." She offered me her hand. "And this is my husband, Mike."

"Charlie Harris," I said, shaking with them both.

I put them in their mid-forties. He was short and stocky—someone who probably spent more time watching sport than actually playing it. She was shorter still, pretty in a faded sort of way, with shoulder-length blond hair, dark roots just beginning to emerge at her scalp, and eyes so pale that they were almost opaque.

"After all their recent bad publicity, you'd think that Ultimate would make the effort to be on time." Mike consulted his watch and tutted, beating an annoying tattoo with the toe on one shoe. "I wouldn't stay in business five minutes if I kept my clients waiting around like this."

"I think we're a bit early," I said. "It's not ten o'clock yet."

"Yes, but even so."

A tall, whip-thin guy of about thirty barged into the office. He had untidy hair, pointed features and uncoordinated limbs that looked too long for his body.

"Is this the Day Skipper course?" he asked.

"Yes." Julie spoke for us all. "Are you on it too?"

"Yeah, I'm Ronnie Gossard. I signed up at the last minute. I only got a place because they'd had a last-minute cancellation."

I refrained from telling him that they'd had several. Mike's complaints about timekeeping were reiterated. Ronnie caught my eye and shrugged. We made desultory conversation until, dead on ten o'clock, a guy dressed in the uniform I recognised from Ultimate's website entered the office and greeted us all in a broad cockney accent.

I knew who he was from the photos Monk had shown me and struggled to hide my surprise. Presumably the big white chief wouldn't conduct something as basic as a Day Skipper course—the lowest of lowly qualifications—himself, would he?

"I'm Wayne Richards, manager of this outfit. For the next four days I'll also be your best mate, and the hardest taskmaster you've ever had." He shook hands with each of us in turn.

I stood back whilst Julie did her gushing bit, wondering if I ought to read anything significant into the man getting his hands dirty. I tried to shake off the feeling that Monk had known in advance that Richards would be, literally, at the helm. I didn't see how that was possible, but it *was* Monk we were talking about.

Richards picked up Julie's bag. "Follow me, guys," he said, leaving the office and causing the pontoon to rock from the force of his steps as he strode down it.

I brought up the rear, still taking stock. Wayne Richards was about my height and build and appeared to keep himself in shape. There was no spare flesh on his frame—just taut, solid muscle. I knew he wasn't yet forty but, unlike me, he'd already parted company with most of his hair. What was left was clipped close to his skull, as though he was connected to the military, or at least wanted to be. There was a tattoo of a scorpion on the back of his left hand and the signs of more body art were peeking out at his nape. His squat nose looked as though it had been broken more than once and his eyes were too small for his face.

Even so, there was a suppressed energy about him and a certain down-to-earth charm that would, I imagined, make him good company in the right circumstances. It wasn't the first time I'd felt a connection with one of the bad guys. A number of the old lags I'd nicked over the years enjoyed more of my respect than some of my ex-colleagues ever would.

At the end of the pontoon a sparkling clean Birchwood TS37 with the name *Gladiator* emblazoned on its hull was moored on the hammerhead.

"This will be your home for the next four days."

Richards tossed Julie's bag onto the deck. "She's a fine boat to learn on and will take good care of you, provided you return the favour and respect her needs."

"Just like a few of the women I know," Ronnie said to me in an aside.

Richards showed us the footholds built into the hull and we climbed aboard one by one. The Birchwood was a fast twin-engine motor cruiser with a full-width aft cabin. The requirement for full headroom in that cabin made the deck higher than on average boats—hence the need for the footholds.

Mike and Julie were allocated the aft cabin, which had its own miniscule facilities. Ronnie and I could look forward to squeezing into the V bunks shaped into the forward hull. This boat was, like the rest of Ultimate's fleet, probably about ten years old but, at first glance, appeared to have been well maintained.

Once we'd settled in, Richards provided us with coffee in the main salon. He asked us all individually what we did for a living and what seafaring experience we had. Julie and Mike ran a bathroom supplies company. They had very little boating experience but, in the process of selling their business, were keen to get more involved with marine activities.

"Being responsible people, we wouldn't dream of buying a boat until we're suitably qualified," Julia said primly.

Noble aspirations, but I could have told them that it would take more than a four-day course to achieve that ambition.

Ronnie was in advertising. He didn't say in what capacity and no one asked. He admitted to having done a bit of sailing on a mate's yacht but had never tried motorboats before.

"I can't hack it in sailing boats. Far too much like hard work," he said cheerfully. "All that tacking, and ducking and diving to avoid getting your bloody head knocked off. Not to mention getting soaked to the skin on a regular basis. Nah, mate, if I'm gonna do any boating, I prefer to rely on something a little more substantial than the wind to get me where I wanna go."

"Then you've come to the right place," Wayne said. "I look forward to converting you to stink boats."

"Stink boats?" Julie looked confused.

"There's ongoing not-so-friendly rivalry between sail and motor," Wayne explained. "Sailboats have the right of way when they're actually under sail. If they tack in front of you, the rules of the sea dictate that you have to get out of their way. Motorboaters think they take advantage of that and deliberately cut us up because we cause unnecessary pollution."

"Ah, stink boats." Julie nodded, deadly serious. "I see what you mean now."

"Right, Charlie, your turn," Richards said. "What about you?"

I stuck to the script I'd agreed with Monk. "I'm an entrepreneur," I said with a vague wave of one hand. "I dabble in this and that. I go with my instincts and take a few risks."

"How exciting!" Julie's eyes glowed. "We must seem very dull by comparison."

I ignored her. What mattered was that I had the full

attention of both Wayne and Ronnie. And Ronnie concerned me. I'd connected with him already, but being a suspicious sod, I had a feeling that his last-minute enrolment on this course was more than just coincidence. Did Richards know who I was? Could that be why he was taking the course himself and had he planted Ronnie as my bunk mate to see what he could find out about me?

"My girlfriend is trying to persuade me to go into the charter boat business." I lifted my shoulders. "I'm always open to new ideas, so I thought I'd consider it. This is the first step to see whether or not I wanna go down that route."

"Have you done much boating?" Wayne asked.

"A little, but I've never had any formal training, just picked up a few pointers when I've been on other peoples' boats."

Ronnie nodded. "They say that's the cheapest way."

"Yeah, I've heard boat ownership likened to standing in a shower and tearing up fifty-pound notes," I said. "Which kind of makes you wonder why people do it."

Wayne chuckled. "Boat ownership seems glamorous but it's not for the fainthearted, or for those with light pockets, either." We all laughed and I felt some of the tension easing as we started to gel as a group. "It's my job over the next four days to convince you that taking to the water can be as rewarding as it is challenging."

Wayne outlined his own career, emphasising a long love affair with boats that had apparently started when he'd been a teenager. It culminated in the realisation of his dream when he'd set Ultimate Marine up. There was no mention of his love/hate relationship with the police.

Once he'd finished blowing his own trumpet, he went on to tell us what we could expect from the course, asking if any of us had experience in navigation.

"Isn't that what GPSs are for?" Ronnie asked.

"What do you do if it fails?"

"Fix it fast," he suggested to a mild chorus of chuckles.

"Well, there is another way, but I'll treat you gently and leave the matter of navigation until tomorrow. Okay, first things first. The rules of living aboard. I'm sure you know this already but I have to run through it anyway. No dark-soled shoes on deck." He looked round at our footwear and nodded, apparently satisfied with what he saw. "Remember you're not in a house. Although we're surrounded by water, the stuff we use for washing ourselves is precious. When it's gone someone has to fill the tank, which is not only laborious but also expensive because the water supplied by the marina is metered. So, short showers please and don't leave taps running like you would at home."

He paused to select a custard cream from the plate of biscuits in the middle of the table and dunked it in his tea. He removed it as it was on the point of disintegration and ate it in two bites.

"It's all common sense, but still needs to be said. Be careful about plugging too many things into the boat's electrical system or the power will flip."

"Where does the power come from?" Mike asked.

"When we're in the marina it comes from the shore. See that box there?" He pointed through the cabin window and we all dutifully nodded. "Once we're at sea, the engines will power the batteries but if we need more power than that, we do have a small generator on board. Okay, any questions so far?"

We all shook our heads.

"Right, now to the most important rule of all. Shipboard toilets, or heads as they're known—"

"Why is that?" Julie asked.

"Why is what?" Wayne flashed her an impatient half smile.

"Why are the toilets called heads? I've always wondered about that."

Wayne rubbed his chin. It was adorned with a least a couple days' worth of stubble, as though he'd dressed in a hurry and hadn't had time to shave. "It dates back to the days of sailing ships when the only place for the crew to relieve themselves was all the way forward on either side of the bowsprit, or the head of the boat. Some ships had grated platforms at the bow for sailors to use as a makeshift bathroom. Being situated so far forward the area was regularly cleansed by waves breaking over the bow, but it also left crew members vulnerable to being swept overboard." He laughed. "Perhaps that's why the officers' heads were located in the stern, on the poop deck."

We all chuckled.

"Ah yes, that makes sense now." Julie scribbled notes in the open pad on the table in front of her. "Thank you, Wayne. Carry on with what you were saying."

"Right." He looked rather taken aback to be given permission but soon got back into his stride. "Shipboard toilets. You need to understand that they're not nearly as robust as their land-based cousins and need to be treated gently at all times. They block easily and nothing, I repeat nothing, that you haven't eaten first goes down any of the heads on this boat," he added with a significant glance at Julie.

"Now then, safety. It's the duty of every skipper to ensure that those on board know where the safety equipment is stowed and how to use it in case of an emergency. Let's have a look at the lifejackets first." He walked us to the locker where the *Gladiator*'s supply was stowed and showed us how to put them on. "It's up to you as individuals whether or not your wear one all the time on board. I'd certainly recommend it."

Julie and Mike exchanged a glance and nodded in unison. "We definitely will," Julie said, a sanctimonious expression on her face as she tied the strings a little tighter around her small waist. "It's as well to be prepared."

"They're probably the type to carry umbrellas in a heat wave," Ronnie said to me in an undertone, spluttering behind his hand.

"I'll take my chances," I said, removing the life jacket I'd just tried on for size.

"Me too," Ronnie said.

Wayne didn't push us. He showed us the flares and the flare gun and explained their use as positioning beacons. He lifted the hatch to the engine room, pointed out the automatic fire extinguishers and promised us a more detailed tour later. Next came the fire extinguishers located in other parts of the boat. I glanced at their labels and noted that their servicing appeared to be up to date. The eight-man life raft was stowed beneath a bench seat on the flybridge. I tuned out whilst Richards explained how it would be deployed.

Having exhausted the subject of safety, Wayne walked us along the pontoon, instructing us on the best way to tie a boat up. He warned us against setting lines to a fixed length if the pontoon was solid. "What would happen then?"

"If they're set at high water, when the tide goes out the boat would be left suspended out of the water. The lines would be too short for it to go down with the tide," Ronnie said. "I've seen it happen."

"Exactly. How much boating did you say you've done?"

He chuckled. "Enough never to forget that. Who do you think the idiot was who set those springs too short?"

I was starting to like this bloke, even though I didn't entirely trust him.

We spent the next hour learning how to tie a bowline and how to affix fenders to the guardrail with a clove hitch. We took turns standing on the foredeck, trying to lasso the bollards on the pontoon with a looped rope. All basic stuff and I found it hard pretending not to know how to do these things, receiving more praise from Wayne than I was comfortable with. I'd have to make amends by screwing up when getting the boat through the lock gate.

Lunch on board was provided by an attractive young girl Wayne introduced as Gail. She was pleasant enough but said little or nothing that was of help to me.

I was assigned to the helm as we put to sea for the

first time. Wayne stood beside me on the flybridge, giving instructions. The others armed themselves with boat hooks to fend us off the concrete pilings inside the lock gate if I allowed the boat to drift too close to them.

I wasn't surprised when disaster struck before we'd even motored into the lock. A fender carefully tied on by Julie promptly fell off as soon as the boat left her mooring. It was one of the most common mistakes made by new boaters. Even so, her embarrassment was way over the top for a situation that most people would have simply laughed off. She'd wondered aloud how she could have tied such a simple knot wrong so many times that by the time we'd manoeuvred into the lock I was ready to throttle her.

"Nicely done, Charlie," Richards said. "But remember, when the gates open we'll be in a strong tidal current. You need to take the direction of the wind and tide into account and be prepared to make the necessary adjustments."

"Got it."

"Where's the wind coming from?"

I glanced at the direction of the flag on the boat immediately in front of us and answered him correctly. To make amends I deliberately fluffed it when he asked me if I was about to confront a wind over tide situation.

We spent the afternoon taking it in turns to be at the helm, holding the boat on a specific course. Julie and Mike agonised over the slightest variation and didn't seem to know how to relax. By the time we'd returned to Hythe, tied the boat up and hosed off the salt water,

I was more than ready for a drink. It was going to be a long four days.

Much to my surprise, Wayne joined us in the pub for dinner, even though he did keep excusing himself to make and receive calls on his mobile. He clearly didn't want to be overheard.

NINE

UP EARLY THE next morning, I eased myself quietly out of my cramped bunk, trying not to disturb Ronnie, grabbed a coffee and headed for the foredeck. Seated as far away from the cabin as possible so as not to be overheard, I dialled Kara's mobile. She'd be wondering how it was going but I hadn't been left alone for long enough the day before to call her.

"Charlie?" She answered on the second ring, still sounding half asleep.

"Hey, you taking good care of that mutt of mine?"

"Sure I am. He misses you and sends his love. He kept me company all night."

"Some dogs get all the luck."

Her voice purred down the line. "Your turn will come."

"That's good to know."

"How's it going?" Her tone lost all flirtatiousness as anxiety took over. "I was hoping you'd call last night."

"Ronnie—a last minute sign-up and my new best friend—stuck to me like glue." It had bothered me then, and still did now. Either the man had an innate sense of curiosity, given the barrage of questions he fired at me, or he was definitely a plant. "Didn't get a moment to myself."

"Poor baby." She paused. "Should we be worried about this Ronnie character?"

Nothing got past Kara. "Too early to say. He does seem awfully interested in me."

"Tell him you're spoken for."

I chuckled. "Richards is taking the course himself."

"Really? That's a bit of luck. What's he like?"

"Surprisingly easy to get along with, and good at what he does. He knows his stuff and doesn't take himself too seriously."

"What about the others?"

I made her laugh by telling her about Mike and Julie and their intense approach towards boating. "Fortunately their attitude is tempered by Ronnie. Whatever his true purpose for being here, at least he's laid back and easy company."

"Watch him, Charlie. Don't be fooled by his Mr. Congeniality act."

"Ah, the woman cares."

"Well, yes," she said, a smile in her voice. "I don't want to have to find someone else to go boating with."

"Damn it, she only wants me for my worldly goods."

"Glad we got that one straight."

"He has a head for the sauce," I told her, going back to the subject of Ronnie. "He really packed some away last night. Can't see him letting go like that if he's out to prise information from me."

"Even so."

"Not sure I can keep up with him when it comes to downing the beer."

"Met your match at last, have you?"

I let out a long-suffering sigh. "The things I do for Monk."

"And me. You're doing it for me, remember?"

"Just as long as *you* remember that. You owe me one, Miss Webb."

"And I always pay my debts," she said, her voice low, husky and full of promise.

"I have to go," I said, hearing the door to the aft deck open. "I'll be in touch again when I can."

"Take care, Charlie." She blew me a kiss and cut the connection.

Much to my surprise it was Ronnie who staggered on the deck, looking bleary-eyed but otherwise none the worse for wear. There was still no sign of Julie and Mike, which I thought strange. I had them pegged as the early-to-rise type.

"Morning," I said brightly. "You look like the morning after the night before."

"God, I feel it too. Don't let me do that again. I tend to get carried away sometimes."

I cocked a brow. "Really?"

"Well, what can I say? I'm a live-for-the-moment type of guy."

"Ready for breakfast?"

"Yeah, if you're offering to cook it." He yawned. "Don't know one end of a frying pan from the other myself."

"That's convenient."

He grinned. "Isn't it just."

I went below and rummaged in the fridge for the necessary ingredients.

"Nothing like a good fry-up to settle the old stomach." Ronnie patted his convex abdomen and winced. "Never again."

"Bet that's not the first time you've sworn off the sauce."

"You wouldn't get good odds." He grinned. "Wouldn't mind a pound for every time I've signed the pledge."

Julie and Mike emerged from their cabin, still rubbing sleep from their eyes. Ronnie glanced at them and turned a guffaw into a cough before they realised he was taking the piss. I could see what had set him off and didn't dare catch his eye. Our fellow students were dressed identically in navy cotton trousers, bright red T-shirts and their fluorescent orange life jackets.

"Something smells good," Mike said.

"Goodness," Julie added. "I can't believe we slept so long. Can I help?"

"No, it's okay, I can manage, thanks."

Even so, she insisted upon joining me in the galley. It wasn't big enough for us both, especially with her wearing a bulky life vest. She kept knocking into me, letting out high-pitched giggles and pretending I was the one at fault. She was seriously starting to get on my nerves.

Wayne arrived at exactly nine o'clock. We'd finished breakfast by then and Mike and Julie were washing up, diligently using just a few inches of our precious water supply to complete the task.

"Morning, campers," he said cheerfully. "Sleep well?"

That was Julie's cue to bang on about how late they'd slept, leaving me to cook breakfast. "Men shouldn't have to do anything in the kitchen," she said earnestly. "It doesn't seem right."

Wayne wisely refrained from comment. "Right," he said, when Julie finally ran out of words. "Gather round the chart table, guys. I'm a man of my word, so here we go." He brandished a pair of dividers in the air. "Navigation."

We spent the next hour manually plotting courses the old-fashioned way on paper charts. When Wayne was satisfied that we'd grasped the rudiments, we put to sea without the aid of the GPS.

"At any given time I'll be asking you to show me precisely where we are on the chart."

"Then be prepared to get comprehensively lost," Ronnie said. "I'm crap at directions."

"Remember," Wayne said, zipping his ever-present mobile into the outside pocket of his cargo pants, "don't put anything in your pockets unless they're secure. That especially applies to money. It might fall out when you bend over to pick up a rope."

Julie and Mike patted their pockets to make sure their possessions were safely stowed away.

"And don't forget, just because the weather's warm, once the boat's under way, it can seem a bit cool. Best prevent the loss of body heat from wherever it's most likely to escape." He grinned and pulled a woollen cap over his almost bald skull. "That's a no-brainer in my case." He glanced at me as I donned a baseball cap to keep my long hair out of my eyes. "Will that stay on?" he asked dubiously.

"Yeah, it should do."

Julie wasn't taking any chances and produced something that resembled a rain hat, with strings which she tied tightly under her chin.

"One more thing before we get going," Wayne said. "Just because it feels cool up there, the sun's still pretty strong. Being on a boat that's under way is a surefire way to get burned."

"Oh my goodness!" Julie dived into her cabin and returned clutching a tube of factor thirty sunblock. She smothered it over her face and arms, not completely rubbing it in and leaving traces of white cream over her chin. She offered the tube to the rest of us but only Mike took her up on it.

The day went okay. Wayne showed us how to identify way-points—something on land like a tall building or outcrop of cliff face, so that when we cut the engines we could use our landmarks to see if we were hypothetically dragging the anchor. We also tackled basic boat handling in the marina. Reversing, splitting the engines to make the boat spin around—the usual. We tried not to wince when Julie made a complete balls-up of reversing into a wide open space and finished up pointing in the wrong direction.

"God help them if they ever decide to go to the Med," Wayne said in an undertone to Ronnie and me. "All mooring is stern-to there. They don't have tides to worry about and can cram more boats in that way. Like bloody sardines, they are."

"Isn't it something to do with the left side of women's brains?" Ronnie asked. "They don't function like ours, which is why they can't be trusted to reverse cars, either."

"Don't let my girlfriend hear you say that," I warned.

The day ended the same as the previous one with us all descending upon the pub, desperate for a pint or two and for something to eat. Ronnie seemed to have forgotten that he'd signed the pledge and was the first to the bar. Wayne joined us and encouraged us to talk about ourselves. Ronnie told us a bit about his not-so-illustrious-sounding career in advertising, making everyone laugh at his self-deprecating insider account of the business.

"What it all comes down to," he said, "is making people think they can't live without something they've never heard of and have managed quite well without for years."

We all laughed, except Julie, who sniffed and pinched her features into a disapproving expression. "I think that's exploiting vulnerable people."

Ronnie ignored her and launched into an advertising joke—something about the pope and a Wonderloaf contract. He was a natural when it came to spinning yarns, and even Julie deigned to smile when he finally delivered the punch line. But every time the conversation veered toward Ronnie's personal life, he countered by cracking another adman joke, of which he appeared to have an endless supply. His prevarication bothered me.

When questioned about my own activities I hinted about the shady aspect of my fictional wheeling and dealing.

"What exactly did you say you do?" Wayne asked me when we found ourselves temporarily alone.

"I didn't, but since you ask, I suppose I'd describe myself as a facilitator." I leaned back and crossed one foot over my opposite thigh. "Ronnie reckons his adverts persuade people to buy things they didn't know they wanted. I, on the other hand, supply goods only in response to demand."

"What sort of goods?"

I shrugged. "What do you need?"

Wayne laughed. "Okay, I get the picture. Sorry I asked. I didn't mean to pry."

"Kate and I are thinking about relocating to the Costa del Sol and running a charter boat business from there."

"Things getting a bit hot for you, are they?"

"Well, you know what they say." I spread my hands. "A change is as good as a rest. Anyway, that's why I'm on this course." I hadn't mentioned my supposed relationship with Danny Baxter yet, still not sure about the wisdom of becoming more deeply entrenched. But, as always, my desire to get at the truth overrode all other considerations. "Actually, I was recommended to Ultimate Marine."

"Oh yeah, who by?"

"A mate of mine, Danny Baxter."

Wayne put his glass down so firmly that beer slopped over its rim. Deep suspicion—and something else, too—etched in his expression. Was it fear, anger or blind panic that he was trying to conceal?

"I had a pint with Danny a month or two back," I said, pretending not to notice Wayne's reaction. "When

I said I was thinking about doing some serious boating, he suggested this course. I gather he works for you. How's he doing?"

Wayne, appearing to be genuinely upset, took a moment to answer. "I'm sorry to tell you that he's dead."

"Dead?" It was my turn to look astounded. "You're kidding me."

He let out a long breath. "I wish I was."

"What happened?" I asked.

"My boat that went down a few weeks back. Danny was the skipper."

"Christ!" I ran a hand through my hair, my shocked reaction not altogether feigned. I sort of felt I really did know Danny, what with me being one of the last people to speak to him. My frustration at not being able to save anyone on board still kept me awake at night. "I had no idea."

"How did you know Danny anyway?" Wayne asked, reapplying himself to his pint.

"Oh, we did a bit of business together a few years back." I paused, looking him straight in the eye as I delivered my next words. "You know he did a stretch?"

"Yeah, he mentioned something about it."

"Well, if it hadn't been for me, he'd have been banged up for even longer. I got word that the filth had him in their sights and shifted a load of hot gear for him before they found it."

"That was you, was it?" Wayne cast me a speculative glance. "He mentioned that he owed a mate big time for helping him out."

I silently blessed Monk for the quality of his information. Wayne trusted me now. Not that I was sure how much good that would do me.

"Yeah well, we have to look out for each other in this game."

"You're not wrong." Wayne handed his empty glass to Ronnie, who'd just rejoined us and was offering to get us refills.

"What other boats do you have at Ultimate?" I asked Wayne, deliberately changing the subject.

"We have a forty-foot sailboat, which is currently out on a coastal skipper course, and a seventy-foot motorboat that does our luxury cruises to France."

"You still getting punters for those?"

"Yeah, like I told you yesterday, safety's our prime concern. There'll be a full investigation into *Mistral*'s accident and we'll cooperate with the authorities any way we can."

Wayne was being economical with the truth. Of course he'd offer his cooperation. How hard could that be? The boat wouldn't ever be recovered and there were no survivors to tell what actually occurred.

The conversation drifted onto other subjects until the lovely Gail appeared, presumably in response to one of the many calls Wayne made on his mobile, and they left together.

"Didn't realise they were a couple," Ronnie remarked. "Not that I blame him, mind. She's a class bit of totty."

No arguments from me on that one. But my mind didn't dwell upon Gail's rather obvious assets. Instead I was trying to figure out how best to get my hands on

Wayne's mobile. He kept it on him at all times and, to his credit, didn't make or receive calls whilst he was running the course. But once we hit dry land for the night it was seldom away from his ear. Although he moved well away from us whenever he spoke on it, I'd been close enough on a couple of occasions to tell from his body language that something heavy was about to go down. That phone was a potential gold mine. If I could nab it for a while, it could just make this whole debacle worthwhile.

My opportunity came the following afternoon when we were practising man-overboard drills. Each of us took a turn at the helm and, at a signal from Wayne, a bucket attached to a rope was thrown overboard. He then shouted "Man overboard," which was the driver's cue to turn the boat in a wide circle known as a Williamson turn. The trick was to bring it back alongside the bucket, without running over the damned thing and killing the unfortunate swimmer with the propellers. Once the engines were in idle, the crew fished out the bucket with a boat hook.

I was the last one to take the controls, by which time I had a plan, of sorts. I'd only get one shot at it and needed to time it perfectly. When the "Man overboard" cry sounded, I threw the throttles forward instead of easing back, and pushed the boat into far too tight a turn, causing everyone on the flybridge to topple over. This produced cries of alarm from Julie and Mike and rather more colourful language from Ronnie. With Wayne standing right next to me, I made sure I fell on top of him, failing to allow for the explosion of pain as the side of my head made contact with the console.

I didn't need to pretend to be dazed and was slow to move off him. In the chaos I unzipped his outside pocket and grabbed his phone, pulling the zip back only halfway to make it look as though it had opened by itself in the melee.

As soon as I rolled away from him, Wayne grabbed the wheel and stopped the boat from spinning out of control. I took advantage of his distraction, shoved his phone into my own pocket and remained sitting on the deck, clutching my head.

"Bloody hell!" Ronnie said, picking himself up and rubbing his backside, on which he'd landed rather heavily. "You got a death wish or something?"

Julie and Mike had been seated together behind the helm position. He'd cannoned into his wife when the boat shot forward, pinning her against the fibreglass bulkhead.

"Are you all right, darling?" Mike eased himself away from Julie and helped her to sit up.

"Sorry, everyone," I said sheepishly. "I guess I got a bit carried away there."

"Is everyone okay?" Wayne asked, once he'd regained control of the boat. Mumbled responses confirmed that everyone was. "You were doing a bit too well on this course anyway," Wayne said to me. "It was about time you screwed up. Hey, you're bleeding."

I brought my hand away from my forehead. It was splattered with blood, presenting me with a perfect excuse to go below. "Yeah, I'm just a bit dazed. I'd best go and clean up. Just give me a moment."

"Sure. Take all the time you need."

As soon as I got below I hastily blotted the scrape on my forehead and then scrolled through Wayne's phone. No names were attached to the numbers in the memory—just initials. I jotted them down as quickly as I could and then made a note of the most recent numbers called. There was one in particular on both the called and received list that was obviously important. After all the trouble I'd gone to, I fervently hoped it wasn't something as innocuous as Gail's mobile. No, come to think of it, it couldn't be because it was prefixed with the code for France.

I'd almost finished extracting all the information when a cursory tap at the door preceded it opening. Julie stuck her head in.

"I say, Charlie, are you decent?" She giggled. "Not that it matters if you're not. I've seen it all before, you know. Do you need help? I'm pretty good at first aid."

She didn't wait for an answer but moved right into the cabin and closed the door behind her. I only just managed to hide my notebook and Wayne's phone under my pillow before she joined me.

She looked round the confined space with interest. "Gosh, you and Ronnie are snug in here, aren't you? I didn't realise what luxury Mike and I are living in by comparison." She insisted upon applying salve to my forehead, telling me to be brave because it was going to sting. "You should wear your life jacket, you know. It would have protected you during that fall."

"Yeah, perhaps you're right. Thanks, Julie." I felt the engines slowing and wondered what was wrong now. "We'd best get back to the flybridge."

"Only if you're sure you don't need to lie down."

I'd never been surer of anything. When Julie wasn't looking I quickly slipped Wayne's phone into my pocket and ushered her from the cabin, keen to know why we were stopping. We climbed the steps to the flybridge to discover everyone on their hands and knees. I didn't need to ask what they were searching for. Damn, I'd been hoping it would take Wayne longer to miss his phone and that I'd be able to drop it on the deck somewhere before he even noticed it was gone.

"What's up?" I asked.

"Wayne lost his mobile when we crash-landed," Ronnie said, grinning.

"He obviously didn't practise what he preaches and zip it up securely," Mike said.

"It's never happened before." Wayne's muffled voice emerged from behind the area of seating he was searching. "I thought that zip was strong enough to survive a nuclear blast but I was obviously wrong." He straightened himself up, looking anxious.

"Well, there's cheap clothing for you, mate," Ronnie said.

"Less of the cheap, if you don't mind. This gear cost me an arm and a bloody leg."

"Yeah, but it's all made in China nowadays, no matter what label they stick on it."

"Well, the phone has to be here somewhere," I said. Nothing could fall overboard from the flybridge because it was completely closed in. "Why doesn't one of us keep watch and the rest take a section of the deck each? I'm sure we'll find it quicker if we go about it methodically."

"Good idea," Wayne said. "Ronnie, take the helm, if you don't mind. Julie, you take the starboard forward quarter, Mike the after and Charlie and I will split the port side."

"You've got it," I said, getting down on my hands and knees and diligently starting to search all the nooks and crannies in my assigned area.

I wondered where to drop the phone so that it wouldn't focus attention on me. My section of the cramped deck bordered the one Julie was searching. I sensed Wayne wasn't altogether convinced his zip had let him down. If the phone was found anywhere near me it would arouse suspicion because I was the one who'd fallen on top of him. He considered Julie to be as harmlessly annoying as the rest of us. If she discovered his precious phone he'd never suspect her of anything underhand. But how to get it into her area without anyone noticing?

Inspiration struck. The console housing the navigation equipment was solid but had a recessed area about six inches high off the deck protecting the screws holding it in place from the elements. The boat was moving at just a few knots, which was actually more uncomfortable than when moving on the plane. I waited until we hit a wave that rocked us sideways, momentarily distracting everyone's attention away from the search. I slipped the phone under the console recess, giving it a hard shove in Julie's direction. Then I turned my back and started searching the area behind me, not wanting to have anything to do with the phone's discovery.

"Can I see something moving about under there?" Mike asked.

We all watched as Julie felt under the console and triumphantly produced the phone.

"Thanks." Wayne checked that it was still working and carefully zipped it into another pocket. "Funny," he said, frowning, "we looked under there first off."

"Well, mate," Ronnie said. "You of all people ought to know how things move about on boats, especially when crashing through a swell."

"Yeah, I suppose you're right." But he didn't sound convinced.

We had sandwiches and Wayne told us we'd be practising night passages that evening.

"Damn," Ronnie said. "There goes valuable drinking time."

"At least your liver'll be grateful for the respite," I told him.

The night manoeuvres went okay and we were all getting tired by the time Wayne told us to turn for home, navigating by the buoys that marked the channel in Southampton water. He let us go several miles out of our way—an error which I saw Ronnie make but kept stum about—before telling him that he should have turned to starboard at the last marker.

"Put your foot down, Ronnie," I said, once we were back on course. "They'll be closing in half an hour."

"Christ, is that the time!" Ronnie was now a man on

a mission. He opened up the throttles, we radioed ahead to get the lock gates opened and were back in Hythe in record time. Amazing what you could do with a little motivation.

Ronnie suggested an immediate adjournment to the local and I said I'd catch him up, making out that I needed to visit the head first. What I actually needed was to retrieve my notebook with the numbers in it that I'd copied from Wayne's phone. I didn't feel comfortable leaving it where it was and wanted it on my person—safely zipped away, obviously. I was perturbed that it wasn't where I'd left it. It was still under my pillow but the cover was facedown, and I was pretty sure I'd left it the other way up. Still, if Ronnie had accidentally moved it, it wouldn't mean anything to him. At least, I hoped it wouldn't. I pocketed the book, shaking my head, as I tried to convince myself I must be mistaken.

The next morning Wayne interviewed us all individually. He went back over what we'd learned, asking if there was anything that required clarification.

"No, I think it's all pretty much in my head," I said.

"I was impressed with your skills, dodgy Williamson's turns notwithstanding."

"Thanks."

"If you're serious about getting into the charter business then you might want to consider doing a few runs to France for me. With your girlfriend, if you like."

"Well, I dunno," I said dubiously. "I hadn't thought about working for someone else. I like to be the one in control of any jobs I do."

"Yeah, I know what you mean, but you have to get experience somehow."

"I hear what you're saying, but don't I need more than a Day Skipper qualification to work on a boat full of paying customers?"

He waved the question aside. "That can always be sorted. Anyway, you'd only be crewing. I'd have a professional skipper in charge."

I felt mildly elated. For the first time he was suggesting doing something illegal, like fudging my qualifications so I could work for him.

"Well, thanks, I'll give it some thought." Not that I had any intention of going through with it. Monk could find another chump to do his dirty work.

"You'd be doing me a big favour. I'm a couple of skippers down right now and I've got trips booked. I don't want to let the punters down, especially not after what happened to *Mistral*."

"Yeah, I can understand that."

He sighed. "I have to put it behind me and try to be positive. If I let it get to me and word gets round about *Ultimate* being unreliable, I'll be well and truly fucked."

"Yes, but I'm not sure I'm the answer to your problems. Besides, I've got some stuff going on right now." I spread my hands in what-am-I-supposed-to-do sort of gesture. "You know how it is."

"Sure but this is a good opportunity that might lead to greater things."

"How?"

"Just think about it, Charlie, but don't take too long." Wayne clearly had no intention of expanding upon his cryptic comment and I didn't push him. He gave me his mobile number and took a note of mine. "I'll get in touch with you about it in a week or two and, if you're interested I'll tell you more about the opportunities available then."

TEN

AFTER A LATE lunch on the final day, Wayne told us our collective boat handling skills had reached the required standard. In a little ceremony presided over by Gail, each of us was awarded the Day Skipper qualification. We sipped at the warm fizzy wine that was produced to fuel the celebration, congratulating one another, laughing about the cock-ups we'd made along the way. Wayne encouraged us to return to Ultimate when we were ready to move on to the next stage.

"What is the next stage?" Julie could be relied upon to ask the questions Wayne wanted to hear.

"Coastal skipper. It's a five-day course, basically more of the same, except more intensive," Wayne said. "You need to satisfy me that you can skipper a motor cruiser on a coastal passage by day and night and are able to handle the situation if the weather turns adverse."

"Sounds a bit too focused for my blood," Ronnie said. "To say nothing about the amount of time we'd have to spend away from the boozer."

"Well, I think it's a sensible suggestion and we'll certainly give it some thought." Julie's head bobbed emphatically.

"That's the spirit," Wayne said, pulling a doomed face at Ronnie and me.

We milled about a bit, cracking corny jokes that weren't funny but which everyone laughed at a little too intently. A gaggle of strangers who'd briefly bonded over a shared activity, our thoughts were already drifting toward the real world as we prepared to go our separate ways. We made vague promises to keep in touch, as you did in such situations, but I was pretty sure we'd never see one another again.

Wayne shot off as soon as Julie and Mike had made their protracted goodbyes. He'd been edgy all day, making me wonder if something had gone wrong with the latest trip to France. Then I got annoyed with myself for even thinking about it. I'd done all I ever would to help Monk combat world terrorism.

I made excuses to hang about in the office with Gail until Ronnie finally left as well. I watched his lanky form stroll away, surprised when he didn't turn into the car park. Presumably he lived close enough to walk here. I didn't actually know for sure because he hadn't mentioned anything about his domestic arrangements. Beneath his life-and-soul-of-the-party front he was either a very private individual or, more likely, just plain lonely. It didn't make sense for him to have been on the course for more sinister reasons, but my thoughts still kept veering in that direction.

Cautious by nature, I didn't want any of them to encounter Kara and her distinctive yellow car. I gave Ronnie five minutes to get clear of the marina before I called her, knowing she'd be hanging about a few minutes' drive away. Then I said goodbye to Gail and set out to meet Kara halfway. As soon as she saw me she waved, pulled over and let Gil out of the back. I whistled and he ran full pelt straight at me, almost knocking me over when he placed his front paws on my chest.

"Hello, mate," I said, rubbing his big head with the back of my hand, sending him into a near-delirious state. "Been behaving yourself?"

Woof! He rubbed himself round my legs, tail wagging furiously. *Woof, woof.*

"That's all right then." I waited for him to water the nearest lamppost from several different angles. About to let him back in the car, I flinched when a heavy hand fell on my shoulder.

"Who the hell..." I turned sharply and found myself face-to-face with Ronnie.

"Bit jumpy, aren't we?" he said, grinning.

"Sorry, mate." I unclenched my fist and paused until my heart rate returned to something approximating normal. "I thought you'd gone."

"So did I, but my lift's let me down." His gaze fell on Kara sitting behind the wheel of her car, and his grin widened. "Don't suppose you and the lovely lady are going anywhere near London?"

"London? Didn't realise you lived in town."

"I don't. I just scrape a humble living there and have to be in at sparrow's fart tomorrow. I thought I'd go up now and spend the night with a mate. There's some sort of crisis on and a deadline looming."

"The place fell apart without you?"

"It seems that some idiot shot an arrow in the air.

Now they're all running round like headless chickens because they can't find a target to catch it with." He shrugged his skinny shoulders. "Still, it makes me feel needed."

"So, how were you planning on getting to London?"

"A colleague was supposed to collect me."

"Sorry," I said, "but we're going in the opposite direction."

"Oh well, the train'll just have to take the strain." He backed warily away from Gil, who was diligently checking out the hems of his jeans.

"Charlie," Kara said, eyeing Ronnie speculatively. She must have realised who he was from my description. The last thing I needed was her plying Ronnie with loaded questions about Ultimate Marine. "Perhaps we could..."

I shot her a warning glare, causing her words to stall. "Don't forget we have an appointment we can't break."

"Hi." Ronnie gave Gil a wide berth and leaned into the open window to check Kara out at closer quarters. He turned back to flash me an approving grin. "I'm Ronnie, newly qualified Day Skipper at your service. And since this oaf clearly has no intention of introducing—" He thrust a hand toward a now rather bemused-looking Kara and she instinctively shook it.

"This is Kate," I said, throwing another significant look Kara's way.

"Pleased to meet you, Kate." Ronnie didn't appear to be in a hurry to let her hand go. "And where has Charlie been hiding you away?"

"Well, I—"

I'd never seen Kara lost for words before, but then she'd probably never had to deal with anyone quite as charismatic as Ronnie. In no way could he be described as physically attractive, but his larger-than-life personally more than compensated for any defects of nature. I could see that Kara was already taken with him.

"Ever considered starring in a TV commercial, Kate?"

I groaned. "Is that the best line you can come up with?"

Ronnie gave me the finger behind his back. "Ignore him, Kate."

"Well, er…no, I can't actually say that I have."

"You'd be a natural. I can just picture you, running through a field of flowers with that lovely hair flowing behind you." He waved his arms about, warming to his theme. "The shampoo you advertised would fly off the shelves. You'll have to let me—"

Ronnie's phone rang, breaking into his enthusiastic pitch. He excused himself, took the call, spoke briefly and hung up.

"Saved by the bell, Charlie," he said, grinning broadly. "That was my lift. He got held up but he'll be here in a minute." He sighed. "Looks like I won't have time to entice the lovely Kate into my clutches. But be warned," he added, wagging a bony finger at me, "I don't play fair."

"See you, Ronnie," I said, shaking his hand and my head simultaneously. I let Gil into the back of Kara's car, threw my bag on the floor and climbed into the passenger seat.

"What an interesting man," Kara said. We both watched him trot over to a Saab that had just turned into the road, his legs so long and skinny I was surprised they could support his weight.

"Yeah, he's a real joker." I kissed her cheek. "Hey, gorgeous, everything all right?"

"Hey yourself." She smiled at me, still looking rather bemused by the encounter with Ronnie, as well she might. "What was that all about, anyway?"

"Oh, that was just Ronnie being Ronnie. And you got away lightly. I've just had to put up with four days of nonstop adman jokes."

"Poor baby!"

"Yeah, you owe me, don't forget." I waggled my brows at her, resting my hand on her thigh as she lifted the indicator and pulled away from the curb. "But I thought he'd already left."

His unexpected return niggled away at me. I was probably just being paranoid, but then I'd be a fool not to treat everything to do with Ultimate Marine with extreme caution. The possibility that someone had looked at the phone numbers I borrowed from Wayne's phone still rankled. Then there was the lack of information Ronnie had supplied about himself. He'd come back on a phony-sounding pretext, seen Kara and her car and made a serious attempt to chat her up. The combination worried me but I didn't let Kara see that. To start with, I didn't have a clue where Ronnie fit into Wayne Richards' organisation, or if he even did. Besides, if I voiced suspicions about Ronnie, there was no way she wouldn't let that information slip to Monk. Then he'd put pressure on me to check him out.

"Why did you refer to me as Kate back there?" she asked.

"No particular reason," I said casually. "I didn't want any of them to see you, but I don't suppose it matters."

"No, I'm sure it doesn't." She reached a T-junction, waited for a break in the traffic and pulled out in front of a people-mover travelling below the speed limit. She glanced at me and frowned. "What happened to your head?"

"Injured in the line of duty."

"It looks nasty."

"Yeah, I'm very weak and need plenty of tender loving care."

She chuckled. "Don't push your luck."

As she drove us back to Brighton I filled her in on all that had happened during the course. Well, most of it. I deliberately didn't mention Wayne's offer of a job, especially since it included her. If she heard about that, she'd never let up until I agreed to do it. I *would* agree if I thought it would get us anywhere, but I honestly couldn't see how it would help us find Gordon Reed.

"Have you heard from Monk?" I asked her.

"Yes, I reported everything you told me on the phone. He's going to come to the boat tomorrow morning to talk to you in person."

I rolled my eyes, in resignation rather than surprise. "No rest for the wicked."

"Oh, I don't know. There's a long time between now and tomorrow," she said, a promissory sparkle in her eye.

"Got any plans on how to fill it?"

"Oh, plenty. Trust me, I don't disappoint."

My hand resumed its favourite place on her thigh. "Let me be the judge of that."

"Oh, absolutely."

The *No Comment* was just as I'd left her, only tidier. There were clean sheets on my bed, the furniture sparkled, the cabin smelled of a fresh fragrance, and she'd obviously started preparing dinner before she'd left to pick me up.

"I could get used to this," I said, nodding to show I appreciated her efforts.

"It was the least I could do, given you only went on that course to please me."

"Come on," I said. "Let's take the monster for a run on the beach and then I'll buy you a pre-dinner drink."

"Okay then, what are we waiting for?"

She grabbed Gil's leash and leapt onto the pontoon. Gil and I followed at a more leisurely pace and the three of us headed for the beach on the eastern perimeter of the marina. Gil chased the sticks we threw until he started to flag, at which point we turned back and I steered her toward the Weatherspoon's pub on the fringe of the marina.

I found us a small table that overlooked the dilapidated floating Chinese restaurant and bought her a large vodka and tonic. She made immediate inroads into her drink but I sipped more slowly at my Guinness. Gil lay spread-eagled on the floor between us, tongue lolling stupidly from the side of his mouth, temporarily worn out after his run on the beach. Kara fiddled with a spare drip mat on the table in front of her and repeated all the questions I'd already answered in the car. She appeared to place great stock by the list of telephone numbers I'd stolen from Wayne's phone.

"Don't get too excited about that," I warned. "I was hopeful at first, but think about it. If they're significant you can bet your life they'll be to pay-as-you-go mobiles, completely untraceable."

"Perhaps, but we ought to have a try." She took another sip of her drink, learned toward me, inhaled deeply and finally asked the question I'd been anticipating. "So, Charlie, what's our next step?" She opened her eyes very wide and fastened her gaze on my face. She seemed touchingly full of faith in my abilities, which made me feel like a bastard for holding out on her.

"I don't see that there's anything else we can do," I said, shrugging. "That course produced precisely zero. We're no better off now than we were before I wasted four days attending it."

"So you think we should give up looking for Gordon?"

I leaned back, crossing one foot across my thigh, hopefully looking more relaxed than I felt. "I understand your need to know what's happened to your brother's friend, Kara, but I just don't see how we can hope to find him if he doesn't want to be found."

"Yes, but—"

"It's pretty easy for people to disappear if they really want to."

"But surely they leave a trace." She sat up straighter, as though she'd just had a light-bulb moment. "What about credit cards? If he uses his, couldn't we trace his location from that?"

"The credit card companies would never tell you anything. Data Protection."

"Yes, but the police could find out."

"Only if they had a valid reason to look, which they don't."

"Won't Monk be able to take a peek?"

"Probably. He seems to have access to just about anything he wants." I paused. "I'm betting that he already has and that Gordon's cards haven't been used."

"Because he's dead?"

"Or not in a position to use them."

"Held against his will then?"

"It's a possibility." I paused to take a swig of my drink. "We can either ask Monk if he's checked, or wait for his next statement to arrive at his flat."

She wrinkled her nose, less than impressed with a suggestion that required more inaction. "Charlie." She spoke my name with a heavy sigh. "If Monk comes up with any suggested ways to continue the search, will you still help?"

No longer looking at me, Kara probably knew her request was unreasonable.

"If he does come up with something, he has people much better qualified to pursue this than I am."

"Yes, I suppose so." Her gaze now rested on the tabletop. "I'm sorry I got you into this and endangered you." She reached out and touched the cut on the side of my head, delicately tracing its contour with her finger.

"It's nothing." I took a draught of my beer to avoid

looking at her. Right now she seemed so vulnerable that I had trouble not blurting out Wayne's job offer, just to give her hope. I picked up my glass, reminding myself that it would be false hope, only making matters worse in the long run. "Kara, sometimes we don't get the answers we want, no matter how many different ways we phrase the questions. In that situation, the only thing to do is let go."

"But you don't always practise what you preach, do you?" I didn't respond because I knew where she was going with this. "I mean, you've never given up on finding your mother's killer."

"That was below the belt," I said quietly.

"Sorry, I shouldn't have said that. Ignore me, I'm just frustrated." She bit her lower lip and then looked directly at me. "Tell me honestly, do you think Gordon's still alive?"

"I don't have a clue."

That didn't prevent me from assuming he was dead, but I wouldn't tell her something she wasn't ready to deal with. She gazed off into the distance, watching a sailboat make a pig's ear of coming in to moor.

"I've made up my mind, Charlie."

"I don't like the sound of that." I bestowed one of my carefully rationed smiles on her, attempting to lighten the mood. She appeared immune to my clumsy charm offensive.

"I've decided that you're right," she said. "There's nothing more you can do and it's not fair of me to ask you to. *But*, if Monk thinks there's anything I can help with, anything at all that might shed light on what's happened to Brett's friend, then I'm going to do it and nothing you say will stop me."

Knowing when I'm beaten, I didn't even try to change her mind. But I'd move heaven and earth to stop Monk putting wildly inappropriate ideas into her head. He owed me at least that much.

We finished our drinks and went back to the boat. Kara produced an extremely good meal and we chatted about inconsequential things as we ate it, not once referring to the subject uppermost in both our minds. We washed the food down with two bottles of wine, both of us in need of the temporary solace that only comes from a bottle.

MONK PRESENTED HIMSELF at the boat in the middle of the following morning. I reiterated my account of my activities and described my fellow students in the meticulous detail I knew he'd expect.

"Ronnie Gossard's a real character," I told him. "The joker of the pack. He kept us all amused and probably saved me from throttling Julie Price."

He smiled in sympathetic understanding. "They were all kosher students, then?"

I hesitated for half a beat too long before saying I thought they were. "Who else would be planting ringers?" But I already knew the answer to my own question. Whoever sabotaged *Mistral* might be trying another way to get at Wayne's organisation.

"I haven't the foggiest idea," Monk said airily. "I was merely asking."

Like hell you were.

"What did you make of Richards?" Monk asked.

"I liked him. He wouldn't be everyone's cup of tea," I added, thinking of Julie's thinly disguised disapproval, "but he's easygoing, plainspoken and a bloody good sailor. If he's using Ultimate Marine as a cover—"

"Which we know he is," Kara said, stirring the coffee aggressively in the French press and pushing down the plunger.

"Well then, he's certainly combining business with pleasure because there's no hiding the type of passion he has for the sea."

"Yes, that's what I've heard about him." Monk paused to thank Kara for the coffee she handed him. "Did you pick up anything that might be useful for our investigation?" I shook my head emphatically, which produced a shrug from Monk. "Well, it was a long shot to ever suppose you would."

"I did manage to get this for you, though." I produced the list of telephone numbers which I hadn't yet mentioned.

"What the—" His expression visibly brightened as he examined the list and realised what it was. "The numbers from Richards' mobile? How did you get it?"

I gave him an abbreviated account.

"Well done, Charlie! This could be the break we've been waiting for."

"I doubt it. They wouldn't be stupid enough to use traceable phones."

"Possibly not, but—"

My own phone rang. Because I was so absorbed with my conversation with Monk, I did something I'd never normally do and answered it without first checking to see who was calling. I regretted the mistake as soon as I recognised the caller's voice.

"Charlie," Wayne said. "Have I caught you at a bad time?"

"Wayne, I wasn't expecting to hear from you so soon." I realised the additional damage I'd done only when it was too late to rectify the situation. I'd stupidly blurted out Wayne's name and no one on board the *No Comment* was even pretending not to listen to my end of the conversation. I considered stepping out onto the deck but that would only strengthen Monk's conviction that there was something I wasn't telling him. Better to try and front it out. "What can I do for you?"

"I know I said I wouldn't pressure you, mate, but I just wanted to let you know I've now got definite confirmation that our trip to France is on for next Friday, a week today. I've got other stuff going on at the same time so I'm really up shit street. If you could help me out, you and your girlfriend that is, I'd owe you one."

"Sounds like we could name our price," I said flippantly.

Wayne chuckled. "I'd show my gratitude by adding to your bank account, if that's what you mean. Oh no, I forgot that you don't place much stock by banks." There was nothing I could say to that. I'd got a bit carried away in my role as a dodgy dealer in all commodities, no questions asked, and implied I had cash in need of a kosher home. "I'll pay you in readies but I need to know if you're in or not, and I need to know soon."

"You'll be skippering?"

"Yeah, how about it?"

"No, I don't think so. I'd like to help you out but my girlfriend's got something else on then." I could feel said girlfriend's eyes boring into my profile like lasers. "Sorry, mate."

"Well look, think about it, talk it over with her and let me know by Monday. If she can't make it but you can that would still help."

"Sure, I'll call you Monday but don't get your hopes up." I broke the connection, aware of two pairs of eyes burning accusingly into my skull.

"What was that all about, Charlie?" Monk asked mildly.

"Yes, Charlie, what?" Kara added. "And why do I get the feeling that it somehow involved me?"

"All right, all right!" I threw up my hands, capitulating because I'd boxed myself into a corner. "You might as well know that Richards offered you and me the opportunity to crew on their next trip to France but I turned him down."

Kara jumped up and stood over me, hands on hips, looking ready to inflict serious bodily injury. "I don't believe you just said that! You've been presented with a golden opportunity for us to do a bit of digging and didn't think it was even worth mentioning?" She exhaled though tightly pursed lips, her cheeks flushed with anger. "Charlie, how could you? You know how much this matters to me."

"Yeah, but what matters more is keeping you safe."

"This isn't the Dark Ages. I can look after myself."

"Not against that mob you couldn't."

"How do you know?" she asked. "You've only met Richards and you said you liked him."

"I've liked a lot of the villains I've nicked. That doesn't change the fact that they're ruthless individuals if they think they've been crossed."

"I still think we should do it."

"And I don't, so that ends the discussion." I headed toward the wheelhouse, intent upon putting distance between us.

"Surely that's for Kara to decide for herself," Monk said.

"It is and I intend to do it."

I hitched a brow. "In between the school run?"

She paused, but only for a second or two. "I can make arrangements for the children."

"And possibly deprive them of the only stability they now have in their lives."

"You're not being fair," she said, looking close to tears.

"Nor are you." I turned to her and softened my tone. "I know you miss your brother," I said, placing my hands gently on her shoulders, "but this won't bring him back." I paused for a beat. "Nothing will."

"We can't stop now," she said, switching from aggression to a soft, persuasive tone, her eyes flooding. "We're so close to getting somewhere, Wayne trusts you and wants you involved."

"It wouldn't get us anywhere. These people are too professional to let us anywhere near to the hub of their operation."

"You don't know that. Besides, if they have illegals

on board a small boat how can we avoid coming into contact with them?"

She had a point. "They have more reason to keep stum than Wayne does," I pointed out, refusing to be swayed by something as inconsequential as logic.

"I think perhaps I'll leave you two to discuss this in private," Monk said, standing. "Do let me know what you decide."

"There's nothing to decide," I told him, infuriated by his obvious belief that Kara would eventually talk me round.

ELEVEN

THE ARGUMENT ENDED an hour later. A loaded silence took its place as Kara packed her bags.

"You're going home?" I was surprised by her easy capitulation. I thought she'd at least take me to bed and work on my more vulnerable places before admitting defeat.

"I have to pick the kids up. They're with Mum."

I pulled her toward me. She let me but her body was rigid and unresponsive in my arms. "Kara, I'm sorry, I know you're upset but there really isn't anything else we can do about Gordon."

She dropped her head against my shoulder and let out a prolonged sigh. "Yeah, you're probably right." She reached up and kissed me lightly on the lips. "I appreciate what you've done, but I guess that's it."

"We can't right all the world's wrongs."

"I know." She shook her head. "But I just feel so useless."

"Come on, you're gonna be late."

Gil and I walked her to her car but there was tension between us. I didn't want us to part on a sour note but had no idea what to say to make things better. In the end I said nothing, waved her away and promised to ring. I didn't regret our exclusive relationship but was still making the adjustment. It wasn't always easy.

I kept busy after Kara left, catching up on the jobs that had accumulated in my absence. I was preoccupied, unable to shake off the feeling that I'd let Kara down. I'd delivered on all my promises but even I was disappointed with the results. And, I'll admit, just the tiniest bit curious. The boat felt empty without Kara. I wasn't happy that we'd parted on the back of a civilized disagreement, so when my phone rang I welcomed the distraction.

"Hey, little brother."

"Paul, how's it going?"

"We're on for the big birthday bash."

"What, Dad's agreed to come down?" I could hear the surprise in my own voice. I hadn't taken Paul's suggestion seriously. "How did you swing that?"

"I didn't. I just suggested it to Mum and she worked on him."

I chuckled. "She probably thinks the earth's stopped rotating if you told her that we're now bosom buddies."

"Steady on, dear. I wouldn't exactly say that."

"No, probably best not get carried away."

"Anyway, I didn't say anything about that. Best to surprise the old dears, don't you think?"

"All right. When's it to be?"

"Two weeks Sunday at mine. Bring Harry and the fragrant Kara."

"She comes with baggage."

"Ah, of course. The more kids the merrier—I think."

"You sure? Sticky fingers all over your prized possessions."

"I'll risk it. Anyway, we don't have much time to practise our party piece. Pop round now if you're not busy and we'll work something out."

I waited for objections—for excuses—to kick in. Nothing happened so I agreed and set off for Paul's flat. Gil was sprawled on the foredeck, enjoying the mild weather. I didn't have the heart to move him so left him where he was. I still felt bad about the accusations I'd thrown at Dad regarding my mother's murder the last time we'd met. If hearing me play jazz again helped to repair the rift between us then who was I to throw a spanner in the works?

He answered the bell as soon as I rang it and buzzed me through the lobby. When I reached the second floor he was already standing in his open doorway.

"Afternoon," he said, nodding but not offering me his hand. "Glad you could make it."

"And I'm glad you didn't give me any time to think about it."

He chuckled. "Why do you think that was?"

"Point taken." I walked past him into his flat. I'd not been in there before and was surprised by his taste. Beautifully decorated, it displayed none of the flamboyance Paul favoured in his clothing and extrovert personality. "Nice," I said, nodding my approval as I stepped into the large, minimally furnished lounge. "Plenty of space."

"Just as well, given that," he said, waving toward

the baby grand piano. "Wouldn't have been room for it otherwise."

I threw my biking jacket over the back of a chair and sat at the piano. Paul's acoustic guitar rested on a stand next to it. I flexed my fingers and ran them over the keys, not surprised to find the piano was perfectly tuned.

"Nice," I said again. "What did you have in mind to wow the old folks with?"

"How about 'Hit That Jive Jack'? If it was good enough for Nat then it's good enough for us."

"Nat played it with his trio," I reminded him, referring to Nat King Cole's excellent rendition in the early forties. "There's only two of us."

"That makes it fair then."

Laughing, I tried a few bars. Paul joined in and we each experimented with variations, taking it in turns to solo. Before I knew it over an hour had gone by.

"That ought to do it," I said, standing up and stretching. "We don't need to be concert perfect."

"Are you sure about that?"

I wasn't sure about anything, other than that it was suddenly ridiculously important to me that I regain my father's respect. Something told me he wasn't long for this world and I'd always regret it if I didn't try to make amends.

"Let me know the arrangements for the party," I said, reaching for my jacket. "And if you need me to do anything."

"God, you don't think I'm doing this myself, do you?" He shuddered. "I'll get caterers."

"Ah, I see."

"I've invited Hal and Gloria and a few of Dad's old cronies."

"Good idea." I zipped my jacket. "Right then, I'm off."

I rode back to the marina deep in thought, parked the bike in the multi-story and nipped into the supermarket for a few supplies. Gil's barks reached me when I was still some distance away. I wondered what had wound him up but wasn't left in ignorance for long. As I approached the *No Comment*, I discovered Chief Inspector Slater, Jimmy Taylor and two uniforms standing on the pontoon. What the hell…

"Chief Inspector, to what do I owe the pleasure?" I nodded toward Taylor. "Afternoon, Jimmy."

"Charlie," he said, shuffling his feet and avoiding all eye contact.

"We have a warrant to search this boat, Charlie," Slater said, unable to keep a gloating expression off her face.

"What?" For once she'd actually surprised me. "What the hell for?"

"We have reason to believe there are stolen goods on board."

I stared at her, my jaw hanging open. "You have got to be joking."

"Do I look like I'm laughing?"

I shrugged. With Slater it was difficult to tell.

"Now, you know how these things work, so I trust you're going to give us your full cooperation." Without waiting for an answer, she moved toward the boat.

"Not in those shoes."

Slater was an attractive woman and she knew it. Good figure, nice face, shame about the nonexistent personality. One of her few physical defects, and one which I knew she was self-conscious about, was her rather thick ankles. She wore high heels to try and disguise them and I achieved a puerile sort of satisfaction from drawing attention to her phobia.

"We've been through this before," I said. "Take them off if you really intend to go through with this charade."

Jimmy was struggling to hide a smile. Slater scowled as she removed her shoes, nodding to the two uniformed constables to do the same.

"Right," she said, stretching the word out until it was longer than a sentence. "Happy now?"

"Delirious."

"Let's start out here," she said to the uniforms. She stood barefoot in the cockpit, staring thoughtfully down at the teak. "What's under there?" She nodded toward the hatch that housed the steering gear. I told her what she'd find. She clearly wasn't about to take my word for it and indicated to one of the plods to lift the cover.

"Hold on," I said. "I'll do that. There's nothing in there except pipes, but if you lot go rooting about you could knock something out of kilter."

"Fair enough."

Slater smiled like she knew something I didn't. I wasn't unduly concerned because I knew she was on a fool's errand. What did bother me was the magistrate's willingness to issue a warrant in the first place. I was a well-respected ex-copper, and the decision wouldn't have been taken without a compelling reason.

And that reason was now staring me squarely in the face. I could only watch, dumfounded, as Jimmy donned a pair of latex gloves and carefully removed a wrapped parcel from the depths of the hatch space.

"Well, well." Slater's eyes glistened with malicious satisfaction as the haul was placed on the deck. "What do we have here?"

"I've no idea," I said, my mind reeling with a thousand possibilities, none of them pleasant.

"Oh, come on, Charlie, you can do better than that." When I didn't dignify that with an answer, she pressed ahead. "So you don't recognise this mystery package that's concealed on your boat?"

"Nope. I recognise the towel it's wrapped in. They're the type I use in my engine room to wipe up oil. I buy them in bulk from the chandlery and store them in that locker over there." I pointed to the one behind her, immediately under the barbeque, still trying to figure who'd set me up like this. And why.

"Open it," Slater said to Jimmy, nodding toward the package.

He did so. Inside was a freezer bag full of jewellery. I'd recovered from my initial shock now, and if the whole episode hadn't been so serious I'd have been tempted to laugh. I'd never seen a more obvious plant. Only problem was, Slater would never recognise it for what it was. She lacked the necessary imagination to see beyond the obvious. Too anxious to score points over me, she wouldn't even consider the possibility that I had nothing to do with this.

"Nothing to say, Hunter?"

"It's Mr. Hunter to you, Chief Inspector."

"Nothing to say, *Mr.* Hunter?"

I leaned against the guardrail, endeavouring to appear unconcerned. "Nothing springs to mind."

"We need to search the rest of this boat," she said, addressing this comment to the uniforms. "Remove the dog please, *sir.*"

"Nope. He lives here and stays put. But don't worry," I added, winking at her, "he's been fed." I led the way into the salon. "And the same goes as before. You can search cupboards and lockers if you must, but hatches or anything in the engine room, I need to be there for safety reasons."

I could see that she wanted to argue the toss but eventually decided against it. She'd got what she'd come for. In fact, she'd gone straight to it because whoever put it there had told her where to look. She probably knew there was nothing else to find but insisted on searching because she was enjoying herself. And because she thought it would humiliate me. She wasn't wrong about that but I was buggered if I'd let it show.

Jimmy and the uniforms searched with more care than they'd ever shown for a suspect's possessions when I'd been on the job. Even finding that jewellery clearly hadn't persuaded Jimmy that I was guilty of anything and he took pains to put everything back as neatly as he'd found it. Slater watched his every move, her expression gleeful when we moved into my cabin and

Jimmy searched my underwear drawer, unearthing a half-empty packet of condoms beneath a stack of clean boxers.

"Glad to see you're practising safe sex, Charlie," she said cheerfully. "Your lady friend not here right now?"

I didn't bother to answer her.

"That's it, ma'am," Jimmy said, crouched double as he emerged from the confined space of the engine room with me immediately behind him. "There's nothing else to interest us."

"That's okay. We already have more than enough to charge this *gentleman* with receiving stolen goods." She attempted to place her hand on my arm to guide me off the boat.

I shook her off, laughing aloud as I did so. "Dream on."

"What's that supposed to mean?"

"You figure it out."

"Hope you haven't got a hot date tonight. You're coming with us and might be gone a while."

I whistled to Gil. "Your concern is touching but quite unnecessary. She knows I'm worth waiting for."

"The dog's not coming to the station."

"If you intend to drag this pantomime out then I need to get him looked after." I waited until they'd all left the boat, locked it up and followed them onto the pontoon.

Gil bounded ahead of me, growling every time Slater stepped too close to him, making her nervous. *That's my dog.* They waited whilst Gil and I detoured along the next pontoon. Sue and Pete, fellow live-aboards, greeted me warmly.

"Do me a favour," I said, indicating Gil, who was wagging madly at them. "I have to go out for a while and he needs company."

"No problem," Sue said, jumping onto the pontoon and kissing Gil and me in that order. They often looked after the mutt, and Gil and Sue had an ongoing love affair. "His food in the usual place, is it?"

"Yeah, thanks." Sue had a key to the *No Comment*. "I might be late."

"No worries, Gil and I will have a great time."

I wished I could have said the same thing.

Talk about *déjà-vu*. Slater had pulled me in once before about something and nothing. On that occasion she'd walked me through the squad room at the end of a shift when it was almost full of my old colleagues. She tried the same thing again today but didn't get the reaction she craved. No one gave me the cold shoulder, which clearly bugged her. By the time we got to the interview room her earlier elation at discovering that jewellery had turned to irritation. I wondered if she was already having doubts about her so-called collar.

"Do you want a brief?" Slater asked, sitting herself next to Jimmy, opposite me.

"Am I under arrest?"

"Not yet."

"Then I don't."

"Okay, you know the drill." She switched on a tape recorder, went through the usual rigmarole of introducing all the people present, and got straight down to business. "What can you tell me about the stolen jewellery which we discovered today on your boat, the *No Comment*?"

"Never saw it before, guv."

"Come on!" She leaned toward me, almost salivating. "How did that stuff get to be on your boat? Who passed it to you?"

I half smiled at her. "It's one of life's mysteries."

"Help me out here, Charlie. What would you think if you were in my position?"

"In other words, you want me to do your job for you." I paused. "Again."

"If I were you, I'd stop trying to be a smart-arse and spare a thought for the dicey situation you're in."

She had a point. "All I know," I said, sighing, "is that someone put a load of stolen stuff on my boat and then told you where to find it."

She twisted her lips into a parody of a smile. "Well, you would say that, wouldn't you?"

I let out a long breath and tried to remain patient, never my strong point when dealing with idiots. "If I *was* you, I'd be asking myself why I found the stuff in the first place I looked. What are the odds on that happening?"

"Nice try, Charlie, but I've got you squarely in the frame for this one."

"Really, Jill?" I quirked a brow. "Let's see if I've got this right. I'm an experienced ex-detective but, for reasons unexplained, I've decided to swap sides. So I receive stolen goods but am daft enough to hide them in plain sight." I paused, waiting to see if she'd realise how impossible that sounded. When her expression didn't alter, it became obvious that she was so anxious to pin this thing on me that the tiny logical part of her brain was closed for business today.

"It's how it looks from where I'm sitting, given the overwhelming evidence."

"Okay, let's look at your so-called evidence. I'm stupid enough to put the stuff in an insecure part of my boat that anyone could have access to but haven't left fingerprints on the freezer bag?" I waggled my brows at her. "Sorry to ruin your day but you know you won't find my prints, don't you, because whoever tipped you off put the stuff there themselves."

"Why would they do that?"

Good question. "That's what I intend to find out."

Slater switched the tape off and despatched Jimmy for coffee. I wondered why but wasn't left in ignorance for long.

"Tell me what you know about Ultimate Marine," she said.

So that was what this was really all about and she didn't want Jimmy to know. It should have occurred to me sooner. She knew something big was going on at Ultimate and was desperate to pin her star to that particular mast. She had a knack for being in the right place at the right time, getting herself noticed and enhancing her career prospects by claiming credit that was seldom due to her.

"What makes you think I know anything?"

"Oh, Charlie, you always did underestimate my intelligence."

"That would be difficult," I muttered.

She frowned and carried on. "First off you witness one of their boats blowing up in the channel and then you take yourself off and enrol on one of their courses using a false name." She twisted a pen between her fingers and smiled at me. It was a tight, vindictive smile that reminded me a bit of a cat stalking its prey. "Why would you do that? That's what I've been asking myself."

"Really?" I offered her a lazy half smile. "I'm flattered that I still figure so prominently in your thought processes."

Colour spread across her cheeks. "You really think you're something, don't you?"

I winked at her. "Just telling it like it is."

Flippancy disguised my annoyance. She must have had me under surveillance—how else could she have known about the course and my enrolling under a false name? I wasn't at all happy about that but didn't want to give her the satisfaction of seeing that she'd riled me. I amused myself by baiting her instead.

"About that course," she said, her lips pulled so taut that I could barely make out the words that struggled past them. "You were about to tell me why you went on it."

I wasn't but I let that pass. "Nothing to tell," I said, shrugging. "I was doing a favour for a mate, that's all."

"What mate? Name?"

"None of your business."

Jimmy returned, the tape was turned back on and there was no further mention of Ultimate.

"That jewellery was stolen from a shop in the Lanes

a couple of days ago," she said, switching tack again. "What do you say about that?"

"Not guilty, guv," I said, causing Jimmy's lips to quirk. "You know where I was a couple of days ago. Do you want me to remind you?" I almost smiled at the ease with which I'd outmanoeuvred her. At first just irritating, Slater constantly banging on about what had to be the clumsiest fit-up known to man, had started to rankle. I had to get this over with so I could find out exactly who was behind it all and, more to the point, why.

But I already had a bloody good idea. I drained the last of my coffee from its plastic cup and stood. "Look, I'm done here and if you're not arresting me I'll be off."

"Sit down, Mr. Hunter," Slater said authoritatively.

I ignored her and remained standing. "Or what?"

"You're not under arrest now but you soon might be if you don't cooperate."

I moved towards the door. "You know where to find me if you ever get enough to bring me in."

She sighed. "Go with him, Taylor, and make sure he leaves the premises."

"Who tipped her the wink, Jimmy?" I asked, as soon as we were clear of Slater. "About the jewellery being on the boat I mean?"

"No idea, mate. Sorry."

"It doesn't matter." I shrugged, affecting casualness. "Nothing will come of it."

"Who would do that to you, Charlie? Who's got it in for you or hates you enough to try and fit you up like that?"

I sauntered through the squad room beside Jimmy

and waved to some of my old mates. Once we were out of earshot of everyone else, I addressed Jimmy's question. "Take your pick out of the hundreds of old lags I nicked. Now that I'm out of the game perhaps they think it's payback time."

But I didn't believe that for a moment. This was personal. Someone was playing games with me, trying to manipulate me into doing something I didn't want to do.

And it didn't take a rocket scientist to work out who that someone had to be.

TWELVE

I COLLECTED GIL but refused Sue's offer to join her and Pete for dinner. I'd be poor company. Besides, I had some thinking to do, which meant Gil got a long walk. I ruminate best when I'm on the move and because I had a lot to deliberate about I was halfway to Hove—or that's how it seemed—before I was calm enough to return to the boat and put in hand the arrangements I'd been coerced into making.

In spite of having all the resources of a desperate government at his disposal, it seemed I was the best option Monk had to get close to Richards' operation. I didn't want to think about what that said for the country's security forces. I should have known better than to assume he'd calmly accept my decision not to go on that trip to France. Even so, it hadn't occurred to me that he might plant stolen stuff on my boat and then tip Slater the wink. He must be under a hell of a lot of pressure to stoop so low, but there was no doubt in my mind that he was the culprit. He knew about the animosity between the two of us, something I'd thoughtfully reminded him about when I asked him to keep Slater off my back.

I kicked at a loose drinks can, furious at the way he'd played me, aware that he wouldn't back off. If this didn't work, he'd figure out some other way to keep me in the loop. Perhaps I should be flattered by his faith in me. Slater couldn't actually nick me for receiving stolen goods. Even she must realise that a good lawyer would drive a coach and horses through her evidence, such as it was. But, given leave to please herself, she could have me formally arrested, even if she subsequently dropped the charges. Inflicting a little humiliation on yours truly and leaving a question mark hanging over my honesty would be time well invested from her perspective. I'd survive the experience but if Emily got wind of it… well, it didn't bear thinking about.

I scowled into the distance, cursing Monk and his interfering ways. As soon as I was back on board I poured myself a very large Jack Daniels and drank it in two swallows. The fiery liquid burned the back of my throat as it trickled down so I added a couple of token ice cubes to the refill and sat with Gil in the cockpit, staring up at the stars. Vince Guaraldi's boogie woogie piano music spilling from the speakers gradually soothed me.

I stayed there for a long time, working my way through the bottle. Absently rubbing Gil's ears with my toe, I wondered what it was that Monk wasn't telling me. I wondered too if there was any way to get out of the mess with Slater without going on the trip to France. I didn't come up with any answers on either count. So how could I go without taking Kara? Every instinct I possessed told me it would be dangerous and I'd rather keep her out of it.

Unfortunately my contrary instincts also told me I

didn't have a prayer of achieving that objective. I sighed, having long ago learned to accept the inevitable. Anyway, I supposed I owed her the chance to find what the so-called experts call closure regarding her brother's friend and, with it, acceptance that her brother was gone from her life forever.

But that didn't mean I had to be happy about it.

I kept busy all day Sunday, catching up with some maintenance jobs I'd neglected. By the time I'd done them all, I'd run out of reasons to procrastinate. I pulled my phone out of my pocket and dialled Kara's number. I hoped she wouldn't answer but people always seem to pick up when you don't want them to. Kara was no exception. She sounded surprised to hear my voice but not unpleasantly so.

"Charlie, I didn't expect you to call so soon."

What she was saying was that she hadn't expected me to be the first one to call after our disagreement.

"How were the lonely hearts?" I asked her. She ran an online agency for singles and had had some sort of event for them the night before. I'd forgotten the details.

"It went well, I think. It was fully subscribed, anyway, and I know of at least two dates that have resulted from it."

"That's good then."

There was an awkward silence, which she broke first. "How's Gil?"

"Missing you."

"Oh, and you know that for a fact, do you? He told you, I suppose."

"Of course, I'm very intuitive when it comes to his feelings."

She laughed. "Why are you calling, Charlie? Has something happened?"

I had no intention of telling her about my little run-in with the law. Desperate as she was to go on that trip, if she knew my hand was being forced, something told me her conscience would baulk. I'd then finish up persuading *her* that we had to do it. Sometimes you had to take life's little vicissitudes on the chin until an opportunity presented itself to redress the balance.

"Well," I said after a protracted pause. "I've been thinking about things and have decided that you're probably right."

"Right about what?" she asked, a note of suspicion creeping into her voice.

"I suppose it won't do any harm to go on that trip to France if you're still up for it. Just to see if anything obvious occurs along the way that will help us find Gordon."

She gasped. "Are you serious? You're not winding me up, are you?"

I pretended to be affronted. "I'm prepared to give up my valuable time to help you and you think it's a wind-up." I huffed down the phone. "Thanks a lot."

"No, I don't think that at all. It's just that you were so adamant you didn't want to get involved. What changed your mind?"

"You cried all over me and ruined my best shirt."

"Charlie, be serious!"

"I am. If you're sure you want to and can make arrangements for the kids—"

"Oh, Mum will have them. Don't worry about that."

"Okay then, I'll ring Richards and say we're on. But, no matter what we discover, we're only doing it the once."

"Of course. Was it really necessary to spell it out like that?"

Knowing how persistent and persuasive she could be, it was definitely necessary. "Just so long as we're clear on that."

"Crystal. Thanks, Charlie, when do we go?"

"There's one problem we need to sort first. I'm not sure what to do with the mutt."

"What about Sue and Peter?"

"Well, they would, of course, but I don't think I could ask them to take him for four whole days. Their boat's smaller than mine and Gil takes up most of the space when he's aboard. It wouldn't be fair."

"Why not ask Wayne if he can come on the trip?"

I grunted. "That wouldn't go down well with the punters."

"Perhaps not, but it's worth asking anyway. We're bound to be stuck in the crew quarters, away from the guest cabins, and Gil needn't venture into the main part of the boat if the customers don't like him. Although how anyone couldn't like him is beyond me."

I thought about her suggestion. "Nah, Wayne would never agree."

"If he's as desperate to have us on board as you suggest then he might."

"Yeah, I suppose it's worth a shot. If you don't ask, you don't get."

"When will you call him? About our going, I mean. I assume we will go, even if they won't have Gil. Surely Monk could find a temporary home for him, given that we'd be doing this as much for his sake as mine."

I refrained from saying I wouldn't trust Monk not to throw Gil straight into kennels the moment my back was turned.

"Possibly," I said, 'but I'll bounce your suggestion off Wayne first."

"Good. Let me know what he says."

I promised I would and cut the connection. Before I could change my mind I then dialled Wayne's number. He answered straightaway.

"Wayne, it's Charlie."

"Charlie, how you doing? Hang on a minute, I'm in a busy pub. I'll go outside." I heard noise in the background, a door banging closed and then Wayne's voice came back on the line. "That's better. Now I'm getting asphyxiated by all the bloody smokers out here but at least I can hear you. What's on your mind?"

"Well, about that trip to France. I said I'd get back to you."

"A man of his word. That's rare nowadays, even if you are going to turn me down."

"Yeah, I was going to pass on your offer but Kate's giving me grief about it. Thinks it will be an ideal opportunity to get a feel for the chartering game and, well, you know how women can be when they get a bee in the bonnet about something. On at me night and day, she is."

"Say no more," he said, chuckling. "I'm ahead of you on that one. Will you do it then?"

"Well, we would but I have one problem."

"Problems are my speciality, mate."

"I have a dog, or should I say, we do and he's Kate's baby."

"And she doesn't want to leave him behind."

"Got it in one."

Wayne grunted. "You should give her a few of the real things, babies that is, and her priorities would soon change."

"Perhaps I will, but not until I feel a little more secure about the future."

"Okay, what can we do about this dog of yours then?" A slight pause. "Is he boat trained?"

"Yeah, and soft as shit. Trouble is, he's a huge and some people find him a bit intimidating."

"Tell you what, I'll have a word with the two couples booked on the trip and see what they think. I'll sell it to them as a unique part of the package and if they're happy with it then the dog comes too. I'll get back to you on it tomorrow."

"Great, that sounds like a plan."

"And if it's a no-go then I'll ask around and see if I can find someone reliable to take care of him for you."

"Thanks but I'd prefer it if he could come with us, just in case...well, just in case—"

"Just in case you decide that it would be in your best interests not to return to these sunny shores for a while."

I sighed down the phone. “Yeah, something like that.”

“You’re not serious, are you? If you can’t do the return trip then you’re no good to me.”

“No, if I say I’ll go, then I will. But I’d still like the dog to go too.” God knows why I was insisting. Perhaps I was just curious to see how desperate Wayne was for my help.

“Good, okay then, leave it with me. I have to run. I’ve got another call coming through. Talk to you tomorrow, Charlie. Oh, and thanks. I appreciate it.”

My next call was to Monk and therefore the hardest to make. I hated capitulating through coercion and found it difficult to be civil when his cultured voice echoed down the line. He didn’t sound surprised when I told him why I’d called, nor did he ask me why I’d changed my mind. Well, he didn’t really need to, did he?

“I trust my affairs will run smoothly in my absence,” I said through gritted teeth.

“Oh, I’m sure they will.” I could hear the sound of cutlery scraping against plates and a voice in the background offering to top up wineglasses. I hoped I’d interrupted him in the middle of something important.

“Kara will need a change of identity,” I said, not trusting myself to dwell upon the subject of his interfering without losing my temper. Monk was a master at using other people’s loss of control to further his own ends and he’d already taken more than enough advantage of me. He knew I was aware of what he’d done and, for the time being, that would have to be enough.

"We can't call her Kara. It's an uncommon name and I don't want it to be remembered. I thought Kate Wilson."

"Fine, I'll arrange it and let you have the appropriate documents in good time." He paused and when he spoke again his voice was so low I could barely make out what he was saying. "Charlie, thank you. I know it's an inconvenience and I wouldn't have asked it of you if it wasn't so vitally important. Anyway, you know my people won't be too far away if you need bailing out of trouble."

Like you bailed Brett Webb out?

"Just so that we're clear," I said. "This is a one-off. Whatever happens, we won't be making a second trip and I don't expect to get any hassle about that."

"You have my word that your decision will be respected."

Having given his word, I knew he'd honour it and had to stop myself from thanking him. Instead I ended the call, thought about things for a moment or two and then called Kara again, telling her what I'd arranged. Her voice was soft and mellow—and far too inviting. I wished she was with me so we could talk it through and make sure we'd got all the angles covered. I couldn't seem to shake the feeling that I was making one massive mistake.

WAYNE RANG ME early the next morning and told me that Gil could join us on the trip.

"One of the couples has two poodles and the woman is delighted that there'll be a canine presence on board. The other two don't mind as long as he isn't in the main salon when they are." He chuckled. "It seems the two men are related but I doubt if either of them is bringing his wife with him."

I forced myself to laugh as well, not altogether surprised that he'd managed to accommodate Gil. It was certainly a measure of his desperation. "Okay, whatever. When do you want us and where?"

"Ultimate's offices, bright and early next Friday morning. I shall be skippering this one and I'll meet you and the lovely lady, not to mention the hairy beast, for breakfast at eight sharp."

"I think there's something we forgot to establish," I said.

"Oh yeah, what's that then?"

"The small matter of our remuneration."

Wayne's laugh echoed down the line. "Must have slipped my mind."

"Fortunately I have a good memory for that sort of thing."

"Okay," he said, "here's the deal."

Wayne named a figure that was pretty generous, but I haggled and got him to up it a bit. It was a measure of his desperation that he didn't put up too much resistance.

"Right, that's settled then," I said. "See you on Friday."

Five days seemed a long time to wait. I'm not the most patient person, and having decided I was going to do this thing, I was now anxious to get it over with. I didn't see anything of Kara for a few days. She was juggling her commitments with the kids against It Takes

Two's schedule of special events. By the time she surprised me by arriving at the boat on Wednesday night, she was exhausted.

"Mum's taken the kids for an entire week," she said, flopping down on the seating unit. "I needed a couple of days with just you and Gil before setting off for parts foreign."

"Glad you could spare the time." I was happier to see her than I was prepared to let on, which probably made me come across as being a bit cranky. If she noticed, she didn't comment.

"I thought you boys might be lonely without me," she said, ruffling Gil's ears.

Woof, woof.

One of us was prepared to admit it. Gil went crazy, almost standing on his head in his desire to get close to her. I watched them playing tug on the pontoon with Gil's webbing strap, wondering what had happened to the quiet life I'd promised myself once I quit the force. It had all been going so well until this lovely creature hijacked it, bending me to her will without breaking a sweat. And the bugger of it was that I didn't appear to have it in me to get upset about...well, the upset.

The time passed a lot quicker now that she was with me. We could always think of ways to fill the days. Thinking of nighttime occupations didn't put any strain on the old cerebral process whatsoever.

I heard nothing more from Slater. I was tempted to ring Jimmy and see what was occurring but resisted. Slater would have been told to back off, so it was a fair bet that she'd now be spitting expletives and making everyone's lives a misery. There was nothing Jimmy could tell me that I couldn't imagine for myself.

We received a couriered package containing Kara's new identity. I flipped through it, noticing that the address on her driving licence was the same as mine. Monk had even included a new tag for Gil's harness, which is something I probably wouldn't have thought of myself. I admired his attention to detail. Monk had also supplied us with passports in our new names—not too new and filled with a variety of genuine-looking visas. I wondered where he'd obtained the pictures of us. He rang me shortly after the package arrived to ensure that Kara left anything else of a personal nature behind.

"Someone will drive you to Hythe and drop you just short of the marina."

"How thoughtful."

"All part of the service."

Harry was off school for the summer break and spent the day with me on Thursday. He was delighted to see Kara; Emily considerably less so.

"I should have thought you'd want to spend time alone with your son," was her acerbic parting shot as she waddled away from the boat, shoulders rigid with disapproval, or jealousy, or whatever the hell it was that motived women to behave so bitchily.

Notwithstanding Emily's fit of pique, the three of us had a great time. Kara needed a break from her two but didn't seem to find Harry a strain, probably because the ultimate responsibility for his welfare wasn't hers. Emily arrived to collect Harry, and her mood wasn't improved when he clung to Kara for almost as long as he did me.

"Bye, Dad," he said, waving madly over his shoulder. "Bye, Kara. See you at Granddad's party."

If looks could kill…

MONK SENT AN anonymous-looking Ford Sierra at the crack of dawn on Monday to collect the two of us and Gil.

"Right," I said to Kara. "Showtime. Last chance to change your mind."

"It's not gonna happen."

"How did I know that's what you'd say?"

"Because you want to go as much as I do."

I shot her a look.

"Don't bother trying to deny it," she said, smiling like she knew something I didn't. "Your interest is piqued and you couldn't back out now if you tried."

"Wrong! What I want to do is spend three nights cooped up in a tiny crew cabin with you," I said, waggling my brows at her. "You realise we'll have to get *very* up close and personal?"

She rolled her eyes and got into the back of the car. We made the journey mostly in silence, Kara and Gil sharing the backseat, me up next to the driver.

Wayne and Gail were already at Ultimate's office when we arrived. They greeted me like a long-lost mate, the warmth of our reception not diminishing when Wayne looked Kara over. He even tickled Gil's ears and I could tell from the way he approached him that he genuinely liked animals.

"I see what you mean about him being a large beast," he said, grinning.

"Yeah, well, he's no trouble really."

"Welcome, both of you." Wayne ushered us to the corner of the office where Gail produced breakfast for us all. "And thanks to you both for stepping into the breach like this. You're really doing me a favour."

"I'm looking forward to it," Kara said.

I refrained from rolling my eyes. She tucked into the fried breakfast placed in front of her. I watched her with amusement, wondering where such a slim creature put it all. I caught Wayne watching her too, looking equally bemused.

"Doesn't do to go to sea on an empty stomach," she said, obviously conscious of our eyes on her.

"No danger of that in your case," I said.

"So, Kate," Wayne said. "Charlie tells me you're quite an experienced boater."

When she didn't respond, I kicked her ankle under the table. That was the problem with changing her Christian name.

"Oh, sorry," she said, looking a little flustered. "Yes, but I'm more into sailing. All this motorboating is a bit soft for my taste."

Wayne laughed. "You won't be saying that if the weather in the Channel decides to play up. The punters will still have you dancing to their tune."

"Oh, I expect we'll manage."

"Where exactly are we going to?" I asked. "And how long for?"

"We start off just doing the hop across to Calais and

put into the Port de Plaisance marina, which is usually our first port of call. It's dead convenient for the usual sights."

"Sights?" I queried sceptically. "In Calais?"

Wayne laughed. "You have no idea!"

"You're right, I don't."

"Don't be such a philistine, Charlie. There is some cultural heritage on offer and, of course, traditional French restaurants to sample. And I've yet to do one of these trips where the punters don't want to go to the hypermarkets." He slurped his tea and laughed at the same time—not a pretty sight. "It don't matter how posh they think they are, or what airs and graces they put on because they're shelling out so much dosh to impress some woman. They still can't resist the lure of cheap booze and fags."

"Figures," I said with cynical resignation, turning my attention back to my breakfast. "Everyone loves a bargain."

"We stay one night in Calais and then it's up to them where we go next. It usually not far because the clients pay for the fuel and it suddenly dawns on them that the boat eats the bloody stuff. Anyway, this lot wanna go down to the Cherbourg peninsula, which'll be a doddle. Then we turn tail and head for home. Three nights away is what they're paying for."

"And what do we do?" Kara asked.

"We supply all meals but they don't always eat on board at night. In fact, I consider it my duty to point out some of the better local restaurants," he added, chuckling, "so that the women can show off their finery. Anyway, I gather you can cook, Kate."

"Yeah, sure."

"Lovely and talented." Wayne winked at her.

She offered him a thin smile but didn't speak. I reckoned it was a testament to how much she actually wanted to do this thing that she didn't clock him one for being so patronising.

"I assume we do the usual deck work, washing the salt off the boat, help you with keeping watch, and do the housework," I said.

"Sure." Wayne looked at me askance. "But I thought Kate would—"

"I'm housetrained and know better than to leave it all to her."

"Good man. I guess I was being a bit sexist there."

"Just a bit." Kara smiled sweetly this time. Presumably he was forgiven.

Wayne polished off the last of his tea and stood up. "Right, if you're all done here, let's get you both kitted out with our uniform. Kate, go with Gail and she'll see you right. Much as I'd like to look after your needs personally, I have a feeling Charlie would have something to say about that."

"Oh, he's very possessive," she said, making it sound like an accusation.

A short time later we were both dressed in the navy cargo pants and white polo shirts that made up Ultimate's uniform.

"Come on then, team." Wayne led us out the door.

"I'll show you round the boat before the paying customers arrive."

The boat in question turned out to be a seventy-foot Ferretti, probably getting on in years, called *Vagabond.* There were three good-sized staterooms and one smaller one, used by the skipper. Kara and I were, as I'd suspected, to live in the cramped crew quarters located in the transom, giving direct access to the engine room. There were twin bunks and barely enough room for us both to stand up at the same time. Lord knows how we'd manage with Gil in there as well. There was a miniscule cubicle housing basic facilities. The interior of the boat had been tarted up to appear luxurious but that treatment hadn't extended to the crew quarters.

"I'm surprised you're running this trip if you've only got two cabins filled," I remarked at the end of the tour. "Is it still worth your while?"

"Barely," Wayne admitted, shrugging. "But after what happened with *Mistral*, I have to make an effort to get back on track. If that means running a few loss-leaders then that's what I've gotta do."

"Yeah, I guess so."

"Okay." Wayne ran through all the navigational equipment with me, whilst Gail and Kara busied themselves preparing welcome bits and pieces in the galley. "The punters will be here in a bit so we'd best get ourselves sorted."

THIRTEEN

We formed a welcome committee on the pontoon as the clients pulled up in a stretch limo.

"I've seen it all now," I said, trying not to laugh.

Wayne chuckled. "No you ain't. Trust me, this is nothing."

"It gets worse than this?" Kara appeared bemused.

As soon as the car came to a stop, the driver jumped out and opened the rear door. Two middle-aged men climbed out. They were dressed to the nines in brand new Musto gear, top-of-the-range sailing kit so stiff it might as well still have the price tags attached. It made them look like complete prats with money to burn.

Two women, half their age, giggled and swayed as they clambered out behind them, both sporting spiky-heeled shoes and skirts that barely covered their buttocks. I understood now why Wayne had Astroturf-type carpeting fitted to the outside decks. He could hardly tell the women to take their shoes off when their blokes were paying through the nose to spend a few nights on board.

"Oh look!" one of them said, pointing at *Vagabond* with an awed expression on her face. "It's a palace! I didn't know it would be so big, Phil."

"Nothing's too good for you, sweetheart." The man

called Phil slipped a beefy arm round the woman's waist and stared, not at the boat but straight down her cleavage. She was wearing a top at least two sizes too small, putting significant strain on the seams as it struggled to cover her unnaturally large breasts.

"I do hope I won't disgrace myself by being seasick," she said, giggling.

"Well, I hope you do, darling."

"What, Phil, you want me to be sick? That's really mean."

He leered at her, his well-lived-in face creasing into a plethora of wrinkles. Thick tufts of hair sprouted from his ears, as though compensating for the lack of substantial follicles on his head. "No, gorgeous," he said, "I want you to be disgraceful."

The woman roared with laughter. "You're terrible!" she said, punching his arm.

"Told you," muttered Wayne out of the side of his mouth. "If she's his wife then I'll do the deckhand's job for the next ten cruises."

"I think your manicure's safe," I said, watching in growing dismay as the chauffeur pulled a seemingly endless supply of baggage from the boot. "How long do they think they're staying for?"

"That's normal too," Wayne said. "I bet you a pint the women will say they didn't know what to bring so they brought a bit of everything."

"Where will they put it all?" Kara asked.

Wayne shrugged. "That's their problem. Come on, it's showtime."

I followed Wayne toward the man with the tufty

ears. He released the woman's waist as we approached, dismissing her with a not-so-gentle pat on her rear and turning his attention to us.

"Mr. Davis," Wayne said, extending his hand. "Welcome to Ultimate Marine. I'm Wayne Richards and I'll be skippering the *Vagabond* on this trip. This is Charlie, who'll be my second in command."

Davis shook with us both. "I'm Phil Davis, and this is my brother Ron." The other man stepped forward and more handshakes were exchanged. "And these lovely creatures are Gloria and Janet."

"Pleased to meet you." The one called Gloria touched her fingers to Wayne's. Her eyes lingered on me for a little too long. Then a slow smile spread across her face and it was my turn to get the finger treatment.

"Hey, don't you go getting no ideas," Phil Davis said, wagging a finger at me.

Wayne grabbed a couple of bags and I did likewise. Neither of the Davis brothers offered to help, which meant at least two more trips for Wayne and me.

"This way, ladies and gentlemen," Wayne said, staggering beneath his load. "If you're ready, I'll show you to your staterooms."

Kara, with Gil sitting smartly to attention at her side, had positioned themselves at the foot of the *passerelle*. She'd found a blue-and-white bandana somewhere and had tied it jauntily round his neck.

Janet came alive when she saw the dog and spoke for the first time. "Oh, isn't he lovely! Look, Ron." She pointed. "He's in uniform too. Doesn't he look sweet?"

"Adorable," Ron Davis said with a marked lack of enthusiasm.

Janet was obviously the one with the poodles. She looked a bit like one herself, what with all that peroxide blond hair piled in curls on top of her head, held back with tiny pink bows that she was at least twenty years too old to get away with.

"This is Kate," Wayne said to the Davis brothers, both of whom perked up at the sight of her.

I showed Phil Davis and the still giggling Gloria to the principal stateroom. It had seen better days—as had the entire boat. Rather than an expensive refit, Wayne had cleverly used loads of striped fabric in rich tones of scarlet and cream to cover the large bed, creating a canopy above it and extravagant swathes to cover the port lights. Strategically placed mirrors were absolutely everywhere, covering the worst of the water stains to the walls and ceiling. Such damage is inevitable, no matter how diligently a craft is maintained, since the corrosive salty atmosphere always wins out eventually.

"Very thoughtful, ah, Gloria?" Phil glanced in the nearest mirror to the bed and winked. "I think we'll be very cosy in here. Home from home, you might say."

Gloria didn't seem quite so optimistic. "Is there a hairdryer?" she asked peevishly.

"Of course," I said. "It's in the head."

"The what?"

"It's a nautical term for a bathroom," Phil told her, looking pleased because he knew.

"Oh, well, why didn't you say so?" She glared at me as though her ignorance was my fault. "Show me. And

I hope there are enough towels. We shall need clean ones every day."

"Naturally." I remained impassively calm, wondering if it was too late to jump ship.

I stood back and allowed her to enter the smaller room first. If this was what I had to look forward to for the next few days—a whinging bimbo with an inflated opinion of her own importance and a sugar daddy prepared to do whatever it took to get his leg over—then I should have stayed ashore and taken my chances with Slater.

"Come to the main salon when you're ready and we'll have a welcome drink," Wayne said from the doorway.

I could still hear Gloria's whining voice even after we'd closed the door on them.

"Phil, there's no storage space. Where the hell am I going to put everything?"

"There's some drawers under the bed, babe."

"But I need hangers. Everything'll get creased and then I'll look terrible."

"Get that Kate to iron anything that needs it. That's her job."

"Yeah, I suppose."

"Good girl. Now, I wonder if I can get an internet connection in here."

"Christ," Wayne said, shuddering. "I hope she's worth it."

The four punters joined us in the salon half an hour later. Both women had already changed their clothes. Kara served canapés and champagne. Gil, much to his disgust, had been sequestered in the crew cabin.

Wayne gave them a watered-down version of the pep talk he'd given us on the Day Skipper course. He focused mainly on not blocking the heads. All the same, I had a feeling I'd be making several trips to the bilges in the not-too-distant future, since neither woman appeared to take in a word he said.

"And I'll take your passports please," Wayne said, winding up his spiel. "I'll have to show them to the port authorities when we reach France."

"Whoops!" Phil spoke with a broad grin on his face. "They'll discover our secret now, darling. We're not married, see. Well, not to each other, anyway."

"I think they've probably already worked that one out." It was clearly a touchy subject from Gloria's perspective, causing me to wonder if she harboured serious ambitions to become the next Mrs. Phil Davis. There was no accounting for taste.

The champagne put the customers in a cheerful frame of mind. They were all on the flybridge, waving to Gail, who stayed behind to man the office, when I let the lines go. We moved towards the lock at a sedate pace, ready to leave Hythe and head across the channel. I was *really* hoping for rough weather. That would give us a break from Gloria's constant demands for creature comforts. Sadly the sea wasn't as turbulent as I'd have liked but the Channel was extremely busy, necessitating a degree of vigilance on Wayne's part. Not that I got much chance to help him keep watch because the guests kept Kara and me on the hop for the whole crossing, always seeming to need something simply because we were there to get it for them.

By the time we reached Calais I wasn't in the best frame of mind. Fortunately the customers didn't want to dine on board. In line with Wayne's prediction, they fell for his lavish description of a very expensive local restaurant. The women would be able to pose and the men could flash the cash.

As soon as they left the boat, so did Wayne, with some vague excuse about having someone to see.

"We need to follow him," Kara said, tugging at my arm.

"And how do you suggest we do that?" I asked as Wayne jumped into the only cab outside the marina and sped away in it.

She sighed. "God knows. But he must be doing something about immigrants. Perhaps he'll be bringing some back on this trip."

"No, he won't do that."

"How can you be so sure?"

"Because if he was, we wouldn't be in the crew quarters. Think about it. It's the only place he could put people and be sure they won't be discovered."

"I hate it when you're always right." She expressed her frustration by puffing out her cheeks and flopping into the nearest armchair.

"Besides, he wouldn't risk doing it with two new crew members on board. This is a test run. He thinks I'm dodgy but needs to satisfy himself on that score before getting us involved."

"If he's desperate to recover ground after *Mistral*'s loss, he could have put us in the spare cabin and taken the crew quarters himself. That way we'd never have known what was going on."

"Until I had to go through the crew cabin to do the engine room checks."

"He could do them himself."

"Yeah, he could, but that would look a bit odd."

"So all this is a massive waste of time, then? Putting up with Phil Davis and his wandering hands, I mean. God, he's such a creep! What does Gloria see in him?"

I rubbed my thumb and forefinger together. "Who do you think pays for all that clobber she wants you to iron?"

"If it was me I'd prefer to dress from a charity shop rather than have his sweaty hands all over me like he owned me. That's what he does with Gloria. He displays her like she's a possession."

I chuckled. "Perhaps that's why they're called trophies?"

"Well, she's old enough to know what she's getting herself into, I suppose." She turned to face me, frowning. "But about Wayne, even if he's not bringing any immigrants back to the boat, he must be meeting his contacts here." She stood and paced about, clearly frustrated. "Unless we're close to him, we won't know who they are."

"I did warn you that it would be a waste of time."

"Charlie, that's not what I want to hear."

"What, you're not even going to let me say I told you so?" I pulled a hard-done-by face, making her smile.

"Go on then, just say it and get it over with."

I winked at her. "Consider it said."

The inertia left her and she was suddenly all activity. She tidied the mess that was Phil Davis's cabin, wrinkling her nose at odours imaginary and otherwise as she remade the bed. "What the hell have they been doing in here?"

I shot her an amused look. "Use your imagination."

"Yuck, no thanks!" She sighed. "How can anyone imagine this is glamorous? Working on a superyacht, I mean. The reality is that you're a glorified skivvy, at everyone's beck and call twenty-four/seven."

"Ah, but you get to see the world."

"From the inside of someone else's cabin? No, thanks."

Between us we restored some order to the chaos and I then suggested we walk Gil. "But there's something I need to do first. Keep an eye out, and if you see Wayne returning, give me a shout."

"What are you going to do?"

"Search Wayne's cabin."

"Good thinking. Do you think there'll be anything in there to help us?"

"I very much doubt it. He's too cautious for that, but it's still worth checking."

I let myself into his cabin, which wasn't locked, and wasn't surprised when I found nothing of a personal nature. I returned to Kara and shook my head.

"Just a few clothes, a novel and absolutely nothing else." I grabbed her hand. "Come on then, let's attend to Gil's needs."

I saw the taxi Wayne had taken return to the marina and take up the same position outside the gate. I knew it was the same one because I recognised the driver. "Do you speak any French?" I asked Kara.

"A little. Why?"

"Our friend the taxi driver has just come back and I reckon, if he was asked nicely enough, he might just be persuaded to tell us where he took Wayne. Now, I could ask him myself but my French isn't very good. Besides, something tells me that you'll stand a much better chance of getting him to open up."

She was heading toward the taxi before I'd even finished speaking. Leaning against the cab's roof, she chatted to the driver through the open window. She had his complete attention and I figured she'd return with the information we needed.

She didn't disappoint. "He went to a bar in the centre of Calais, about a fifteen minute drive away."

"You have the actual address?"

She looked offended. "Of course! I wrote it down, just in case I forgot."

"Good girl."

She handed me the address but it meant nothing to me.

"Shall we go there?"

"And do what?"

"Well, I don't know. You're the policeman." She waved her hands about. "Investigate. Ask questions. Get a feel for the clientele." She expelled a frustrated sigh. "Something."

"If Wayne's still there, he'll see us. If that happens, he'll wonder why we chose the exact same bar as him when there are dozens of others in Calais."

"Yes, but—"

"And if he's not there, then we'll be no further forward. It's not a risk worth taking. Besides, we're supposed to remain close to the marina in case the punters come back."

"But we might find out who he's meeting."

"Too dangerous," I said firmly.

"But—"

I held up a hand. "No buts. You agreed to do as you're told on this trip." She glowered at me but couldn't deny it. "That cab seems to be the only one that serves the marina. We've already taken a chance, asking the driver where he took Wayne. If we then get him to take us there as well, it would be asking for trouble. No, we stay put. I'll pass the information to Monk and let him make of it what he likes."

I pulled out my phone, rang Monk's number and did precisely that.

"Thanks, Charlie. Shame you couldn't follow him but I guess you know what you're doing." I was glad he thought so. That made at least one of us. "Let me know if anything else comes up."

Kara and I walked along together in companionable silence as Gil made the most of his freedom. We found a small waterside bistro and enjoyed an excellent meal of seafood, washed down with Chablis Premier Cru.

"I'll say one thing for the French." I set aside my cutlery and sighed with contentment. "They certainly know how to produce decent food. And they don't put up silly objections to having dogs in their restaurants."

"That's two things," Kara pointed out. "But you're

right, that was lovely." She pushed her empty plate aside and leaned back in her chair, a soft smile dancing about her lips. "The perfect end to a shitty day."

I signalled for the bill. "We'd better get back. Our lovely guests could return at any time and no doubt there'll be something they need."

"Don't remind me, I was just starting to enjoy myself. We've never been abroad together before, Charlie."

"This is hardly abroad." I tweaked her nose. "When I decide to whisk you away from it all, I hope I can do a little better than Calais."

"That's sweet of you," she said, linking her arm through mine as we stood up to leave. "But I'll settle for just being with you. I don't care where it is."

"Why are you being nice to me? Are you after something?"

She offered me a tantalising smile. "You'll just have to wait for the cramped crew cabin to find that out."

"Beware what you wish for," I warned her, swooping in for a kiss.

Laughing, we strolled the short distance back to the boat. Wayne was already there.

"Good meal?" he asked.

"Yeah, great. We went to the little waterside bistro just over there." I pointed in the general direction of the establishment in question.

"Good choice. It's one of the best around but the punters don't usually go for it. It's not upmarket enough for their tastes. Besides, there's nobody there that they'd want to be seen by."

"That must be why we enjoyed it so much," Kara said.

"You've done a good job tidying up, guys," he said. "Sorry they're so messy."

"Are all your customers as bad?" Kara asked.

"Always!" Wayne laughed. "But, believe it or not, you get used to it."

"That's hard to imagine." Kara shuddered. "Is there something wrong?" she asked Wayne, who was looking at her rather intently.

"No, it's just something...are you sure we haven't met before?"

"Yes, why do you ask?"

I could see panic in her eyes and said the first thing that came into my head to divert attention away from her. "You mean you would have forgotten?"

I feigned mild surprise, forcing myself not to look at Kara. She'd assured me that although Brett worked for Wayne once or twice, she'd never met him before. Had she lied?

"No, you're right." He laughed and the tension left him. "But there's something familiar about you, Kate. Something about your facial expressions that puts me in mind of someone else. I just can't think who."

"Perhaps you're mixing me up with someone famous," she said jokingly.

I was actually glad that the guests chose that moment to return. They'd obviously eaten well and were in excellent spirits. Kara served drinks for us all.

"Excuse me, ladies and gentlemen," Wayne said, having had just one glass of wine and clearly feeling he'd more than done his duty. "I'd best start planning our route for tomorrow. I assume there's nothing more you want to do here," he said to Phil Davis, "and that we'll head for Cherbourg straight after breakfast."

"Well, I—"

"What about those hypermarket places?" Gloria asked. "I reckon there're some great bargains to be had there. They have lovely shopping arcades and my friend Celia got some really good designer gear dead cheap. Can we go there, Phil?" She wrapped her arms round his thick neck as she spoke, her voice an irritating wheedle.

He sighed, feigning indifference. "Well, I suppose, if you really want to, love."

Wayne shot me a look. "We can arrange that if you like," he said to Phil.

"Well, it's not really my cup of tea, but if the ladies want to shop—" Phil lifted his shoulders in a *what-can-you-do* sort of gesture and left the words hanging.

"I'll arrange a taxi to take you there," Wayne said. "Now, if you'll excuse me."

He headed for the chart table forward of the salon, making a big pretence of measuring distances. It was all for show since there wasn't actually any planning required to remain in Calais the following day.

Phil Davis was in an expansive mood. He sipped at a large brandy and bragged about the cost of the trip. "It was a steal. Half the brochure price. I thought about flying the ladies off somewhere exotic for the weekend but this was too good a deal to pass up. Besides, it's a bit different and, best of all, there's no hanging about in bloody airports."

The price he'd paid surprised me—and got me thinking. I knew how much Wayne was paying Kara and me, roughly how much the mooring fees would be, insurance, wear and tear and all the rest of the costs that had to be factored in. By my calculations he was running this trip at a whopping loss. I could understand him trying to rebuild his reputation, but if he carried on at this rate it would bankrupt him. The only feasible explanation was that he was trying to convince his paymasters he was reliable. I didn't imagine they'd taken too kindly to losing their last lot of illegals, who were presumably vital to whatever plans they had in the U.K. Why else did they go to so much trouble and expense to get such a small number of people into the country?

"What business are you in, if you don't mind my asking, Mr. Davis?" I didn't think they had anything to do with Wayne's activities, but it didn't hurt to make sure.

"Call me Phil," he said with an airy wave of his hand. "Every time someone calls me Mr. Davis, I expect my dad to pop up." He chuckled. "Gawd knows what he'd make of things if he could see me now. Very religious man, was my dad, worked hard all his life and never looked at another woman."

"A bit like you then, Phil," Gloria said, slipping onto his knee.

He roared with laughter. "Yeah, well, I saw what a life of hard work got him. Fuck all, that's what. Anyway, to answer your question, Ron and I are into gaming machines. Supply a lot of the casinos and other venues. Very lucrative it is too."

The brothers banged on for ages about their trade before eventually deciding to call it a night. Kara and I tidied the salon in record time, eradicating all traces of their messy presence, and turned in ourselves—or tried to. When we entered the crew cabin we found Gil in occupation of the lower bunk, stretched full length, snoring peacefully. I rolled my eyes, trying not to laugh.

"What do we do?" Kara asked. "It would be such a shame to disturb him."

"Seems to me there's only one thing we can do." I climbed up to the top bunk and offered her a hand up. I lay flat on my back, shoulder against the bulkhead, and pulled her against me. "As long as you stay really close and don't move a muscle all night, I'm sure you won't fall out."

"Charlie!"

I strived for an innocent look. "Well, you said it yourself—we can't disturb Gil. Besides, you mentioned you had a surprise for me."

"Hmm, that's true, but in this cramped space?" She shook her head. "Not sure it's possible."

I set about proving to her that it was.

"Charlie," she mumbled drowsily into my shoulder a little later, "what was that with Wayne thinking he knew me? We've never met before, I'm sure of it."

"I was going to ask you about that."

She huffed. "You thought I'd lied to you."

"It crossed my mind."

"Well, I didn't. I wouldn't put us in that position."

"No, sorry." I thought for a moment. "You probably share a few characteristics with your brother. Facial expressions, turns of phrase, stuff like that you're not even aware of."

She thought about that for a moment. “I suppose it’s possible,” she conceded.

“I wish he hadn’t noticed,” I said. “We need to be extra careful now. He’s still not entirely convinced that his phone fell out of his pocket on the Day Skipper course, and now this. Which is why it’s a good job we didn’t follow him this afternoon. If we’d been caught, then that would have been our lot.”

FOURTEEN

KARA EXPELLED AN elongated sigh of relief as we waved the Davis brothers and their lady friends away.

"They were even more demanding than the usual type," Wayne conceded, "but still fairly typical. You guys handled them brilliantly, though."

"It was either that or throttle them," I said.

Wayne chuckled. "Never mind, Davis showed his financial appreciation and there's a share of that for you two. You sure as hell earned it. I'll settle up with you now and then I'd suggest adjourning to the pub for a well-deserved pint or six."

"Those are the first sensible words I've heard you utter in four days." I whistled to Gil, who was taking avid interest in some evil-smelling spillage on the pontoon, and followed Kara and Wayne to the office.

"I've got another lot booked for next week," Wayne said when we were on the second round of drinks. "Don't suppose I can tempt you two to do it again."

"Well, I suppose we could think…" Kara glanced at me and as quickly looked away again, her words stalling.

"Don't think so, Wayne, thanks all the same." I gave Kara's fingers a warning squeeze, annoyed but not surprised that she was already prepared to renege on our agreement.

"But, Charlie, it was fun, really, and—"

"Give me a break! You never stopped complaining about how messy they were, to say nothing of dodging wandering hands."

"Yes, but looking back it wasn't all bad, and we did get to sample some good food."

"Hindsight's a wonderful thing."

"I don't want to cause friction between you," Wayne said, "but at least say you'll think about it." He clearly set as much stock by Kara's powers of persuasion as Monk did. "I won't be able to do this one myself and I'd feel better having two people who know the score helping the skipper out. He's fairly new, see. I've only used him a couple of times before."

I knew then that we'd passed whatever test Wayne had set for us. If he wasn't skippering the next trip, illegals would almost certainly be aboard. And we'd make perfect fall guys if something went wrong.

"Sure, we'll give it some thought," I lied, "but don't hold your breath. Surely any decent crewing agency would find you the right people easily enough."

"Don't get me started on those bloody barracudas!" Wayne scowled off into the distance. "There are hundreds of people out there who romanticise the idea of working at sea but can't hack it when reality sets in. Besides, most of them don't know a bowline from a bloody granny knot. Those agencies charge a fucking fortune to supply a load of rubbish." He paused mid-rant and grimaced. "Trust me," he said in a more moderate tone, "I know about what I speak."

And I knew he was lying. Respected crew agencies vet their applicants thoroughly. They don't take anyone on unless they can prove they have both the appropriate qualifications and the necessary practical experience under their belts. Marine industry employees keep logbooks signed by the skippers of the boats they've worked on to back up their credentials. That Wayne wished to avoid taking on such people reinforced my suspicions. Shame that, under different circumstances we might have been friends.

Kara was uncharacteristically quiet on the way home, not trying too hard to talk me round. Monk was less circumspect when he heard about Wayne's offer, but his subtle arguments fell on deaf ears.

Kara dashed off not long after we got back to Brighton to collect the children from her mother. I should have felt relieved but perversely I missed her lively company and found it hard to settle back into any sort of routine.

As I walked back to the boat with Gil after his evening constitutional a couple of days later, my path was blocked by two tough-looking individuals. At first I thought one of them had bumped into me accidentally. When the other put out a hand to prevent me moving round him it became obvious the encounter was deliberately contrived. Gil sensed it too. He growled, hackles raised, and looked as though he was seriously contemplating attacking. I held on to his harness to prevent him from doing anything rash. These two louts looked as though they wouldn't think twice about putting the boot in, and I'd grown too fond of the big guy to put him at risk.

I stared at the goons, and they stared right back at me through flat, unblinking eyes. The smaller guy was my height, with close-cropped hair, a vicious expression and forearms the size of mature tree trunks. This bloke knew how to handle himself and, I'll admit, he intimidated me. Until I looked at his oppo, that is. Well, everything's relative. The second guy was even taller, and completely bald. Whether his head was shaved in a deliberate ploy to project a hard image, or whether he was naturally lacking in the follicle department, I couldn't have said right then. I had more pressing matters on my mind. Like how to get out of whatever was going down with the requisite number of limbs still in good working order.

I focused my attention on the larger guy, guessing he was the boss. The bowling ball that passed for his head was attached to one of the largest pairs of shoulders I'd ever seen, bypassing the need for a neck. Amazingly, both men were fully suited and booted—neckties, the works. They looked completely out of place in the relaxed environs of the marina. What was that all about?

I took all this in as the standoff continued. Gil growled, I held him back, and the two goons attempted to stare me down. It seemed to go forever. Someone had to break the stalemate and since I'd never been big on passivity, I took the initiative.

"Something I can do for you gentlemen?" I asked.

"Indeed there is."

Bowling Ball spoke just the three words but it was enough to shock me into temporary silence. I'd been expecting threats and bad language, but the man spoke politely and with an educated accent. Goons with a proper command of the English language. Whatever was the world coming to?

Once I recovered from the initial shock, I felt a bit better about the situation. Whatever it was they wanted, something told me they'd only fall back on violence as a last resort. But that didn't help me figure out who they were or why they'd specifically come looking for me. Had I got it wrong, about Monk, that is? Had he sent these louts to change my mind about the trip to France, or were they connected to my previous occupation? That was always a possibility that no copper could afford to ignore, even in retirement. No one on this planet harboured grudges like ex-cons—the inevitable result of having few other productive ways to pass the time inside.

Bowling Ball watched my reaction and appeared to find it amusing.

"I'm pushed for time," I said, "so perhaps you'd spit it out."

"Let's walk."

It wasn't a suggestion. Besides, what choice did I have? I moved off, Gil still with a growl rumbling in his throat, sticking close to my heels. The goons took up positions on either side of me.

"I have a simple request to make of you, Charlie," Bowling Ball said in beautifully enunciated Queen's English.

So they knew my name. "Call me in office hours."

"I wouldn't trouble you like this if it wasn't a matter of some urgency." He paused, presumably so I could ask what was so urgent. I'm a contrary sod and didn't oblige, forcing him to forge ahead. Round one to me. "We need you and Kara to go on that trip to France next week."

I stopped dead and glared at him, disappointed that Monk *was* behind this after all. Stooping to such low tactics was a measure of his desperation, but I was through with being manipulated.

"You can't be serious!" So much for playing it cool.

"I've never been more serious about anything. You and Kara will make that trip and when you get to France, someone will contact you with further instructions."

"And I would do this because…"

"It would be in your best interests."

I stopped walking, turned toward the goon and thrust my face up close to his, inchoate anger winning out over caution. I was outnumbered and out-muscled but I was also in a public place and had a large dog that appeared ready to fight my corner.

"Don't threaten me," I said, my voice a belligerent rumble. Probably not the smartest reaction but just recently people had been queuing up to make me do things I didn't want to do. I'd had just about enough of it.

"Let's just say that we're asking you politely and leave it at that," Bowling Ball said calmly. "You'll be well paid, and once it's over we won't trouble you again."

Where had I heard that before? I elevated my brows

in a show of sardonic disinterest, as though I was threatened every day by two quietly spoken men-mountains and didn't give a toss. But inside my guts churned as fast as my mind. A feeling of self-preservation kicked in as I tried to think of a way to extract myself from this situation without blood being spilled—especially not mine.

"Sorry, but I'm a bit stretched at the moment," I said, trying to sound casual. Judging by Bowling Ball's amused reaction, I didn't come close to pulling it off.

"So will your credibility be if Richards finds out what your previous profession was."

I grunted. "Is that the best you can do?"

"A word to the wise. Don't be fooled by his public persona. Wayne Richards is a vicious individual, especially if he thinks he's been played. Who do you suppose would be directly in the firing line if he discovered he'd been set up?" Bowling Ball shook his head, sighing. I wondered how he managed it without the services of a neck. "Trust me, Charlie. It would be a massive mistake to underestimate him."

"I'll take my chances."

"Not the answer I was looking for."

"It's the only one I have for you. Now, if you *gentlemen* will excuse me."

Bowling Ball drew a deep breath and expelled it slowly, like a teacher expressing disappointment at a star pupil's inconclusive answers to a key question.

"Well then, let's see if we can change your mind." He stopped walking and his partner, who had yet to speak a word, grasped my forearm with surprising gentleness, making sure I stopped too. I wasn't stupid enough to mistake that gentleness for weakness and did the sensible thing. "Now then, Miss Kara Webb." I felt my chest tighten as he reeled off her address, telephone numbers and car registration, all from memory. "Such a lovely young lady, so full of life. And as for her nephew and niece—"

I lost it then. My fists clenched of their own accord and I aimed an ill-thought-out blow towards Bowling Ball's shiny pate. A band of steel gripped my wrist when my arm was still in midair and brought it back to my side. I waited for the inevitable blow, which didn't come. Instead Bowling Ball nodded to his oppo to release my wrist and carried on talking as though nothing had happened. Well he could afford to. He'd got to me and I'd stupidly allowed it to show.

"And Harry," he added in a conversational tone. "Remind me, how old is your son?"

I ground my teeth, seriously considering releasing the still-growling Gil to see what damage the two of us could inflict upon this infuriatingly polite thug and his sidekick. Common sense prevailed in the nick of time.

"Leave my son out of this," I said, knowing how pathetic that must have sounded. To give Bowling Ball credit, he didn't sneer at my predictability. Instead he reached inside his jacket and produced a photograph. He passed it to me, watching me closely as I took in the image of my son leaving school in the company of his classmates. The photo was date-stamped the previous day.

"He's a nice-looking kid, Charlie. He does you credit."

I was beaten and we both knew it. I'd agree to just about anything now to get rid of them, but no way was I taking this lying down. My first port of call would be Monk. Not that I thought it was his doing. He could be a manipulative bastard when it suited his purpose but I didn't think he'd be this crude. If push came to shove he might threaten me, but never Kara, and especially not Harry. Monk was old school, and innocent women and children weren't used as bargaining tools.

Even so, I was willing to bet he'd know something about these goons, and who'd sent them. Monk always had more information than he was willing to share. Well, all that was about to change, and the first question I needed answers to was why these thugs wanted an ex-copper on the run to France.

"What do you want me to do?"

"I believe I've already told you. Simply go with Kara on the next trip to France and await instructions."

"And finish up like those poor sods on *Mistral*?"

"Ah yes, you witnessed that unfortunate event. That was an accident." *Like hell it was.* "It shouldn't have come to that, but you just can't get reliable staff nowadays. The idiot we had on *Mistral* exceeded his brief, but I'm confident someone of your calibre won't make the same mistake."

"Who do you represent?" I asked, knowing full well they wouldn't tell me. "What do you hope to achieve by all this?"

We'd reached the land side of the marina, by the

parking spaces for the occupants of the waterside apartments. The two goons headed for a silver Mondeo illegally parked there. The silent man opened it with a remote control.

"I know I can rely on you, Charlie," Bowling Ball said politely, almost as though he were making small talk at a high-end cocktail party. "But, needless to say, we'll be watching you."

"Well," I said, determined to have the last word. "Everyone needs a hobby."

Still reeling from the encounter, my police training kicked in and I memorised the licence number of the car as it sped away.

Back on the boat I poured myself a large drink and tried to calm down. I needed to think about this.

If Monk hadn't sent the thugs, then who the hell had? And more to the point, why?

Before I did anything else I needed to see what I could find out about that Mondeo, and to do that I needed the cooperation of my ex-colleagues. Difficult, given Slater's determination to paint me as one of the bad guys, but I knew I could still rely on Jimmy. I called his mobile and caught him off duty, at home.

"Slater's hopping mad because she's been told to back off you," Jimmy said, chuckling. "Someone in high places is looking out for you, mate."

Someone in high places had got me into this mess in the first place but I didn't bother to put Jimmy straight on that. "She'll get over it."

"Yeah, but you don't have to work with her in the meantime."

"There are some benefits to early retirement then." I listened whilst Jimmy let off a bit more steam about Slater, making appropriately sympathetic noises until such time as I could interrupt his flow. "Jimmy, I wondered if you could do me a favour."

He guffawed. "You've got one hell of a nerve."

"Yeah, I'm sorry about before, but this time all I need is a trace on a car registration."

"Why?"

"Someone's been seen around the marina harassing some kids and I want to make sure it's not some nonce."

"Call it in and we'll deal with it."

"I will if it proves to be kosher, but if it's perfectly innocent, I don't want to cause the guy any grief. You know how word tends to get out. It would blight the guy's life, perhaps needlessly."

It was a pretty thin story but Jimmy appeared to buy it. That perhaps was one of the reasons he'd never rise above the rank of detective sergeant. He simply lacked the ability to ask the right questions and was altogether too trusting. He ran the Mondeo's number the following morning and supplied me with the name of a company in Ramsgate it was registered to. It meant nothing to me but that situation would change soon enough.

First, I had more urgent priorities.

It was time to extract a few home truths out of Monk, but before I did that I rang Kara. We chatted for a minute or two, both studiously avoiding the subject of the trip to France.

"Can you get a sitter and come round tonight?" I asked her.

"Sure." She sounded surprised but pleased by my request. "Any special reason?"

"Do I need one?"

"Of course not. I'll be there around seven."

"See you then."

I rang Monk and asked him to come as well, but an hour later. I'd mulled things over and decided that Kara deserved to know everything that had happened so we could decide between us how to react before confronting Monk.

"I wasn't expecting to hear from you," she said when she arrived, only just remaining on her feet in the face of Gil's enthusiastic greeting. "I thought you'd had enough of me for the time being."

I affected bemusement. "I thought so too, but apparently not."

"So," she said, settling into the corner of the seating unit with her bare feet tucked beneath her and Gil's head resting in her lap, "what's on your mind?" When I didn't immediately respond she tilted her head, subjecting me to a thoughtful appraisal. "Something tells me there's more to this invitation than an overwhelming desire for my scintillating company."

"You underestimate your charms, sweetheart."

She took a sip of her drink and smiled at me over the top of the glass. "Come on, Charlie, give. Don't keep me in suspense."

Now that she was actually here, telling her that she'd been threatened seemed like not such a good idea, but I had no choice. I refreshed her drink, warned her to prepare for a shock and told her what had gone down the previous evening. It was the first time I'd ever seen anyone genuinely rendered speechless. Her mouth fell open, her eyes doubled in size and a series of trembles reverberated through her body. Whether occasioned by rage or fear, it was hard to say.

I took her hand and squeezed it. "Hey, don't get upset. It'll be okay."

"No it won't," she said vehemently. "It's very much not okay and it's all my fault. I got you into this but it was never my intention to endanger the kids."

Typical Kara. She hadn't spared a thought for herself.

"Of course it wasn't. And as for dragging me into it, I'm a big boy and I make my own decisions."

She offered me a wan smile. "Why were you threatened like that, Charlie? Who do you think was behind it all? It doesn't make any sense. Do you think Monk might have something to do with it?"

"It's hard to see how?"

"Even so, I blame myself."

I caught a tear as it trickled from the corner of her eye and arrested its progress with my forefinger. Then I slipped a comforting arm round her shoulders and pulled her close. "Don't cry, sweetheart, it's not your fault and we'll get something sorted."

Kara managed a watery smile. "What are we going to do about all this then?"

"That's more like the fighting spirit I've come to know and fear."

"Well, you can't keep a good woman down for long."

"I don't have any interest in restraining good women."

"Thanks."

"You do realise that it's not only the kids' welfare that's at stake." I needed to stop this exchange of flirtatious banter and make her understand precisely what we'd be up against if she insisted upon charging headlong in. "Those thugs threatened you as well."

"Yes, but if we do as they say then they won't hurt us." So much for the cautious approach. "What choice do we have?"

I sighed, wondering what other response I could have expected from her. And she was right, of course. Much as I hated to admit it, the only way we could guarantee our safety was to go on that bloody trip to France.

"I think it's a little more complicated than that."

She blinked up at me. "What do you mean?"

"Well, we know Wayne's up to his neck in this but we don't know who the men who accosted me are. Nor do we know who was behind the sabotage to *Mistral*. They may not be one and the same, so by doing as the thugs asked, we might be transferring ourselves from one dangerous situation to another."

"That's possible, I suppose." She nibbled the end of her index finger as she thought it through. "But I still don't see what choice we have."

"Monk's due shortly and we might get a clearer picture after we've spoken to him."

Kara's face expressed shock. "You think he's behind this?"

"I don't want to think so. Threatening children isn't his style. But I do think he knows a lot more than he's let on so far. We'll confront him and demand a full explanation. If he didn't send those men we'll have the element of surprise on our side and he won't have had time to concoct a convincing story." Not that that would stop him for long. Monk was a master at thinking on his feet. "If we're gonna put our lives on the line, then we deserve to know what we're up against. Whether or not we actually go on that trip depends largely upon whether he tells us everything he knows."

"I agree."

I made a big show of gaping at her. "So that's what it takes, is it? I've finally discovered how to get you to agree with me."

Instead of laughing at my clumsy attempt at levity, she surprised me by wrapping her arms round my neck. "Charlie, I seem to make a habit out of making life difficult for you." She traced the contour of my face with her forefinger. "I'm surprised you put up with me."

"Sometimes I surprise myself." I gave her a brief kiss. "Let's have another drink before Monk gets here." I extracted myself from her grasp.

"If these people have been watching you then they must know about Monk's visits to the *No Comment*," she mused as I opened another bottle of wine. "If they don't work for him then presumably they're the enemy. Won't his coming here only complicate matters?"

"I doubt if they know who he is or who he actually works for. It's top secret, remember, and even we don't know who he reports to."

She made rapid inroads into her fresh drink. I took my beer a little slower. I would need to keep my wits about me when confronting Monk.

Monk arrived dead on time, accepting the glass of single malt I offered him with a nod of thanks. "This is an unexpected pleasure."

"Is it?"

He seemed genuinely surprised by the question. "Well yes, I assumed our business dealings were at an end."

"Something's happened that you need to know about." I told him the same story I'd related to Kara a little earlier.

Monk listened intently, not once interrupting. He appeared interested but not particularly surprised. "Ah, now I understand why you're so angry."

I wasn't aware that my anger had been on open display, but then not much got past Monk. "So who were they?"

"What do you intend to do?"

"I asked first." When he hesitated, I really lost it. "Come on, guv, you got us into this, so I don't think it's unreasonable to expect a few honest answers. My son's been threatened, so has Kara and her two, all because someone's smuggling illegals into the country. What's so important about a few more when the place is already overrun with foreigners seeking a new start in life?"

"I understand your anger. In your position I'd feel the same way."

"Is that why you sent those men?"

A quirk of an eyebrow was the only indication that I'd surprised and probably offended him. "Not my style, Charlie. You should know that."

"Then who were they?" I sat beside Kara and took

her hand. It was trembling. "There's more to this than you've been letting on. If we're going to remain involved then we deserve to know what we're up against."

Monk paused for a protracted moment but I felt no compulsion to fill the ensuing silence. Eventually he spoke. "Yes, you very likely do." He let out a breath in one long whoosh. "All right, I'll tell you what we know, but before I do I'll need a little more sustenance, I think."

He held out his empty glass and I got up to refill it. With a nod of thanks he rearranged his legs into a more comfortable position and took a sip of his new drink.

"What I told you before about election issues was true. The red-hot topic all the parties are pinning their hopes on is immigration. They're piously vowing to sort the problem and blaming each other for it having got so out of hand in the first place. The Labour Party's open door policy has permanently altered the cultural mix of this country, and there's no going back on that now. Their reason for allowing it to happen isn't particularly transparent, but anyone who might have questioned it held back for fear of being branded a racist." Monk paused again, making me wonder where he was going with this. He sighed as though the weight of the entire world rested on his shoulders. "And so, out of the chaos emerged the growth of the British white extremist parties."

"Those so-called national supremacist parties," Kara said, wrinkling her nose. "Their party leaders causing outrage by guesting on respected political TV shows."

"Quite. Few people would have imagined such a

thing as recently as a couple of years ago. The fact that men of that ilk get invited onto such a high-profile TV show indicates how strong feelings are amongst the electorate regarding the whole issue of immigration."

"Rightly or wrongly, it's been brewing for a long time," I said.

"Yes." Monk nodded. "It wasn't so bad when times were booming. I mean, someone had to do all the dirty minimum-wage jobs that Joe Average wouldn't even contemplate." His words were accompanied by an eloquent shrug. "But we're in recession now and all people see are foreigners with barely a grasp of the English language filling jobs they now wouldn't mind doing themselves. They see their culture being eroded, mosques outnumbering Christian churches, whites becoming the minority group in certain cities, immigrants living off benefits when they've made no contributions toward the state in the first place...the list goes on." He placed his empty glass aside and appeared not to know what to do with his hands. He settled for waving one about and resting the other on his thigh. "In a nutshell, the silent majority has been nudged out of indifference."

"Yes, a lot of ill-informed people feel that way. But surely your average *Daily Mail* reader isn't voting BNP." Somehow I couldn't see *Outraged of Tunbridge Wells* resorting to such extremes.

"Probably not but someone sure is, which is what's finally got the politicians admitting there actually *is* a problem. This little island of ours is overcrowded and it's easy to blame people with a different skin colour for that because they're running scared. Although most people are disgusted by their policies, the white supremacist parties have had successes in local elections and, significantly, in Europe, which has been a real wakeup call." Monk paused, as though trying to decide how much more to say. "Enter stage left the English Patriotic Party. What do you know about the EPP, Charlie?"

I shrugged. "Only what I've read in the press. They're a less extreme version of the white supremacists. They want to stop further immigration, offer voluntary repatriation, allow people to use the word *Christmas* without fear of offending other religions, blah de blah. A common-sense approach to the problem that's hit the spot for a lot of people, apparently."

"You see, they've got you half convinced too."

"No, not me. I take people at face value and don't begrudge the less fortunate for wanting a better life."

"Even so, the pendulum had to swing back sometime or other," Kara said.

"Yes, and what sets the EPP apart from the other extremist parties is their leader, Peter Elliott. Have you seen him on TV? Don't see how you can have failed to," he said, not waiting for me to respond, "because he's seldom off our screens these days."

"He's the blond, good-looking ex-public schoolboy, isn't he?" Kara asked.

"A very accurate description," Monk said, smiling. "Not difficult to see why he's got half the female voters in the country already eating out of his hand, is it? He comes from an upper-class family, attended Eton, has a degree in politics from Cambridge and boasts strong Christian beliefs. Not only that, but he's exceedingly intelligent, photogenic, mild-mannered and entirely plausible. He's also a natural at playing the media, and his common sense attitude appeals to people across the political divide. At last voters have someone they can support without it troubling their consciences. Elliott makes it okay to be proud to be British again without worrying about offending the politically correct brigade."

Kara frowned. "Hasn't Elliott starting saying that the U.K. is under imminent threat of attack from extremists opposed to his views and popularity?"

"Yes." Monk looked at me rather than her as he spoke, leaving me with the impression that I'd missed something obvious.

"I can understand why the big parties are getting worried," I said. "Elliott is doing what they should have done themselves years ago if they'd had the balls to tackle the issue."

A boat passed the end of the pontoon too quickly. Its wake rocked the *No Comment*, pressing the fenders against the dock, causing them to squeak in protest.

I waited for the boat to settle again before asking my next question. "But what has that got to do with Ultimate Marine's little game?" I had a feeling I already knew the answer to that but wanted to hear it from Monk.

"Intelligence sources believe that the illegals being brought in by Richards are the key to a terror plot against the U.K."

"Suicide bombers, you mean."

"Yes, brainwashed young men and women who think

they will receive their reward for making the ultimate sacrifice in the next life."

"With their virgins already picked out and waiting patiently," I said, rolling my eyes in cynical resignation.

"The sad part of it all is that they honestly believe in their cause. They think it's right and just. But then, if you take kids young enough, people who have so little to lose in the first place, and paint a brighter picture for the future of their people if they help to overcome the wicked infidels in the west, what else can you expect?" Monk readjusted his position and didn't speak for a moment or two. We waited him out in silence. "We believe that Peter Elliott's party know about Wayne's operation as well and are trying to intercept it so they can take the credit for foiling the plot. A surefire vote winner, in other words."

I thought I was in danger of exploding with anger. "And you placed Kara and me in the middle of two warring factions without thinking it worth mentioning."

"We don't know for sure that Elliott's party is in any way involved."

"Bullshit!"

"Truly, Charlie, we know nothing for definite." Not many men can face me down when I get as angry as I was then but Monk, infuriatingly calm, didn't even seem to notice how wound up I was. "Our intelligence is sketchy because Elliott is paranoid about security, and it's impossible to penetrate his inner circle. We had high hopes of Gordon but…" He glanced at Kara, his words trailed off, and I really lost it.

"Sorry, guv, but I'm not buying that. You don't give

a shit about Richards. All your paymasters want to do is catch the EPP at its dirty little game so that they don't steal its glory in exposing the suicide bombers."

"We'd rather like to get everyone involved."

"Why did the EPP deliberately sabotage *Mistral*?" I asked. "Surely their objective would be the same as the government's. They'd want to bring the boat into port, loaded with idealistic young men primed to blow the country to kingdom come."

"We've been brainstorming that one and can only surmise that the EPP didn't actually destroy *Mistral*—"

"You think someone else was responsible?" I didn't attempt to hide my surprise. "I know the Channel's a pretty crowded place but this is rapidly becoming farcical."

"We think it was an accident. The fire deliberately started in the engine room was only supposed to halt the vessel. It got out of control quicker than anticipated, people panicked and, well…you know the rest."

"But I was there," I said, scratching my head, still uncomfortable whenever I thought about my inability to help the poor sods concerned. "That cigarette boat could easily have rescued the survivors. Instead it deliberately ran them down."

"It looks that way."

"Tell me more about the EPP," I said, still trying to separate the truth from any fiction Monk might be attempting to weave.

"The party's strong Christian foundation finds favour with a surprising number of people in this country. In spite of what you might think, religion still plays a strong part in a lot of British lives, even if the churches are no longer full. Everyone falls back on their faith in times of stress. It's a kind of comfort factor, I suppose. Anyway, the EPP has renounced violence as a means of achieving their objectives."

I shot Monk a look. "If those two goons who accosted me are part of their organisation, then you could have fooled me."

"I didn't say they don't use threats and intimidation, I merely said they don't resort to violence and actively speak out against its use. You did say that they were polite and didn't back up their demands with a show of strength."

"True, but they certainly looked as though they could handle themselves if it came to it."

"That's all part of their image. I bet there were no tattoos or piercings or any of the other symbols you'd expect from a white extremist party."

I admitted I hadn't seen anything of that nature. "But I would recognise them again. If you have pictures of the main players I could pick them out and that would give you grounds to bring them in."

"On what charge?"

I knew where he was going with this and conceded the point with a reluctant nod.

"It's their word against yours, Charlie. We wouldn't be able to hold them and that would make things worse for you in the long run."

"Not if they're only posturing and are nonviolent."

"You want to put that to the test?" Monk held my gaze. "It's Harry's welfare we're discussing here, to say nothing of Kara's and her nephew and niece. And, of course, there's your own skin to consider."

I dropped my eyes first. "Yeah, okay, point taken."

"I have no evidence of them resorting to violence but it's hardly the sort of thing they'd advertise. It goes against everything they stand for. However, I think your gut reaction is right, and if it came to it they'd be willing to put the boot in."

I nodded, stretching my legs in front of me as I tried to assimilate all I'd just heard. "But, if what you've told us is accurate, how will our going to France help your cause? Presumably the EPP will want us to do their dirty work for them. They'll probably get me to disable the boat somehow mid-Channel. But what then?"

"Well, Charlie, if you did decide to go, we'd give you a mobile phone with a state-of-the-art tracking device in it. We'd know where you were at all times. We'd have a boat out there as well and as soon as yours slowed, we'd be there to overpower the EPP's rescue craft."

Why did my gut tell me that it would never be that simple?

"So, let's see if I've got this right," I said caustically. "What you're really telling me is that you never expected us to get near the people behind the business and don't really care about them. All your paymasters want is your help to win them the election by foiling the EPP's attempts to steal their glory."

"Well, that's a rather simplistic explanation, but basically true, I suppose."

"Presumably the EPP plan is to leak the interception of the boat to the press, who'd be there in numbers when it's towed into port. The government would have a hard time recovering from such a coup, besides looking pretty stupid for letting it happen, of course, especially when the EPP have been warning for months that something of that nature was afoot."

"Pretty much," Monk agreed. "But if the government can intercept the boat before the EPP does, they can claim that they were on top of the situation all along. They'd be able to disparage the EPP's predictions without letting them have their moment in the spotlight."

"Yes, I suppose that would make people think twice about the EPP's scaremongering."

"Exactly. Bear in mind that the pundits predict this election will be a very close run thing, almost certainly won or lost on the race issue. Worst case scenario, we'll have a hung parliament again, requiring another coalition, and that would be in nobody's best interests."

"But if the incumbent majority government pull this off, they'd be virtually guaranteed success without a need for a coalition partner?"

Monk inclined his head. "More or less."

"Why don't you simply shadow the boat when it leaves France and intercept it when it slows down?" Kara asked. "Why do you need us?"

Good question.

"Because we have to assume that the boat the EPP plan to use to intercept *Vagabond* will be following her closely on radar. If another boat is sitting in her slipstream, they'll not risk going through with the sabotage."

"But that's good, isn't it? That way, you could simply be waiting when the boat gets to England and nab the stowaways yourselves."

When Monk merely raised a brow and said nothing.

"Oh, but I was forgetting. It's like I just said. Your masters don't just want to intercept the suicide bombers, they want to expose the EPP's role in it, albeit privately, and crush them once and for all."

"Something like that," Monk said with the ghost of a smile. "But one thing that isn't in question is the danger these young people pose to the country. We know for a fact that they're planning a coordinated attack on mainline railway stations during the rush hour."

"Christ!"

"Exactly. Security at airports is too tight for them to be targeted but they can arguably do more damage on the trains."

Kara and I exchanged a glance. "Yes," I said quietly, "I'm sure they could."

"The terrorists have won in the airports anyway," Kara said. "They need never attack another plane or terminal again because they've made every traveller's life a misery with all the extra security."

"That's true."

Kara expelled a long breath. "All I wanted to do was find Gordon and we don't seem to be any further on in that respect."

"So, Charlie, will you do it?" Monk asked, not addressing Kara's frustration. He didn't look at me as he spoke, his excessively casual tone indicating just how important my answer was to him. He concentrated his attention upon straightening the already razor sharp creases in his trousers whilst he waited for me to respond, extending his legs in front of him to examine his handwork and nodding in apparent satisfaction at the results. "Will you help us by going to France?"

FIFTEEN

"HAVEN'T DECIDED YET," I told Monk before Kara could jump in and commit us. "We'll talk about it and let you know."

"Fair enough," he said, standing up. "You know, of course, that there isn't much time so hopefully you'll be in touch soon." He had the sense to leave it at that and headed for the door, ruffling Gil's head as he passed him. "Thanks for the drink, Charlie. Goodnight, Kara."

Monk had barely left the boat before Kara let rip. "I can't believe he didn't bother to tell us about the EPP!"

I could. Monk operated on a strictly need-to-know basis and he clearly didn't think we qualified. I let her rant on, figuring that once she calmed down she'd bring up all the reasons why we still ought to go on the trip. Instead she kept glancing at her watch.

"Do you need to be somewhere?"

"The kids," she muttered.

I'd forgotten about them. I guess I still wasn't into this full-time parenting thing. "Then Gil and I'll walk you to your car."

"It's just as well that I have to go," she said, gathering up her bag. "I don't very often get angry, but when I do, I'm not the best company."

"We'll talk about this on Thursday. You'll have calmed down by then, with a bit of luck."

"I hate to admit it, but Monk's right about one thing. Time is short." She let out a long, frustrated sigh. "Despite what I think of him, we ought to make up our minds. Why don't you come round to me tomorrow night?"

"I'm busy tomorrow."

"Oh." She glanced up, her expression wary. "Anyone I know?"

"Sweetheart, there's no one in my life but you." I wiped imaginary sweat from my brow. "I'm not that brave. You're more than enough for one man to handle."

She grinned. "Just checking." I helped her over the gunwales and we followed Gil up the pontoon. "So, are you going to tell me what you've got planned for tomorrow then?"

"Nope, not until I see how it pans out. You'll just have to trust me until Thursday."

"Thursday it will have to be then," she said, clearly not happy about my reluctance to confide in her. "Wayne and Monk can dance to our tune for a change."

I shot her a look, wary about her easy capitulation. "Why not?"

"Perhaps Wayne will find someone else to crew if he doesn't hear from you before then."

"He rang me today and I said I'd get back to him by Thursday. He obviously hasn't got anyone else he can trust to do this, which is why he's worked so hard to cultivate us." I nodded emphatically. "He'll wait."

Back on the boat, I decided against calling upon the

long-suffering Jimmy, instead doing an internet search of the business address in Ramsgate that the goons' car was registered to. If it was connected to Monk's operation, however tenuously, I couldn't risk Slater finding out about my interest in it and causing me more grief.

The property in question housed an import-export business called Gatestone Enterprises. Presumably the import-export umbrella was broad enough to encompass people smuggling. *What is it you'd like us to import for you today, sir? Furniture, machine parts, guns, knocked-off designer gear, suicide bombers? No problem. Just sign on the dotted line.*

I reined in my imagination, concentrating on my search for information about Gatestone Enterprises. I wasn't altogether surprised when I found absolutely nothing. No website, no advertisements, not even a phone number. Zero, nada, zilch. The company simply didn't exist. I leaned back in my chair and thought about that. What company operating in today's fiercely competitive market did so without a website? It just didn't happen—not if it was kosher. A search of Companies House might lead me to the names of the directors behind the corporation but somehow I doubted it. An operation not in business to make money legitimately would hide its origins behind a maze of offshore shell companies. Anyway, time was of the essence so a more direct approach was called for.

Early the following morning, I left Gil with my neighbours for the day, fired up the Harley and headed for Ramsgate. After several wrong turns I found Gatestone Enterprises in a dingy backstreet of terraced residential houses, many of them converted into flats. It wasn't the sort of street in which you'd expect to find thriving business premises, but then I already knew Gatestone Enterprises didn't match that criteria.

In books there was usually a convenient cafe in which to kill time, stay warm and keep the target premises under surveillance. Hiding behind a newspaper whilst sipping industrial strength tea would have suited me just fine. In reality it seldom worked out that way and today was no exception. Resigned to the inevitable, I parked the Harley a safe distance away and did a slow walk-by before taking up a position at the head of an alley opposite. The front door of the house that interested me was painted blue. And firmly closed, with nothing outside to identify it as a place of business. No brass plaque or sign advertising its presence, no staff coming and going, no cars parked outside. Even so, I was pretty sure someone was home. The window blinds were all closed but every so often I saw a shadow move across the first floor front.

It was gone midday and presumably whoever was inside would feel the need for lunch sometime soon. An hour later I was starting to doubt that assumption because no one had gone in or out. I stretched to relieve the stiffness in my joints, tried to ignore my desperate need for a pee and continued with my vigil.

I was on the point of giving up when the front door opened. Bowling Ball appeared in company with another man who looked vaguely familiar. The thug punched in an alarm code, double locked the front door, and the two men walked away in different directions.

They parted without shaking hands or saying a word of farewell. I wondered if I ought to follow Bowling Ball but quickly dismissed the idea. He was a professional and would be on to me in a flash. By then the other man was heading towards the busier road abutting the one I was in, so I followed him instead. It was crowded with pedestrians and heavy through traffic. I glanced in both directions and swore. He'd already been swallowed up in the crowd and I didn't stand a hope in hell of finding him again.

But I didn't need to because I'd just remembered why he looked familiar. The mystery man was Ramsgate's Conservative MP, a shadow minister widely tipped to be the next leader of the party.

His name was Andrew Dannett.

I took one last look at the house before walking slowly back to the bike, my head whirling with a whole new raft of possibilities, none of which made any sense. What possible reason would a respected Tory MP have for conducting a secret meeting with one of the EPP's thugs?

Realisation came crashing in, causing me to stop dead in my tracks and swear aloud. The Asian man walking behind me cannoned into my back. I apologised absently, still trying to untangle my thoughts. A disused military base in Dannett's constituency had been earmarked for conversion to house the largest number of asylum seekers in one place in the entire U.K. It was all over the press and, not surprisingly, his constituents were up in arms about it. If Dannett's party was to have any chance of an outright victory in the election, keeping alive his personal ambitions to lead that party, then he clearly needed to find a way to scupper the immigration camp PDQ. And since he was on the intelligence committee, what better way to go about it than to use the confidential information that came his way? He could steer the EPP in the direction of the people smuggling, hardening public opinion against the whole business, all without getting his own hands dirty.

I shook my head, wondering why I should be surprised at the depths that supposedly respectable politicians were prepared to plummet to further their own ends.

Even if I was right about Dannett's intentions, it still didn't explain why he'd taken the EPP into his confidence. They would want their share of the glory so how would that help the Tories win the election? The answers might well lie in the house I'd spent most of the afternoon watching. I needed to get in there to see what was what and I knew precisely whose help to enlist. Having ex-cons owe you a favour was sometimes a useful thing.

Alf Vickery was one such and this was right up his street. Instead of riding the bike back to the marina, I headed for his office, more commonly known as the Blacksmith's Arms, a rundown backstreet pub in a less salubrious district of Brighton. I pushed through the door. Sure enough, Alf was propping up one end of the bar, a half-empty pint of bitter in front of him. The place was almost empty. There were just a few other customers, all men, sitting in solitary isolation from one another as though the idea of social networking had passed them by. The old-fashioned decor and air of shabby neglect perfectly suited the establishment's clientele.

"How you doing, Alf?" I plopped down onto the vacant stool beside him, trying not to let the depressing atmosphere seep into my bones.

"Hello, Mr. Hunter." His world-weary expression didn't change at the sight of me. "Long time no see."

I motioned to the barmaid, who was as well-worn as her place of employment, ordering a pint for myself and a refill for Alf.

"I heard you'd retired."

"I have."

"So, you felt the overwhelming urge to offer your patronage to this fine establishment and buy me a pint, is that it? Not that I'm not grateful, mind." He drained his old drink and took the top off the new one as soon as it was placed in front of him. He wiped the froth from his lips with the back of his hand and offered me a toothy grin. "How's things?"

"I have a bit of a problem, Alf, and thought you might like to help me out."

He chuckled. "You don't say?"

"How's June?"

This time his grin was filled with paternal pride. "She's doing great, Mr. Hunter, thanks for asking. Got herself a job in Boots."

"That's good."

"Yeah, but she says it's only temporary." He pulled a doomed face. "She wants to be a model. She's got the body for it an' all, so I'm hoping she don't get talent spotted, or whatever it is that gets 'em on their way."

"It probably won't happen."

June was Alf's daughter and the apple of his eye. His wife died when June was a baby and she and her light-fingered dad had coexisted since then to the exclusion of the rest of the world. When I last nicked Alf, June had been fourteen. Alf looked upon doing time as an occupational hazard. His only concern was for June. It had got to the stage where some of the dodgy boys hanging round his good-looking daughter were a real worry for him. Like all parents, he wanted better for her than the hand life had dealt him. June, in turn, felt let down by her dad, who'd promised to go straight. She was perpetually angry with a world that had done her few favours—a disaster in the making that wouldn't happen if I could prevent it. I promised Alf I'd see what I could do and got her placed with decent foster parents. They'd obviously kept her on the straight and narrow and it seemed the story had as happy an ending as the Junes of this world could ever hope for.

As a consequence Alf felt indebted to me and I was about to call in that debt. He was the best I'd ever met at picking locks and disabling alarms, which was one of the reasons why he'd so seldom been captured during a long and illustrious career as a burglar. Okay, so he helped himself to stuff that wasn't technically his but, as far as I knew, he'd never trashed the places he broke into and had never used violence or hurt anyone during the execution of his crimes. Alf was an old-school type of thief for whom I felt a grudging sort of respect.

"I need the benefit of your expertise, Alf." I sipped at my pint, wondering if it was such a good idea since I hadn't eaten much all day.

"Yeah, well, you know I'll do anything I can for you, Mr. H."

"I need to get into a property in Ramsgate."

He didn't bother asking me why. "Type of locks?" he asked, switching to business mode.

"A standard Yale and a mortis."

He wrinkled his nose in obvious contempt. "You insulting my talents?"

"There's an alarm with a keypad."

That got his interest. "What type?"

"Wireless."

"Best forget it then 'cos there ain't no way round them buggers," he said gloomily. "Cut the phone line or the power and it goes to battery. If the battery fails the alarm goes off. Cunning bastard who invented 'em killed off my trade."

He wasn't telling me something I didn't already know, but I was still disappointed. "So you can't get me into that house then?"

"Did I say that?" Alf smacked his lips together, justifiably affronted. "I can get you in but I can't stop the alarm going off."

"Ah, well then."

"It'll go straight through to the alarm's control centre and they'll ring the householder, and probably the old bill too." Alf scratched his chin. "But, unless the householder lives nearby, I reckon you've got twenty minutes before anyone'll turn up to check it out. I mean, no offence, Mr. H, but your lot have never been that hot on responding to ringing alarms, have they now?"

I conceded the point. "Other priorities, Alf. They're usually false alarms anyway. But still, someone will know we've been in there if the alarm goes off and I'd like to try and avoid that."

He looked at me askance. "I assume you ain't gonna nick nothing."

"Correct. I just need to have a look round."

"Well then, they'll just think it's a false alarm." Somehow I doubted it. "Anyway, if we're gonna do this, is there a back entrance?"

"Yes, leads straight into an alleyway."

"Well, I could get you in but, like I say, the alarm'll ring immediately. To be on the safe side, I'll give you five minutes to look for what you need and then we're out of there. Will that be long enough?"

I didn't have a clue because I didn't know what I was looking for. I nodded anyway.

"Okay, Mr. H, whilst you having a shufty, I'll make sure we've got an escape route out back in case it goes pear-shaped."

I realised then just what I was asking him to do. It was a harebrained scheme, the chances of getting caught were infinite and if that happened Alf, with his previous, could look forward to a long stretch. I didn't even want to think about the consequences for me. But in spite of the dangers, Alf didn't hesitate to offer his help. I felt an overwhelming sense of gratitude towards him, at the same time sorely tempted to call the whole thing off. What could I possibly achieve in five minutes?

"Are you sure you're up for this, Alf? Don't feel obliged. The risks—"

He waved my objections aside. "When do you want this done?"

"Right now. Come on, drink up."

"Blimey, you don't give a bloke much notice, do you." But he drained his glass and followed me willingly enough. "I'll need to stop at my place and pick up a few things."

"No problem."

"Where's your transport?" he asked, looking round when we got outside.

"Here." I nodded at the Harley and threw my spare helmet in his direction.

He looked horrified. "I ain't getting on that death trap."

"Course you are, Alf. Where's your sense of adventure? Come on, I'm in a hurry."

He clung to my waist for the entire trip to Ramsgate, and I could hear his muttered complaints even over the rumble of the engine. It was gone eleven o'clock when we arrived, a busy time for the local plod so, hopefully, ringing alarms wouldn't feature high on their list of priorities. I parked up in a different spot and we walked the short distance to the house. There were a few people about but, as in any busy town, everyone was minding their own business and not paying any attention to us. Alf rang the bell, just to make sure no one was at home. Not that I imagined there would be. There were no lights coming from inside, but it paid to be cautious.

Alf pulled on a pair of gloves and flashed me a

grin, already enjoying himself. The downside of going straight was that he missed the crack, and my request had obviously cheered him up no end. He insisted upon looking round the back first, scoping the place out.

"I do like nice quiet back alleys," he said, rubbing his hands together when he returned.

"Glad to oblige."

Alf applied his attention to the front door. Less than two minutes later we were standing in the hallway of Gatestone Enterprises with the door closed behind us and the alarm ringing loud enough to wake the dead.

"Well done, Alf!"

"Piece of piss." He looked round with a professional eye. "Blimey, looks like someone beat us to it."

He was right. The hall and the two rooms on the ground floor were completely devoid of furniture, the bare floorboards creaking with age every time we took a step. The entire place smelled mouldy and unused, the only recent investment apparently made on the thick blinds pulled closed across the windows, assuring absolute privacy. The kitchen was antiquated, the only concession to modern living a brand new kettle sitting incongruously in the centre of the pitted wooden surface.

I noticed all this in the first few seconds and then headed for the stairs, using a torch to light my path. Alf disappeared into the scullery to effect an emergency escape route. I was more interested in the room I'd seen movement in that afternoon. If there was anything to interest me, it would be up there. I almost had a heart attack when a disembodied voice echoed through the wall. It hadn't even occurred to me that someone might actually be in the property. Only when my heartbeat returned to a more normal rate did I realise it was the alarm company, talking through the speaker on the wall, asking if everything was all right. I froze to the spot, anxious not to make any noise that would alert them to a genuine break-in. After what seemed like an eternity of wasted opportunity the static died away and it was safe to move again.

The upstairs room was furnished with two old settees, a glass coffee table separating them. There was also a wooden dining table and four chairs but absolutely nothing else. Dannett obviously only used this property for meetings with his EPP buddies. Now that I was actually inside I wondered what I'd hoped to find. A smoking gun in the form of detailed written accounts of their exploits would be useful, but that was probably too much to expect.

Alf joined me and prowled about, muttering to himself. A jubilant exclamation alerted me to the fact that he'd found something of interest. It was a locked cupboard, but wouldn't stay that way for long. A bit like a compulsive gambler being unable to walk past a bookie's, so Alf couldn't see a lock and not wonder what was behind it.

"What's the point of locking anything away in an empty house?" he asked, standing back as the door to the cupboard swung open on squeaky hinges.

There was a laptop computer inside. I felt vindicated in breaking in now that I'd found something of potential value but my sense of triumph was short-lived when I fired the machine up and it asked for a password.

"Damn!" I tried Dannett's name, then his wife's name, and came up blank.

"What are you doing?" Alf asked.

"Whatever I want is on this computer but I can't get by the bloody password."

"I have absolutely no idea what you're talking about, Mr. H." Alf sat himself down on one of the settees, not having found anything worthy of his professional attention in this empty shell of a house. "I reckon the whole world has gone off its rocker with this computer stuff," he said morosely. "Nobody talks to anybody face-to-face anymore. It's all email, and Twitter and blogs, whatever the fuck they are. It ain't healthy, if you ask me."

I barely listened to him as I racked my brains, trying to figure out what word Dannett would have used to protect his secrets. I read somewhere that people use the most obvious passwords, like abcde or 12345. Not Dannett, though. He'd gone to extreme lengths to hide whatever was on the computer and had been a little more inventive than that. I tried a few more obvious combinations and swore in frustration when they failed.

"We ain't got much longer, Mr. H."

"I know, Alf. Just give me a minute or two and then we'll go." It wouldn't be long enough but the stubborn corner of my brain refused to admit defeat. I was sorely tempted just to take the computer, but that wasn't really an option. It would be missed, Dannett would be given advance notice to cover his tracks and he'd get away with his dirty deeds.

"Not if I have anything to say about it," I muttered, as keen now as Monk was to expose him for the fraud that he was.

"Mr. H!" Alf said again a minute later, an urgent edge to his voice this time.

"Just one minute more." What the hell were the names of Dannett's kids? He had a daughter and two sons and I was willing to bet that his little girl was the key to this bloody password. Sandra? Serena? Neither worked. Why the hell hadn't I taken the time to do a little research on Dannett and come better prepared?

"Did you 'ear that?" Alf was on his feet, peering round the edge of the blind. "Christ, it's the filth!" He shot me a panicked look. "How did they get here so quick?"

I switched off the computer and threw it back in the cupboard exactly where I'd found it, snapped the door locked and joined Alf at the window. My heart was literally in my mouth. Sweat trickled down my spine and I'm ashamed to say I had to clasp my hands together to stop them from shaking. We were cornered up here and I doubted whether we'd be able to creep downstairs and reach Alf's escape route without being detected. The coppers were bound to check round the back, looking for any signs of a break-in, and we'd be caught red-handed. I should have listened to Alf and got out whilst we had the chance. And it was all for bloody nothing anyway because I didn't have a prayer of cracking that password.

Alf and I remained stock still at the window, straining to hear what the coppers were saying. One rattled the front door but we'd locked it behind us and it didn't budge.

"Door's locked," he said, shining his torch over the windows, "and it doesn't look as though any windows have been forced."

"Probably another false alarm," said his mate. "Still, I'd better check the back since we're here."

He returned mercifully quickly and said nothing was disturbed. I didn't know what Alf had done back there but whatever it was, the copper clearly hadn't taken much of a look. I offered up a silent prayer of thanks for his lack of diligence.

"Shall we wait for the key holder, just to be sure?" said the first guy. I heard the sound of a match being struck and guessed he was a smoker grabbing the opportunity for a fix.

"Suppose it wouldn't hurt. He said he'd get here sharpish, didn't he."

Alf and I shared an anxious glance, neither of us daring to move or speak a word aloud. The coppers settled against the front wall immediately beneath us, talking amongst themselves. The road suddenly seemed a whole lot quieter than when we'd arrived, but as long as we didn't make a sound, we might just remain undetected. For now, at least.

Then my phone rang.

"Here, what was that?"

I sensed the policeman who'd asked the question glancing up at our window as I scrabbled to shut the phone off. Alf fixed an incredulous gaze on my face, his disgust alleviating the need for words. "Sorry," I mouthed.

"I didn't hear anything," the other copper said.

This was a stalemate and I was all out of ideas. If the coppers accompanied the key holder into the house, then we were stuffed. If he came in alone, on the other hand, we might just have a chance. Either way, Dannett would know someone had been nosing around.

I heard a crackle of static emanating from the police car and the sound of one of our coppers speaking into the radio.

"Come on," he said to his mate. "We've got a shout. A domestic in Queens Road."

"Bugger it, not again."

To our relief we heard the doors slam and the engine start. As soon as the car took off we ran down the stairs like our lives depended upon it. Alf disappeared into the scullery to re-secure the rear escape route and we let ourselves cautiously out of the front door, Alf resetting the mortise after us.

"Fuck me, that was close!" he said, wiping sweat from his brow.

I heard a car approaching and pushed him across the road, into the alley I'd spent most of the day hiding in. "Quick!"

A familiar silver Mondeo pulled up at the house and Bowling Ball emerged from the driving seat, a set of keys in his hand. He was alone. And he didn't look happy.

SIXTEEN

I DROPPED ALF back at his place with my heartfelt thanks and a few bob in his pocket.

First thing in the morning I collected Gil. I could have done with more sleep but couldn't afford the luxury. I had work to do. I took Gil for a shorter walk than usual and, forgoing breakfast, took off on the Harley. My destination was a half-decent block of flats on the outskirts of Brighton. The person I intended to visit didn't currently enjoy gainful employment so my chances of finding him at home this early had to be good.

I knocked several times and was on the point of giving up when the door was wrenched open by Ben Pocock wearing a pair of boxer shorts and nothing else. It wasn't a pretty sight, especially on an empty stomach.

"Mr. Hunter?" He peered myopically in my direction, rubbing the sleep from his eyes. "What have I done this time?"

"I'm not here in my professional capacity, Ben. Can I come in?"

He shrugged. "Suppose so."

He opened the door wider and I followed him into a cluttered kitchen. He put the kettle on, yawning and muttering beneath his breath.

"Black, no sugar," I said when he waved a jar of instant coffee in my face. "Thanks." I took a sip of the resulting brew and got right down to business. "I've got a job for you, Ben."

"Oh yeah. What would that be then?"

Ben was another ex-con who owed me a favour. He'd been a private detective before he let his personal ambitions override his professionalism. He was following a guy's wife, the guy suspecting her of having an affair. It turned out that she was, but before Ben could report back to the husband the woman clocked him. She was attractive and, by all accounts, very persuasive. Not only did she convince Ben not to let on to her husband that she'd strayed but also used her feminine wiles to get Ben to knock off her old man's safe. Supposedly they'd ride off into the sunset with the proceeds and live happily ever after.

There's no fool like a man thinking with his prick. He was caught, the wife denied all involvement and Ben finished up doing two years. Slater was under pressure at the time to do something about clear-up rates and, unable to get anywhere with her own cases because she was basically crap at detective work, she started dabbling in mine. She had a personal dislike of PIs, but Slater had personal dislikes about most professions, so that didn't say much. Anyway, she tried running behind my back to the superintendent and pinning a load of other shit on Ben, implying that I'd ignored it. I made sure she didn't get away with it, further souring my relationship with Slater but earning Ben's gratitude.

"I need you to follow this bloke." I handed him a picture of Dannett I'd downloaded from the net. "I want to know everything about him. Where he goes, who he talks to, the works."

"Here, isn't he that toff politician?"

"That would be him. He's attending a rally in his constituency this afternoon. If you get your skates on you'll be able to pick him up and tail him from there."

"What do I do about transport?"

"Hire yourself a car," I said, passing him an envelope with some cash in it.

"Fair enough." He looked almost cheerful. "It'll be like old times. How long do you want me to watch him for?"

"Say until the end of the weekend." That would mean I'd hear from him before I went to France with Kara. *If* I went to France with Kara. "That should be long enough."

He laughed. "The old bill on a budget nowadays, are they?"

"Er, this isn't anything to do with the job, Ben. You'd be doing this for me as a personal favour. If you're uncomfortable with that, you don't have to—"

He waved away my explanation. "Say no more."

I could see that he was pleased to be working again. It must be tough for someone with a lively mind like Ben's to be unemployable because of his record. If it had been down to me I never would have done him for breaking into that guy's safe. He'd been led by the balls by a woman who wanted revenge against a violent husband. I couldn't prove it though because when Ben got caught in the act, she and the husband were magically reconciled. Upshot of it all was that she walked away from the wreckage she'd caused of Ben's life without a stain on her character. I felt for Ben but Slater would have carried on snitching to the super, trying to push on with the other stuff she'd supposedly dug up on Ben, if I hadn't charged him.

"How do I get in touch with you?"

I gave him my mobile number. "If you can get any pictures that would be even better."

"Consider it done."

I hadn't been back at the boat for long when Gil started creating a ruckus, warning me I had a visitor. Kara's voice called to me from the pontoon. She was early. Our date was for tonight.

"Can I come aboard, Charlie?"

"Sure."

It was sweet that she still bothered to ask, given our exclusive relationship. I'd offered to go to hers but she preferred getting away for a while and coming to the boat. Perhaps the time had come to give her a key. But was I ready to go that far? It seemed like the ultimate commitment.

Probably better not to rush into it.

Out in the cockpit, I stretched to remove the kinks that had accumulated after hours of sitting in front of the computer. She threw a large holdall on the deck before stepping on board. So much for discussing the possibility of going to France.

"Just in case we decide to go," she said sweetly, following the direction of my eyes.

I kissed her and carried her bag through to the salon. "And the kids?"

"Sergei is at boys' camp this weekend. Saskia's with Mum."

"Have you had lunch?"

"No, now that you mention it."

"Soup and warm bread?"

"Sounds good. Can I help?"

"I think I can manage, thanks."

Once we'd eaten and cleared away I told her all about my little trip—well, trips actually—to Ramsgate.

"You should have told Monk. He'd have been able to look into that house without you putting yourself at risk." She wagged a finger beneath my nose. "I don't like to think of you encouraging reformed criminals to break and enter. What if you'd been caught?"

"We weren't." She didn't need to know how close to the wind we'd sailed. "And Alf would be most put out if he heard you calling his professional expertise into question."

"Well, if you put him in prison he can't be that good."

"Oh yes, he can, trust me. Much as I'd like to claim that catching him was the result of brilliant detective work, in actual fact it was nothing more than a piece of luck. And to answer your first assertion, Monk definitely didn't need to be told. He's not the only one who can withhold information. But, as it turned out, it was all a pointless waste of time because I couldn't get past that bloody password."

"Shame you couldn't have copied the hard disc."

My expression probably told her what I thought of

that suggestion. "Even if I'd thought to go prepared, I didn't have enough time."

"Hmm, shame." She tiled her head, regarding me with suspicion. "Why that house anyway? What took you there?"

"Does the name Andrew Dannett mean anything to you?" I asked her.

Her eyebrows shot upward. "The next Conservative Party leader, you mean?"

"So he'd like us all to believe."

"What's he got to do with all this?"

"That's what we broke into that house to find out. I saw him there with one of the men from the EPP who accosted me. They left together."

"Blimey, this gets weirder by the minute. We've got the Labour government, the EPP and now the Tories all involved in this." She turned towards me, frowning. "How does it all fit together?"

I shrugged. "Beats the hell out of me."

"Do you think Monk knows about Dannett?"

I nodded. "I'm sure he does."

"So why didn't he tell us?"

"Why indeed." I paced the wheelhouse, glad for the opportunity to bounce my increasingly wild ideas off her. "Monk is basically a civil servant, but that doesn't mean his loyalties necessarily lie with this present government."

"They probably do." She paused, plucking at her lower lip as she thought about that. "I can hardly imagine him wearing a flat cap and reading *The Sun*."

"No one reads *The Sun*, darling, they just look at the pictures."

She pulled a face at me.

"And just so that you know, New Labour followers wouldn't be seen dead in flat caps anymore. They're just glorified Tories in red coats."

"I didn't know you were such a political cynic."

I winked at her. "There's a lot you don't know about me."

"Well, I still don't see what Dannett hopes to gain from an alliance with the EPP."

"Me neither, but whatever was on that computer has to be crucial, otherwise why keep it hidden in an empty house with state-of-the-art alarms? Dannett must have loads of computers, in his offices, at his home. What can be so important that he won't trust it to any of those?"

"Other people could access it, I suppose," she said. "His staff, his family…has he got a family?"

"Yeah, a wife and three teenage kids. The perfect family unit according to the media, who love him, by the way."

"Then why would he risk it all by getting involved with the EPP? They might be less extreme than the neo-Nazis but they're still considered racist by a lot of people. Unless…"

"Unless what?"

"Well, perhaps he isn't—involved with EPP. I mean. We don't know for definite that those men who accosted you are part of the EPP. Monk just assumed they were because it fits with the information he has, but what if they're really Tories?"

"Unlikely. If they were bona fide colleagues then why meet them in secret?"

"Yes, there is that, I suppose." She looked deflated. "So we're back to why Dannett hid stuff on that laptop. His staff and kids probably have access to his computers and the kids in particular wouldn't be able to resist rooting about to see what he has on them. If he couldn't afford for this to be found then he obviously had to hide it somewhere safe."

"Yes, and we know where it is, much good that'll do us."

I considered telling her I'd set Ben to keep watch on Dannett but in the end kept it to myself. Whatever the politician was up to, it was unlikely to involve Gordon Reed.

"So," I said with a dramatic sigh that made her giggle. "Still want to go to France?"

"I don't see that we have any choice, not really."

Neither did I. After all the risks I'd taken recently I was too involved to back down. Besides, the policeman in me wanted to see Dannett get his comeuppance. "Okay, if you're sure then I guess we'll do it."

"That's good." She frowned. "I think. And since the kids are accounted for, I can spend the entire weekend with you."

"Oh no, anything but that!"

"What will we do to pass the time?" she asked, fluttering her lashes at me.

"Play scrabble," I said, reaching for her and pulling her onto my lap. "Only this time, no cheating."

"Charlie, I swear to you on the children's lives that *ablatively* is a genuine word."

"I ablatively don't believe you."

"As if I'd lie to you."

I rolled my eyes. "As if you would."

"Well, anyway, I'm sure we'll think of more interesting games to play."

"That's my girl! You dream up entertainments and I'll call Wayne." I picked up my phone and, with Kara still on my knee, did just that. "As long as the mutt can come too, then we're on."

THE FOLLOWING AFTERNOON, Monk received a pandemonious welcome from Gil. I'd been feeling edgy ever since agreeing to do his bidding, so his immaculate trousers getting covered in dog hairs improved my mood a little.

"Drink?" I waved a bottle of single malt in front of his face.

"Thank you, Charlie." He sat down and Gil, suddenly on his best behaviour, sank to the floor next to him.

"Anything for you, Kara?"

"White wine, please."

Once we'd all got our drinks, Monk got down to the reason for his visit. "I've brought you the mobile I promised you." He handed me a Blackberry. "It's fitted with a GSM tracker. Provided that you keep it charged and switched on at all times, we'll know where you are and if you've stopped." He smiled. "You'll even be able to use it to pick up your email."

"That's comforting."

We spent another half hour talking through every

likely scenario that might result from the trip. Monk constantly reassured us that help would never be far away, and that we were in no real danger.

I didn't believe a word of it.

That evening I told Kara I needed to go out alone for an hour.

"Okay." She was immersed in some work for her lonely hearts on her laptop and didn't ask me where I was going. "I'll have dinner ready for when you get back."

"Sounds good."

We were starting to act like an old married couple, and the bugger of it was that I actually didn't mind.

I met Ben in one of the bars abutting the marina and bought him a beer.

"What have you got for me?" I asked, once we'd settled at a quiet corner table.

"He's squeaky clean," Ben said glumly, making inroads into his drink. "I didn't think that was possible for a modern politician. It's a bit of a contradiction in terms, isn't it?"

I agreed. "But you found something?" I suggested, alerted by his expression of barely suppressed excitement.

"I'd almost given up hope, that's not to say the will to live. Well, following a politician does that to a body. All those insincere smiles and back-patting. Made me nauseous, it did."

"I can imagine."

"Yeah, well anyway, late last night he left wife and family and called at an upmarket block of flats in Ramsgate. I didn't dare get too close to see which flat he went into, so I thought I'd lost him." He leaned back in his chair, legs stretched out in front of him, dragging it out. Since he'd clearly discovered something important, I let him enjoy his moment of glory without urging him to get to the point. "Anyway, I was just trying to decide what to do next when two men emerged, neither of them Dannett. Or so I thought at first." He paused and took a long, irritatingly slow swig of his drink, grinning at me over the rim of his glass.

"But?"

"Okay, Charlie, keep your hair on, I'm getting to the best bit."

I refrained from asking if he planned to do so before we both died of old age.

"There was something about one of those men. The way he walked with a swagger, like he owned the world, but also kept glancing around as though worried he might be seen. I didn't recognise the face but there was no way he could disguise the body language."

I felt my heart rate increase. "It was Dannett?"

"Yeah, it was him." Ben smiled complacency. "He was wearing glasses and a hat that covered most of his face, but it was definitely him."

"Do you know who he was with?"

"No, but I know where they went." He named a restaurant. "It's a quiet place but expensive and serves good food."

I pondered this information for a moment. "I wonder why Dannett needed to entertain another man to dinner without wanting to draw attention to himself?"

"Perhaps because they returned to the flat and Dannett stayed until the early hours," suggested Ben smugly.

The penny finally dropped and I shot upright in my chair. The staunch family man, the honest politician who wanted to be the next prime minister, was having a relationship with another man.

"I've got pictures," Ben said, handing me a sheaf, "but some of them are a bit blurred. Sorry, but I couldn't risk being caught."

"No worries," I said absently, my mind still reeling after Ben's discovery. "You've done more than I could have hoped for."

I leafed through the photos. The disguise was effective and I wouldn't have recognised Dannett had I not known it was him. Only problem was, I didn't recognise the man with him either so I wasn't really any further forward.

SEVENTEEN

"This is a bit like groundhog day," Kara muttered as we were again greeted by Wayne early on Monday morning at the offices of Ultimate Marine.

"Come on in, Charlie, Kate," he said, shaking my hand and giving Kara a smacking kiss. "Morning, Gil," he added, patting the dog's big head. "I'm really glad you decided to do this one."

"Happy to oblige. What's on the agenda this time then?"

Wayne didn't respond immediately. There was no sign of Gail and so he made coffee and assembled breakfast himself, waving away Kara's offer of help. "Okay," he said, placing steaming mugs and platefuls of bacon sandwiches in front of us. "Get that down you."

"Thanks."

"Like I said," Wayne continued, speaking round a mouthful of bacon and tomato sauce. "I won't be coming this time but Tim Bolton will be the boss. You'll like him. He's competent, good with the punters and has done this jaunt a few times before."

"What are you up to then?" I asked.

"I've got a half-dozen wannabe sailors to take care of." He made it sound like a fate worse than death. "There's no one but me available right now that's qualified to take that particular course. Tim only does motor."

"I see. Well, never mind. How many punters this time round?"

"A full complement. Three couples, but none of them are connected to each other, as far as Gail knows, anyway. She handles that side of things and tells me they all booked separately."

"I'm surprised they all agreed to have Gil on board then," Kara said. "I'd have thought there'd be at least one person allergic to dog hair, or something equally ridiculous." She stroked Gil, just to make sure that he hadn't taken offence, and sneaked him a piece of her sandwich under the table when she thought I wasn't looking.

"Yeah well, we struck lucky I guess because nobody objected. Mind you, the discounts I'm still having to offer probably helped to overcome any canine hang-ups. Ah, here's Tim." Wayne waved to the guy who'd just walked into the office. "Come on in, Tim. You're just in time for a sarnie, but let me introduce you to your crew first."

Tim Bolton was a clean-cut guy of about thirty. At first glance he was the last person I'd have figured to be involved in something shady, but after all my years on the force I knew better than to make snap judgements. He shook our hands but didn't make eye contact, which told me a lot. He took the last seat at the table and picked at a sandwich.

"Does anyone know what the weather has in store for us?" Kara asked.

"It looks like it won't be quite as straightforward as last time, I'm afraid." Wayne grinned. "The hot spell is forecast to break and you might catch a squall or two on the way across. Get the sick bags ready," he added, chuckling.

"Oh God!" Kara shook her head. "Is it too late to change our minds?"

"Get seasick, do you, love?" Wayne asked.

"No, but clearing up other people's puke doesn't exactly fill me with joy."

"Ah well," I said, "what else can you expect in this country? We've had almost a month of good weather now. It had to come to an end sooner or later."

"Especially as it's the start of the school holidays," agreed Tim gloomily. "That's the most reliable weather indicator I've ever come across. It's in the eighties whilst the kids swelter in the classroom, but as soon as school's out, the heavens open."

"Got school-age children, Tim?" I only asked to get a handle on what tempted such a decent seeming guy to get involved with Wayne's shenanigans.

"Yeah, two." His smile was broad and I feared he was about to produce photos. Mercifully he didn't, but he was clearly a besotted father. "A boy and a girl, seven and five."

"At least you don't have to keep them occupied for the next few days."

"Nah, he'll be looking after the customers instead, which is probably worse." Wayne glanced at his watch and pushed himself to his feet. "Look, sorry, but I've gotta run. I'll leave you in Tim's capable hands. Have a good trip and I'll see you when you get back. Keep in touch, Tim," he added with a significant glance over his shoulder, "and if you have any problems at all you know where to find me."

"So," Tim said, wiping sauce from his mouth with a paper napkin. "If you're finished let's make sure the boat's all ready. The customers will be here soon and it'll save us a lot of grief if everything's in good order before they start finding things to complain about."

We cleared away the debris and then went aboard. Everything was it should be. The fridge and freezer were fully stocked and, naturally, the drinks cabinet boasted every imaginable alcoholic drink, presumably courtesy of the boat's frequent trips to France. Those fabric scrunchy things that women use to hold their ponytails back were wrapped round the bottles, preventing them from hitting against each other in big seas.

"We'll establish ourselves in the crew quarters, shall we then?" I said to Tim. "Get settled before the punters arrive."

"Well actually, I was thinking," he said, stuttering slightly, a pink blush spreading upwards from his neck. "As there's three of you, why don't you take the skipper's cabin on board and I'll go in the back?"

"Oh no!" Kara's expression was convincingly shocked. "That's not right. You're the skipper so you get to sleep in comfort. We don't mind cosying up in the transom and giving you some space."

"No, no, I insist." Tim managed to dredge up a tone of authority. It would have been quite convincing if his face wasn't now burning bright red.

"Well, if you're sure," I said.

Kara was right to protest, and we all knew it. There was a strict pecking order on board any professionally run boat, status attaching to the level of accommodation allocated to each member of the crew. These things mattered and, by giving way to us, any lingering doubts about Tim's involvement were dispelled.

"Oh yeah, don't worry." He ushered us into the captain's cabin and hovered in the doorway. "I've slept in worse places than the crew cabin."

"What about Gil?" I asked, determined not to make it too easy for him. "Won't he be in the way if he's on the main deck?"

"Nah, Wayne says he's well behaved. Just make sure you use the side door to let him onto the deck, don't take him through the salon, and it'll be fine."

"Fair enough."

"I'll leave you to get sorted then." Tim looked relieved to have got the accommodation issue out of the way. "Let's reassemble in ten."

Kara and I looked at each other when the door closed behind him but waited until Tim was well out of earshot before sharing our thoughts. The cabin was a very small double—little more than a large single really—but luxury compared to the cramped crew quarters. We'd be able to get very comfortable in that bed, provided that Gil didn't requisition it first, of course.

"Shame," Kara said quietly, sitting on the side of the bed and bouncing up and down to test the quality of the mattress. "He seems like a decent bloke. Wonder what persuaded him to get involved?"

"He's a young man trying to make a living out of the sea in times of recession." I shook my head. "He's got two kids and presumably a mortgage to pay." I left her to connect the dots.

"Yes, I suppose Wayne would have sold it to him as easy money for minimal risk. It probably proved irresistible at first and now he's in too deep to back down." She stashed the few bits and pieces we'd brought with us and turned to face me, frowning. "But why do you think he's so nervous?"

"He probably can't stop thinking about what happened to *Mistral*."

"Nor can I." She shuddered. "Come on, let's go and face the music before I lose my nerve altogether."

We assembled with Gil at the bottom of the *passerelle*, much as we'd done on the previous occasion. Two middle-aged couples arrived separately and we showed them on board. Quietly spoken and appreciative of our service, the only thing they had in common with the last lot was that they were clearly not married to their respective partners. The sideways glances and frequent hand contact gave them away but, unlike the Davis brothers, they seemed reluctant to flaunt their relationships. Even so, I figured we wouldn't be seeing too much of either pair during the crossing.

We were on the point of giving up on the third couple, who were over half an hour late, when a car screeched to a halt directly behind the dock and a familiar-looking couple rushed toward the *Vagabond*. My mind reeling, I could barely believe my eyes.

"What the hell are they doing here?"

I'd been wondering if the EPP would have a presence on board to make sure this trip didn't end up the same way as *Mistral*'s. Had Ronnie shown up, I'd have had no difficulty believing it of him. But these two…?

"Who are they?" Kara asked, peering inquisitively at the approaching pair. "And why have they made you so agitated?"

Before I could respond, Julie and Mike Price were upon us, looking very different to the bumbling incompetents who'd taken the Day Skipper course. Gone were the his-and-hers outfits. Instead Julie looked almost sophisticated in tailored linen trousers and a smart top. Mike was dressed in expensive casual gear and wore an air of self-confidence that belied the henpecked-husband role he'd assumed on the course. They both stopped dead in their tracks when they saw me.

"Charlie, what a coincidence!" Julie kissed my cheek and passed me the hold-all she was carrying. The put-down wasn't lost on me. "I didn't know you'd be crewing on this trip."

Like hell you didn't. "Hello, Julie. Mike." We shook hands. "Kate, this is Julie and Mike Price, who were on the Day Skipper course with me a few weeks ago."

Kara recovered her poise with commendable speed and shook hands with them both.

"We did tell Wayne," Mike said, sliding an arm round Julie's waist, "that we might take one of these trips. It's our anniversary this month and the price was so good that we thought, why not?"

"Why not indeed?" Tim came forward and introduced himself. "And it's my job to ensure that you don't regret that decision. I'm Tim Bolton, your skipper, and you've obviously met the rest of the crew. Now, do come aboard and I'll introduce you to your fellow passengers. I believe we're about to serve welcome drinks in the salon."

They disappeared on board, leaving Kara and me to struggle with their luggage.

"Are they part of it?" Kara asked, staring after them. "They don't seem the type."

I grimaced. "They must be."

"I thought you said they were complete imbeciles."

"That's obviously what they wanted me to believe."

And I'd fallen for it. I tried to think of signs I might have missed but I'd been too busy avoiding Julie's clumsy attempts to flirt with me to notice them. I thought of her visit to my cabin shortly after I'd snaffled Wayne's phone and was convinced now that she knew exactly what I'd done—although hopefully not why.

"So what happens now?"

"We wait and see, I suppose," I said, unable to shake the feeling of unease that had gripped me since the Prices showed up. "There's not much else we can do, short of jumping ship."

Kara and I served drinks and then prepared the boat for sea. I could smell rain in the air as I let the lines go and suspected that Wayne was right about the weather.

It broke not an hour after we left Hythe. All the way across the Channel the boat was lashed by torrential rain and buffeted about by a huge swell. It was at times like this that the *No Comment* came into her own. She was made for these conditions. The same couldn't be said for the *Vagabond*, and Tim was forced to retreat to the lower helm position to save himself from a drenching. He slowed us down to eight knots, taking the powerful boat off the plane. She wallowed about and made slow progress in the big sea.

As predicted, the first two couples stuck to their cabins but Mike and Julie were obviously much better sailors than they'd previously let on and seemed unaffected by the conditions. They led Kara and me a merry dance, politely asking for a full lunch service—next to impossible under the circumstances but Kara rose to the challenge. They were charming but demanding for the entire crossing.

Once we arrived in Port de Plaisance, the rain stopped and a weak sun made a half-hearted attempt to penetrate the gloomy skies. The other two couples emerged from their cabins, whey-faced and full of apologies. After a short discussion with Mike and Julie it was decided that the cruise would begin and end here. The non-sailors had had more than enough and were happy to spend the next couple of days exploring the questionable delights of Calais. That clearly suited Mike and Julie, which was perhaps why I'd overheard her putting the idea into their heads.

"What now?" Kara asked as we prepared for bed that evening.

"Now," I said, slipping between the sheets and pulling her against me, "we wait."

"I'm scared," she mumbled into my shoulder.

We'd been in a number of dangerous situations during the course of our relationship and she'd never once admitted to being scared. That she did so now bothered me. Had we done the right thing, coming here? Not that Kara would have taken no for an answer, but if I really hadn't wanted her to come, I could have stopped her somehow.

WE GOT THROUGH the next day but it was a strain. Tim was a nervous wreck. Several times I noticed him talking animatedly on his phone, gesticulating wildly. The two older couples spent the entire day and most of the evening off the boat but Mike and Julie were never far away. The atmosphere was tense, the strain of keeping up the pretence until they spelled out their demands telling on both Kara and me. I was determined to play them at their own game and not let them see that I was on edge, but Kara had remembered she had responsibilities and found it more difficult to behave normally. When she dropped a full serving bowl of potatoes all over the galley floor that evening, I knew she was close to her limit.

"Are you all right, Kate?" Julie asked. "Can I help?"

"No thanks." I answered for Kara. "It was just an accident. We have everything under control."

We were about to turn in when Tim cornered us in the now empty salon.

"Can I have a quick word?" he asked, twisting his hands together nervously.

"Sure thing," I said, confident I knew what was coming. "What's on your mind, Tim?"

Kara and I had speculated upon whether or not he'd tell us about the illegals. I reckoned he'd have no choice.

I *had* to go into the engine room to do checks during the trip home, and I'd have to be blind not to notice any extra bodies littering my path. Kara argued that perhaps Tim would find an excuse to do the checks himself but I didn't see how he could be sure I wouldn't go down without telling him. If he locked the crew quarters to keep me out of the engine room, it would not only be dangerous but also highly suspicious. No, I was convinced Wayne had told him to enlighten us just before the illegals were due on board. It looked like I'd been right about that. Now I was interested to hear how he'd dress it up.

"There's something you need to know," he said. "We'll be…er, that is to say, we'll be taking a couple of extra passengers back with us."

"Oh really." I feigned surprise. "And you need our cabin, is that it?"

"No, not exactly. They'll be in the crew cabin, out of sight. They don't exactly have up-to-date passports, you see."

"What, you mean they're illegals?" Kara said, her expression of wide-eyed shock pretty convincing.

"Something like that," he said, gesturing vaguely. "It's probably better that you don't ask too many questions."

"That's easy for you to say," I pointed out. "We're part of the crew and didn't sign up for this. If we get rumbled, no one's gonna believe we didn't know what was going down."

"Nah, that won't happen. We've done this before and the system's pretty slick."

"All the same, Wayne should have warned me, instead of just assuming I'd go along," I said, feigning anger.

"Well, I'm sure he would have done but—"

"I've got enough problems of my own." I pointed a finger in Tim's face, like I blamed him. "I don't need this."

"That's what I told him." Ah, so that's what all the animated phone calls had been about. "He said to tell you that there's a good bonus in it for you both."

I glowered at him. "So I should bloody well hope."

Kara turned on him, also frowning. "You say it's safe but what about *Mistral*? Did she have illegals on board when she went down?"

"I…I don't, er, I'm not sure."

"Wonderful!" I rolled my eyes. "You just wait until I get my hands on bloody Wayne."

The following day saw the return of the good weather, and Mike and Julie asked us if we'd accompany them ashore to help with some shopping. I knew then that the time had come and made sure the Blackberry was in my pocket, fully charged, in case I needed to contact Monk in a hurry. It made me feel slightly better about a situation which was rapidly slipping beyond my control.

Mike hailed a cab and climbed in the front seat. I was sandwiched in the back between Kara and Julie. We sped off along the main road that would take us to the hypermarket but I figured that probably wasn't our destination. I was proven right when the taxi took the next exit. We were in the suburbs of Calais—not the sort of area on the tourist trail. A warren of smaller and more rundown streets took us to an empty warehouse close to the port.

"What shops do you think you'll find round here?" I asked.

No one answered me. Mike paid the driver and ushered us towards the prefabricated building, which looked long disused and decidedly neglected. I had absolutely no intention of walking into a trap and figured it would be easy enough to overpower Mike, even if I didn't know where the hell we were and had no means of transportation.

Kara nudged my arm and nodded towards two well-built but decidedly dubious-looking characters leaning against the doors to the warehouse like breathing statues, arms folded across massive chests. Thoughts of overpowering Mike evaporated at that point. I'd never get us past them all. And even if I did, what then? We trudged across a path made of cracked paving stones, weeds struggling to reach daylight between the joins, unfiltered cigarette ends, and fast-food wrappers scattered just about everywhere I looked.

"Must offer pretty decent discounts to encourage punters to come here?" I quipped.

No one bothered to respond.

I tried to figure out where we were but quickly gave up. I didn't know the area well enough. The taxi ride had been short but we'd taken a confusing route along a number of similar-looking back streets. To admit to being lost went against the male psyche, but there came a time in every guy's life when he just had to bite the bullet and come clean. I consoled myself with the thought that it didn't matter much anyway. If they wanted us to dance to their tune they'd have to take us back to the boat unharmed.

So why bring us here? They could have simply confronted us on the boat and been done with it.

It didn't occur to me until it was too late that it would only take one of us to do their dirty work.

Julie led us into the cavernous interior of the warehouse. Mike struggled to roll the door shut, his efforts meeting with shrill protests from the rusting wheels as he jerked them across the tracks bolted into the crumbling cement floor.

"Isn't it rather dishonest?" Julie said. "What we've done, I mean." Neither of us said a word, which clearly annoyed her. "I asked you a question?"

"Did you?" I shrugged, feigning disinterest. "When I know what you're talking about, I'll try and answer you."

"I was talking about Wayne Richards giving us all Day Skipper certificates. It's dishonest because we're all much better sailors than we let on, with the exception of Ronnie, obviously, and Wayne must have known it."

She had me there. I recalled her inept attempts to affix fenders to the guardrail. I'd put it down to her not knowing one end of a boat from the other. And that, of course, was precisely what she'd wanted me to think.

"It's harder to pretend not to know what you're doing than I thought it would be," she said. Okay, so she was a mind reader as well. "But still, I managed it better than you did, Charlie."

"Congratulations."

"Oh, now don't be such a sore loser." She led us toward some old crates and motioned for us to sit down.

The human statues had followed us inside and stood directly behind us. With no alternative open to us, we sat.

"It seems he was the only genuine candidate. Ronnie, that is." Julie appeared determined to keep harping back to the bloody Day Skipper course, rubbing my nose in it. "Mike and I were there to check Wayne out and I guess you were as well, Charlie. We know you were doing it as a favour to Kate, trying to find out what happened to her brother's friend. Did you have any luck, by the way?" When neither of us answered her, she merely smiled in a superior way that was really starting to get on my wick. "I'll take that as a *no* then, shall I?"

"Do you know where Gordon is?" Kara asked.

Julie merely smiled.

"What's this all about?" I asked. "Why have you brought us here?"

"I mean, why else would an ex-detective inspector, who lives on a boat and has been associated with the sea for years, want to go on a course like that?" Since she knew who I really was, I didn't see any point in saying anything. I showed no reaction and left her to her gloating. "What, nothing to say, Charlie? God, you really are an arrogant prick, do you know that? You couldn't stand air-headed Julie on that course and thought yourself above the company, as my old Mum would have said, but all the time Mike and I were laughing at you. You didn't have a clue, did you?"

I fiddled with the loose change in my pocket, refusing to look at her. "If you say so."

"Oh I do. Your face when you saw Mike and I arrive the other day. It was priceless." Her ensuing laughter was generated by spite rather than humour. When I again failed to respond she turned away from me and looked directly at Kara. "And as for you, Kate. Or should I say Kara."

Kara sat a little straighter and I could tell she intended to indulge in a spot of verbal sparring. I shot her a warning look and she got the message. When a person was intent upon demonstrating just how clever they think they are, there was seldom any point in trying to interrupt their flow. Best let them get it over with and see what you could learn from the things they didn't say.

"You'll do anything to find your brother's friend, won't you dear, even shack up with Charlie here."

"Oh, that's no hardship." Kara's casual words produced an irritated frown from Julie. "I gather you tried hard enough during that course."

"It might have been an easier way to get him onside." She shrugged. "Never mind, you'll just have to make do without him whilst he does as he's told. You'll be staying here with my friends." She indicated the men still holding up the wall, both of whom showed a flicker of interest now that they'd seen the subject of their assignment.

"What!" we said together. So much for keeping our cool.

"I don't trust you to play fair, Charlie, and so Kara

will stay here. When you've done as we ask, she'll be released unharmed."

"And if I don't do as you ask?"

"Take my advice and don't even think about it," Mike said in a steely tone. "This isn't a game. There's too much at stake for us to let you and your girlfriend mess it up."

"I don't have a clue what's going on here," I lied. "All I did was take the job Wayne offered me in the hope of finding out a bit more about Kara's friend. What's your interest?"

"You don't know?" Mike and Julie shared a glance.

"Not about your agenda, no." I paused, pretending to mull things over. "Why don't I tell you what I do know and you can fill in the gaps?"

"Go on," Mike said, folding his arms across his chest and eyeing me with suspicion.

"Well, a few weeks back Kara persuaded me to look for her brother's friend."

Julie offered Kara a twisted smile. "You were rather careless with your own siblings, weren't you, dear?" Kara drew in a sharp breath but wisely held her tongue. "Perhaps you thought you could make amends by looking for this Reed character, is that it? And Charlie, thinking with his dick, was ready to go along with anything you suggested."

"Trust me, Julie, the rewards are worth it." I knew I'd scored a direct hit when she glowered at me. "I went on the Day Skipper course to see what I could find out. When Kara heard that Wayne had offered me a job crewing for him, she used her persuasive powers on me until I agreed. She thought it might throw some light on Gordon's disappearance." I lifted my shoulders and looked each of them straight in the eye. "That's it as far as I'm concerned. Wayne's clearly a bit of a dodgy character but if there's anything off about these trips to France, other than over-enthusiastic purchases of alcohol from the hypermarkets, then I sure as hell don't know what it is."

"You *know* there's a lot more to it than that," Mike said. "No one's that naive."

"You know about the two thugs who accosted me last week and threatened my young son if I didn't come on this trip?" I feigned surprise. "They said I'd be contacted and I assume that's what this is about. I just didn't consider that you two would be—"

"He's a smart boy, Mike," Julie said sarcastically. "I knew he'd catch on in the end."

"So what's your interest in Wayne's business and why are you making ridiculous comments about keeping Kara with you?" I asked, switching to the offensive.

"Oh, come on, Charlie, don't stop now," Julie said. "Not when you're doing so well. You must know that we'll be taking a few extra passengers back with us."

"We've just been told," I said. "I'm not happy but I don't see what we can do about it."

"Well, that should make it easier for you to help us then."

"Help you do what?"

"We're British Patriots," Mike said, puffing out his chest.

I looked at him askance, wondering if he realised just how pompous he actually sounded. "Come again."

"We belong to the EPP," Julie explained. "The silent majority are at last making their feelings felt. Decent, law-abiding citizens like us have had enough of watching this great country of ours being flooded by the dregs of just about every third-world society. Instead of sitting about, complaining, we've decided to do something to redress the balance."

"By joining the EPP." I shrugged. "That's your prerogative."

"We want to expose the country's porous borders by capturing *Vagabond* with a hold-full of would-be suicide bombers on board. That's what they are, you know." She paced in front of us like a lecturer with all the answers, attempting to recruit us to her cause. "We've tried telling the powers that be but they just think we're extremist nutters. They've ignored everything we've told them and so the time has come for direct action."

"So those *gentlemen* who had a word with me and threatened physical bodily harm to my young son were colleagues of yours, I take it."

"I hope they were polite."

"Count me out." I sneered at Julie—the woman was demented. "I have no axe to grind with anyone."

"Don't you care that whites are becoming the minority group in some of our cities? Don't you care that our taxes are being haemorrhaged to support their burgeoning families—families who've never given a thing but know too damned well how to take, take and take some more? Don't you care about rising crime, about—"

"I don't judge people by their colour, gender, age, sexual orientation or even the colour of their god-damned eyes." Her mind was closed to reasoned argument but I still felt the need to make the point. "I take or leave them on their individual merits," I added more moderately. "You should try it sometime."

"There's no talking to him," Julie said to Mike. "It just shows how much work we still have to do, fighting against such apathy. But never mind." She shook her hair away from eyes blazing with fresh determination. "You will help us out, Charlie, whether you like it or not. And we'll keep hold of Kara to make sure that you do."

"How do I know you'll release her if I do as you ask?"

"You're just going to have to trust us on that. We're not killers. In fact we need everyone on board *Vagabond* to come through alive to strengthen our hand when we expose the illegals."

They had a point, but I wasn't reassured because I didn't think that requirement necessarily extended to Kara and me. I also didn't think now was the time to mention *Mistral*.

"Violence is not our way."

I glanced at the thugs still lining the walls and decided not to put that assertion to the test. "As a matter of interest, how did you know illegals would be smuggled back on this particular cruise?"

"We knew Richards was running this show, which is why we went on the Day Skipper course." Julie was clearly the boss in this relationship because it was she who answered most of my questions. "When you thought we were safely tucked up at night with cocoa and a good book, we were actually listening to you and Richards chatting in the salon. Those walls are very thin and a strategically placed upturned glass still beats your most sophisticated listening devices, you know. Anyway, after the loss of their last boat, we knew he'd need new crew. We weren't surprised when we heard him offer you a job so we kept tabs on what was happening. We suspected he'd do a test run with you aboard before exposing you to his real agenda, and that if you crewed for him again it would be for real. When we learned that you'd be doing this one we booked ourselves in at the last minute."

It made sense. I didn't bother to find out how they knew we'd be crewing. Wayne would have had to add our names to the crew manifest and I dare say, with their connections, the EPP could get their hands on it.

"Right then," said Mike, holding out a hand. "Your phones, please."

Damn, I should have left the Blackberry on the boat but then hindsight always has been a bloody irritating little sod. I reluctantly extracted it from my pocket and indicated to Kara that she should do the same with her mobile.

Julie and Mike's revelations had been interesting but hardly unexpected. The biggest weakness in any megalomaniac's psyche was his inability to resist bragging when he thought his position was unassailable. If Julie and Mike knew about Monk's operation they would have mentioned it, so perhaps there was still hope. But all that could change in the blink of an eye, or rather the touch of a button. If Monk called the Blackberry for any reason, curiosity would cause Mike to answer it. Monk would know at once that it wasn't my voice and that something had gone wrong, but would he send in the cavalry? Somehow I doubted it. He had too much riding on this whole operation to abandon it because of us.

We were now very much on our own.

"Now then, Charlie," Mike said. "On the return journey, once I give you the word, you're going to add water to the portside fuel tank. I'm sure you can manage that without Tim noticing."

"That will kill the engine stone dead."

"Of course it will."

According to the forecast there would be a big sea running tomorrow. With only one engine operational, Tim would have to bring the boat off the plane. Progress would be slow, making it comparatively easy for a rescuing craft to take control of it. They'd chosen a clever way to do this, because most twin-engine boats had fuel tanks that could switch from port to starboard engines. *Vagabond* didn't. Each fuel tank was peculiar to its allocated engine.

"How will I explain it to Tim?"

"You won't. He'll be too busy keeping the boat under control to worry about what's happened."

Good point. "Sure, but you could do this yourself. Why do you need me?"

"Insurance," Mike told me. "We're just innocent punters enjoying a mini break to celebrate our anniversary and have nothing to do with anything. We're not even registered members of the EPP so no suspicion will fall on us."

I was heartened to hear it. Perhaps they really did mean to release Kara and me if we did as they asked. But even as the thought flickered through my head, I knew I was deluding myself. They couldn't take that risk. They were aware of my previous occupation and must realise I couldn't keep quiet about something like this.

"Let me go back with him," Kara said. "I only care about my brother's friend. We'll do whatever you like to the engine and let matters play out your way."

"Do I look that stupid?" Julie asked with a withering smile. "Apart from anything else, I wouldn't put it past Mr. Heroic here to try and warn Tim what we're planning to do. The only thing likely to prevent him is concern for your welfare."

"How am I supposed to explain Kara's sudden disappearance to Tim?"

"Oh, I'm sure you'll think of something."

"Tell him she's upset about the illegals and has jumped ship," Mike said. "You had a row over the ethics of it and she's gone home on the ferry. That should work."

"All it will do is make Tim more uptight than he already is."

"Then you'll just have to reassure him that you can do your job as well as Kara's. It's only tonight and the trip back tomorrow to get through."

"Only!" I shook my head, defeated and all out of arguments. "Just make sure you take very good care of her. If any of those goons lay so much as a finger on her…" I abruptly stopped talking, belatedly aware that it would be unwise to reveal the extent of my feelings for Kara. "And before I do anything to the fuel tank, I need to talk to Kara to make sure she's okay."

Mike exchanged a quick glance with Julie and nodded. "Fair enough but just remember, once we get back to the boat we'll be watching you all the time. Don't try anything stupid and we'll all come though this unscathed."

"How do we know this won't end up the same way as *Mistral*?"

Mike sighed. "We're on board to make sure that it doesn't. The idiot we had on the crew of *Mistral* clearly got over-enthusiastic and fucked the whole thing up." He shrugged, as though it was no big deal that all those people had died. "It won't help our cause if *Vagabond* blows up as well."

"So, Charlie," Julie said, sliding a hand playfully up and down my arm. "Do we have a deal?"

I wanted to tell her to go to hell. "Do I have a choice?"

"No, dear," she said sweetly, "not really."

EIGHTEEN

I HUGGED KARA, furious with myself for not anticipating that we'd be separated and planning for such an eventuality. In hindsight it was so bloody obvious—precisely what I'd have done in Mike's position. We'd played straight into their hands. *Face it, Hunter, you've underestimated them every step of the way.*

Although Kara was putting on a brave face, her entire body trembled against mine. Clearly, she was terrified. I whispered that I'd find a way out for us, just to give her hope, but they were empty words. Even if I could get a fix on our current location, there was no guarantee they'd keep Kara there once I'd gone. Besides, we'd be putting to sea first thing in the morning and I'd never be left alone for long enough to launch ill-thought-out rescue operations.

Rough hands pulled us apart and I was bundled out of the warehouse into a waiting car. Mike and Julie climbed in behind me. Julie smiled at me with smug satisfaction. The temptation to forcibly wipe that bloody grin off her face and release some of the tension that had me coiled tighter than a hungry boa constrictor was compelling. I resisted, but only because breaking the habit of a lifetime and hitting a woman wouldn't do anything to get me out of this mess. I forced myself to sit on my hands, metaphorically speaking, and stared out the window, rebuffing all efforts at conversation.

Once we got back to the boat I told Tim that Kara had abandoned ship. With Julie loitering close enough to hear every word, I pretended to be annoyed about it.

"Dunno what got into her, mate," I said with an apologetic shrug. "She's not usually so moody, but that's women for you."

"I ought to let Wayne know," Tim said nervously, pulling out his phone.

"Why?"

"Well, you know…" He indicated the door to the crew quarters by shifting his eyes sideways.

"Best not to worry him." I moved closer and lowered my voice. "Kara got a bit upset about our extra passengers but she won't say anything. She knows better than that."

He thought for a moment. "Yeah well, if you're sure she'll keep her mouth shut, perhaps I won't ring Wayne after all. I mean, there's nothing he can do, is there?" He looked as though he was on the point of bottling it himself, causing me to wonder why Wayne had trusted him with such a high-risk assignment in the first place. He had to be really short of reliable people, hence his unseemly haste to recruit me. "Are you sure you can cope without her?"

I nodded but he still dithered for an age before returning his phone to his pocket.

"Okay, well, I'll lend a hand if you need it."

"Nah, should be all right." I gestured towards our

cabin, where Gil was waiting patiently to be liberated. "I'd better walk the mutt before I get stuck in, though."

"Fair enough."

"I'll keep you company," Mike said. "I could do with stretching my legs as well."

I'd taken note of the route we took back to the boat but any vague idea I'd had about trying to relocate that warehouse withered when Mike stuck closer to my heels than Gil did for the duration of our walk. I maintained a dignified silence, pretending he didn't exist, all the time cursing my stupidity in not bringing my own phone with me. What had I been thinking? Just because Monk's Blackberry was our lifeline, there was no reason not to have a backup. Kara had a pay-as-you-go and we'd thought two phones between us would be enough. *Stupid, stupid, stupid!* Mike and Julie were bound to have searched our cabin. They'd had plenty of opportunities whilst we'd been busy waiting on the guests. But that didn't make me feel a whole lot better, even if it did explain how they knew we were only carrying one phone each.

Julie and Mike kept me within their sights that evening. Even so, several opportunities arose when I could have used the satellite phone in the lower helm position to call Monk. I kept thinking about Kara and how alone and scared she must be feeling, wondering how she was being treated and whether I'd ever see her again. That was what decided me against actually making the call. I'd already reached the conclusion that Monk wouldn't do anything to jeopardise this operation, so what was the point in further endangering Kara?

Tim told me the illegals had been smuggled on board during the early hours, otherwise I never would have known. They were crammed together in the crew quarters but didn't give their presence away by making the slightest sound. Presumably a spot of physical discomfort didn't matter too much when committed to a greater cause.

The weather deteriorated overnight and there was a force six forecast for the Channel that day. It was overcast and drizzling when we left Calais—the weather a perfect match for my mood. The two couples who were innocent bystanders—give or take a spot of mindless adultery—used the conditions as an excuse to adjourn to their cabins, unwittingly playing straight into Julie and Mike's hands. They would want as few people around as possible when they put their plan into action. Well, to be more accurate, when I kick-started it for them. They hung about the lower helm position with Tim and me but Mike kept a close eye on the GPS. I figured it would be about another hour before I was called on to act.

"Time for coffee, is it?" Mike asked when we'd been underway for exactly that amount of time.

"Certainly." I turned towards the galley, grim-faced, Mike on my heels.

"Time to go to work," he said quietly.

"When I've spoken to Kara."

Without a word he produced a phone from his pocket. I was disappointed that it wasn't my Blackberry, but that would have been too much to hope for. He scrolled down the pre-recorded numbers and selected one. He exchanged a few words with the person who answered and then handed the phone to me.

"Kara?"

A prolonged pause. "Charlie?"

"Are you all right? Has anyone hurt you?"

Another pause. Why wasn't she answering me immediately? My anxiety increased as the conviction that she was hiding something took root in my brain.

"I'm fine."

Then it hit me and a surge of euphoria caused adrenaline to shoot through my bloodstream. She was talking on a satellite phone. There was always a delay before your voice reached the person at the other end of the line, hence their delay in responding. The EPP had made their first mistake. Instead of leaving Kara ashore, they'd taken her aboard the boat they planned to use to intercept *Vagabond* when she developed engine trouble. Presumably they were currently farther out to sea than we were, in an area outside mobile phone signals, so they had to use the satellite phone. Kara was probably only on the boat so they could despatch us both when we'd outlived our usefulness, but that was neither here nor there. If we were in the same place it would give us a fighting chance of survival, and the EPP had carelessly given me advance notice of the fact. All I had to do now was figure out how to use that knowledge to my advantage.

We exchanged a few more stilted words before the phone was snatched away and the connection broken.

"Tell Tim you're going to do the engine room checks," Mike said in my ear.

"Why? I don't need to go near the engines to get to the fuel tanks."

"If you don't do them, he might leave the helm and do them himself. I want him to stay where he is."

"You're the boss."

"Just do it and don't try anything smart."

Give me one chance, I silently begged, and I'll show you how fucking smart I am. Aloud, I called out to Tim that I was doing the checks.

"Okay." There was uncertainty in his tone. Obviously, he didn't want me anywhere near the illegals but couldn't leave the helm when the sea was so rough and I was supposedly inexperienced. "Take care back there."

He wasn't referring to the engine room checks and we both knew it.

Six brown faces peered at me from the gloomy depths of the crew cabin. There was insufficient space for so many people, and no ventilation worth speaking of. This was borne out by the mingled aromas of unwashed bodies, fear of the unknown and the physical results of good, old-fashioned seasickness. My first impression was that they were little more than children, which saddened me, but I had too many problems of my own to dwell upon their misguided intentions. They'd been told to expect my visit and, once I indicated the door to the engine room, they visibly relaxed.

I closed the door on their faces, donned earphones to block out the noise of the engines, and thought about what I ought to do next. Perhaps there was something I could do to the engines to stop the boat ahead of time. It would be too risky for Mike to come and check what

I was up to. Even if Tim didn't see him, the non-fee-paying passengers would be sure to mention his unauthorised visit, which might cause an already nervous Tim to abort the trip and return to Calais.

The engines thrumped away as I stared at them for what seemed like an age, thinking about my options. There *had* to be something I could do, but no brilliant solutions magically sprang to mind. Should I accept that I'd been well and truly boxed into a corner, or do something to fight back?

My hand hovered over a spanner but I didn't pick it up. For a moment I was sorely tempted to play things differently, every bone in my body balking at being so easily manipulated. But then I thought about Kara and my rebellious turn of mind gave way to dull acceptance as I reluctantly afforded Julie and Mike the credit they deserved. They'd read me exactly right. By holding on to Kara, they'd done just about the only thing that would guarantee my cooperation. I'd agreed with Monk to sabotage *Vagabond* anyway but I hadn't bargained on Mike and Julie forcing my hand. That rather changed the way I felt, especially since Kara and I would never be permitted to walk away.

To be honest, I didn't much care about the fate of the illegals crowded into the room next to me. That might sound callous but then, if they really were prepared to blow themselves up for the greater good of their beloved cause, taking a load of my innocent countrymen with them, they didn't deserve my compassion. I'd save them if I could but my first and only priority was Kara. Tim was a decent guy but he'd gone into this with his eyes open and would just have to take his chances.

I completed the engine checks, wiped my hands on a rag and returned to the aft deck. Mike had considerately left a bottle of water on the table. Before I could change my mind, I slid along the side deck, unscrewed the cap to the port fuel tank and tipped the water in. Before I'd even got back to the lower helm and joined Tim, the alarm on that engine rang a stark warning just before it conked out.

"What the hell?" Tim glanced at the gauges, then at me. "What did you do?"

"Nothing, mate." I spread my hands. "Just the usual checks. What do you think's wrong?

"Dunno, but that port engine is buggered."

"Everything was fine when I checked just now. No overheating or anything." The conditions had worsened, and Tim had been struggling to keep the boat on course even before the engine gave out. "Could it be something to do with the weather?"

"No, it's either mechanical or somehow connected to the fuel." He removed one hand from the autopilot controls and scratched his head. "Could be dirt in it."

"Wouldn't that affect both engines?"

"Depends."

"Won't you try starting it up again?"

"Not until I know what's wrong." He seemed lost in thought. "Look, can you manage here for a moment?"

"Yeah, what are you going to do?"

"I'll just go and check the engine room myself. You might have missed something."

"That's possible, I guess, but I don't think I did."

"Won't be a moment."

"You ought to join our side, Charlie," Julie said with an admiring smile once Tim left us. "You were very convincing. We could use cool heads like yours."

"I'll pass, thanks."

Mike produced his phone and made a call, presumably to the boat that would rescue us. Occupied with trying to keep us on course, I didn't hear what he said.

In spite of my best efforts, the boat wallowed about, slamming into deep troughs and then pitching back out of them with the velocity of a cork flying from the neck of a champagne bottle. Cresting the next wave, we teetered on its edge before plummeting into a seemingly bottomless void. Water was thrown all over the boat, and I had trouble staying on my feet as I fought a losing battle to keep us stable. The sea was all over the place, which didn't help matters. One minute it was hitting us directly abeam so the boat lurched violently and dangerously sideways, the next it was on the nose, pitching us in and out of those huge waves.

Tim returned and shook his head.

"Any clues?" I asked him.

"Nothing obvious. It must be related to the fuel but I don't see how it could have affected one engine and not the other."

"Just be glad that it didn't," I said, ceding my place at the helm to him.

The boat floundered in the big sea as he fought to keep us pointing in the right direction.

"Should we put out a Mayday?" I asked.

Tim shook his head emphatically. "I need a moment to think this through."

I was guessing he'd already factored *Mistral*'s ill-fated Mayday into the equation, wanting to believe it was mere coincidence that two successive runs with illegals aboard had hit trouble. His eyes frequently darted towards me, as though he suspected I'd somehow been responsible for the engine room problems. I could almost hear his mind whirling as he tried to figure it out. Fortunately he wasn't into lateral thinking and decided to give me the benefit of the doubt.

"Perhaps I didn't tighten the screw to the fuel tank properly when I checked the levels in Calais?" I suggested apologetically. "With water being thrown all over the place, some might have got in the tank."

"Yeah, it's possible, I suppose."

"Sorry," I said meekly.

"We need help," Tim said after a few more minutes of silent struggle.

"Is that a boat on the radar there?" Mike asked, pointing to a fast-moving dot on our starboard bow which had conveniently just appeared.

"Yeah. Where did that come from?"

"Does it matter?" Julie had reverted to the scatter-brained female routine she'd used on the Day Skipper course. "We need help and they're the closest vessel to us. I don't like this. I'm scared."

Tim responded in the way most men do when a woman loses it. "Don't worry, we're not in immediate danger of anything other than seasickness." He flashed a brief reassuring smile. "I'll give the vessel a call on the radio."

Before he could do so, the boat in question—a forty-seven-foot Sealine open sports cruiser—pulled closer to our position and called us on Channel 16, asking if we needed help. Upon learning we had engine problems, they offered to give us a tow.

I could see Tim mulling over the offer. On the one hand he needed rescuing, but there was the small matter of a half dozen illegals hidden in his crew cabin to be taken into account. If they were discovered he'd be the one who'd have to face the music. But on the other hand he knew only too well what had happened to *Mistral*, and by now even he must have come to the conclusion that our problems were no accident.

If conditions had been calmer we could have staggered back to Calais on one engine, but if we arrived in broad daylight with obvious engine problems, the chances of the illegals going unnoticed were minimal. Without punters on board, Tim would probably have toughed it out and carried on for England but with Julie throwing a wobbly, he obviously couldn't do that. He eventually decided that the money involved wasn't worth dying for. Without even asking where they were bound for he accepted the Sealine's offer of help, sending me onto the foredeck to organise the appropriate line.

Gil and I left the warmth of the lower helm position and cautiously made our way across the rolling deck. Even though it was made treacherous by a combination of the water crashing over the side and the heavy rain still pouring down, a feeling of implacable calm engulfed me. The next half hour or so would be crucial but we were now in my environment, a factor which I was depending upon to give me the edge. My seamanship was superior to that of anyone aboard *Vagabond*, and possibly the Sealine too. The current conditions would make everyone clumsy but, being accustomed to boating in British waters, I was able to deal with them. That had to count for something.

The other two couples finally emerged from their cabins, probably wondering why the boat had slowed. I dismissed them from my mind, needing to remain focused. Given the sea state, it took a while to set up the tow line. All the time I was trying to peer into the cabin of the other boat as it drew closer to ensure that Kara was actually on board. Frustratingly there was no sign of her familiar red hair. The disappointment was acute. Either I'd got it wrong or they were keeping her well out of sight until I'd done as I was told.

The rescue craft was now directly alongside. If we were uncomfortable in these conditions on board *Vagabond*, God knows how they must be feeling in a small open sports cruiser. Presumably it had been chosen because they were a common sight, much favoured by recreational boaters during the summer months, but only when conditions were set fair. Obviously the people behind this weren't regular boaters. If they were, they'd know better than to assume the weather wouldn't change in the blink of an eye. It made the Sealine stand out and rendered her a much less suitable craft to use for rescue purposes. All I had to do was figure out how to use their stupidity to my advantage.

The two boats were now pitching and rolling within a few feet of one another. I placed a long row of fenders out, taking my time, assessing my chances of pulling this off. The manoeuvre I was contemplating was sheer stupidity—or desperation—but I wasn't about to dwell upon the spectacular possibilities for failure. Skill, patience and a big chunk of luck might, against all the odds, just see it through.

Hold that thought, Hunter.

I felt my chin tighten with grim determination as two of the crew from the Sealine signalled that they intended to board *Vagabond* via the cockpit. It made sense since it was the lowest point to the water, and the gap between the two boats would be slightly easier to span. But still, rather them than me.

They took advantage of a brief lull in the conditions and, swearing and complaining, narrowly avoided being crushed between the two wallowing boats as they hauled themselves athletically into *Vagabond*'s cockpit.

It came as no surprise when I was invited to take their place on the Sealine. No one was pretending anymore. I was simply told with an abrupt jerk of a thumb to move my arse. Jesus, that flimsy little boat looked miles below us. One slip and I'd be in the drink.

I knew that if I didn't go voluntarily, they wouldn't be beyond offering a little unfriendly persuasion. Without giving them a chance to object, I motioned to Gil to go first. It was a testament to his faith in me that he didn't hesitate to make the leap into the Sealine, landing in the open cockpit with a heavy thud.

I lowered myself a little more carefully, using the rope attached to the nearest fender as a safety line. I inched my way cautiously down and began to think I might actually make it unscathed. Then a monster wave rocked the boat so violently that I lost my footing. The full force of a freezing spray of water smacked me directly in my face. I gasped, swallowing a mouthful of salt water that made me gag. *Great!* My feet slipped on the slick hull and I finished up dangling over the caldron-like sea. My arms screamed at me as I held on to that slender rope for dear life.

I took a moment to regain my breath and composure, taking my weight off my weakening arms by again bracing my feet against the hull. I waited for the next lull, said a silent prayer to a God I didn't actually believe in, and somehow made the final leap without breaking my neck.

As Gil and I stood there, wondering what would happen next, the glass door to the salon slid open and Kara launched herself into my arms.

"Charlie, thank God!"

I cuddled her close, barely aware of Gil's scrabbling claws scratching my gloved hand as he jumped up, attempting to get to her as well.

"Are you okay?" I asked, releasing her so I could look at her face. "Did they hurt you?"

"No, I'm fine, really." She bent to give Gil some attention. "What now?" she asked in an undertone.

Good question. "How many are on board?"

"The guy at the helm and two others. I think they're the ones you met in Brighton."

The men in question emerged from the salon, confirming her suspicions. Bowling Ball had a red fleece hat pulled over his bald pate and a thick jacket zipped up to his chin. But there was no doubting that it was him.

"Ah, Charlie," he said, his well-modulated voice removing any lingering doubts. "Good to see you again."

"Wish I could say the same."

"Perhaps you two would be more comfortable if you sat down," he suggested. His face had turned a sallow shade of green. This guy was no sailor so had to be struggling with the conditions.

"What? Out here?" I wasn't about to let on that sitting in the open suited me just fine. "It's bloody freezing."

"You're well dressed for the weather."

The other guy also looked uncomfortable but seemed to be bearing up a little better than Bowling Ball. He nodded toward the bench in the stern of the cockpit, not looking averse to forcibly making us sit if we didn't do so of our own accord. I grasped Kara's hand and made a big show of reluctance as we sank onto the wet bench.

There was nothing to protect us from the wrath of the elements, and water was already seeping through the seat of my jeans. We were both dressed in thick sailing jackets but neither of us was wearing waterproof trousers. Not that it mattered much because I doubted that our discomfort would last for long.

I made eye contact with each of our captors in turn but refused to give them the satisfaction of asking what was going to happen to us now. Given that they wanted us to remain in the open. I probably wouldn't want to hear their answer anyway.

We were now towing *Vagabond* 150 feet behind us, heading slowly toward England. The rain, thankfully, had eased off and I caught brief glimpses of the coastline taking shape through gaps in the clouds.

I held Kara, looking for break clauses in a contract I didn't recall signing. It didn't look too hopeful. Since no emergency signal had been sent, no one knew that *Vagabond* was in trouble. There would be no helping hand from the Coastguard.

Monk would have his suspicions, of course, but the Channel was a big place and he'd have no idea where to start looking due to my careless loss of the Blackberry. Any search he did instigate would be hampered by the conditions.

We were in a busy shipping lane but no one would notice if two people and a dog fell from the back of an open boat—at least not quickly enough to save us. We could try to persuade Bowling Ball that we didn't represent a threat to him and his organisation, but I saw little point appealing to a fanatic's better nature when it clearly didn't exist.

There had to be another way.

Hopeless as things seemed, I was damned if I'd go down without a fight so I forced myself to assess the situation dispassionately. I glanced about the cockpit, taking stock of its contents without making my interest obvious. There were always useful weapons on boats if you know what you were looking for. And what I was specifically looking for was encouragingly close at hand. I stored that information away and turned my attention to the three men on board.

The guy driving the boat was about twenty feet in front of us, kept more or less dry beneath the canvas canopy that covered the forward part of the cockpit. Bowling Ball and his oppo were sitting on a bench, also under cover of the canopy, at right angles to him. Both were staring fixedly at the horizon, confirming my suspicions that they were feeling seasick. Good! I hoped the bastards really suffered.

The rain was more of a drizzle now, cold and uncomfortable for Kara and me as it laid siege to our already damp clothes. I gave no indication that I was affected by it. Gil huddled beneath our legs, his coat too thick for water to penetrate as far as his skin.

I forced myself to be patient, waiting for the right moment to launch my rather desperate plan. But would the opportunity come before they decided they no longer had need of us? Every time one of them moved, my heart hammered and I thought I'd left it too late. I couldn't figure out what they were waiting for. In their position I'd have acted long ago but didn't fool myself into thinking they'd had a change of heart. No way could they allow us to walk away from this, so the only explanation for their inertia had to be that they were getting some sort of perverse pleasure out of keeping us guessing. Either that or they'd been rendered temporarily immobile by seasickness.

I was suddenly grateful for the conditions, which were almost certainly responsible for their decision to sit outside. Men in particular didn't want to display weakness by admitting to feeling ill so they did as these two currently were and sat stock still, staring fixedly at the horizon, swallowing down bile and praying for a quick and painless death.

I would endeavour to oblige.

After about fifteen minutes of our getting drenched to the skin, Bowling Ball's oppo got up, mumbled something incomprehensible and staggered below. Presumably he needed the head, either to throw up or for more traditional purposes, I didn't give a toss which.

"Don't be long, Dave," Bowling Ball said, glancing significantly at the man.

Take all the time you need, Dave.

My pulse rate increased. This was it—the only chance I was likely to get. I swung straight into action.

"Oh Christ, that hurts!" I clutched my stomach and fell dramatically to my knees on the wet deck.

"Charlie, what is it?" Kara was beside me in seconds, her face full of concern, as well it might be since she had no idea I was acting.

"It's my stomach. You know how it's been playing me up ever since I ate that monkfish in Calais. Argh!" I writhed about, confident when I saw comprehension flicker in her eyes that she'd caught my reference to Monk. She had to remember that we'd tried a similar ploy in another tight situation and would be ready to follow my lead.

"Can you get up?" she asked. "Let me help you."

Bowling Ball's hand reached towards his pocket but

he made no move to intervene, seasickness rendering him clumsy and slow to react.

"Let me try."

I put one hand on the bench and pulled the webbing strap attached to the inflatable life raft located beneath it with the other, letting out a soft whistle between my teeth. My entire plan hinged on Gil associating that whistle with playtime. Thankfully he didn't disappoint. The strap was the same as the one he used as a toy on the *No Comment*. Regardless of the conditions, he was always ready for a game. He grabbed the strap between his strong teeth and put all his pent-up energy into tugging as hard as he could.

I moved with lightening speed for a man supposedly crippled with stomach cramps and kicked the life raft clear of the bench that was restricting it. Gil wagged his sodden tail and tugged harder still. His position above the life raft made his teeth act as though the webbing strap had been attached to the guardrail, causing the raft to inflate under the pressure, right there in the restricted space of the cockpit.

It all happened so quickly that Bowling Ball only realised what was going down when it was too late to prevent it. He jumped clumsily to his feet, only to be knocked straight off them again by the expanding life raft. He fell to the floor, hitting his head hard against the console, and didn't move. I kicked him to make sure he was still breathing. Unfortunately he was, but I could tell at a glance that he'd be out of it for some time.

One down, two to go. I reached across Bowling Ball's inert form and hit the button to activate the EPIRB, transmitting an immediate emergency signal to the rescue services.

Bring on the cavalry!

Dave, presumably alerted by all the activity, appeared at the door to the salon, still zipping his fly with one hand and wiping his mouth on the back of his hand with the other. He took in the scene at a glance and abandoned all attempts at modesty. Demonstrating a little more savvy than Bowling Ball, he approached me by walking across the bench that separated us, elevating himself above the inflating life raft, and swung a meaty fist with considerable force behind it as soon as he was within range of my head. He caught me totally unprepared, leaving me with no time to take evasive action. His series of vicious follow-up blows sent me sprawling backwards.

I fell awkwardly, the confined space now acting against me. I was acutely aware of the sound of the angry sea crashing all around me, the noise ringing in my ears, far too close for comfort. We hit a big wave, and freezing water washed over my body, threatening to take me with it as it rolled slowly off the deck again. I didn't think I was still in the cockpit and it took me a moment to realise that the force of Dave's punches had sent me straight over the transom.

By rights I should have been swallowed up by the sea but instead I'd landed on the tiny bathing platform, mere inches from the churning water and the vicious propellers driving the powerful Volvo Penta engines. I was holding on to the transom with the frozen fingers of one hand. One shove and Dave's work would be complete because I was too exhausted to put up any resistance.

Kara's anxious voice was slow to penetrate my fuzzy brain. She was kneeling on the bench in the cockpit, reaching down with both hands to help me, shouting encouragement.

"Charlie, grab my hand!"

I couldn't seem to move.

"Do it now!"

I was aware of the urgency in her tone and of her frequent glances over her shoulder. Presumably Dave was struggling through the crowded deck to get to me and finish off his assignment. She was right, I had to move. But my body, battered and bruised, soaked through and frozen to the core, refused to co-operate. I closed my eyes in weary resignation and conceded defeat.

"Charlie!"

The naked fear in Kara's voice roused me from my semi-conscious state. I mustered what little strength I had remaining, snaked out the hand not frozen on the transom and grasped the back of the bench in the rear of the cockpit. I knew Kara wouldn't have the strength to pull me out, and if I took her hand she could well finish up joining me on the bathing platform, being swamped with water every time the boat hit a wave. My ribs protested as I slowly pulled myself to my knees, but the discomfort was nothing compared to the sharp pain ricocheting through my jaw.

Cracked ribs and a broken jaw, I decided, doing a quick assessment of the damage. Still, I wasn't dead yet.

I finally pulled myself back into the cockpit and lay

prostrate on the bench, gasping for breath, taking a moment to regain my senses. Fortunately that was a luxury I could afford because, by knocking me backwards, Dave had also put me out of his range. His attempts to reach me had been frustrated by the fully inflated life raft which now took up almost the entire deck space.

Less fortunately, I was still well within range of his gun—a very obvious possibility that I hadn't stopped to consider.

Dave was smiling as he trained that gun on me.

NINETEEN

I STARED INTO the barrel of the gun, my mouth dry, heart palpitating, and accepted there was no way out of this for Kara and me. I lifted my chin, attempting to retain a modicum of dignity, and drilled Dave with a cold, defiant stare. His lips twitched, as though he found my efforts amusing. He had a point. The hell with my pride. Begging suddenly seemed like a more viable option than saving face.

I'd talked down any number of criminals during my time on the force, but I'd rarely found myself at the business end of a gun. I swallowed against the ache in my throat, not ashamed to admit I was scared shitless. Disjointed images flashed through my mind, rather like a film spiralling on fast-forward. I wanted to focus my final thoughts on Harry but couldn't seem to summon up an image of his face.

Sitting beside me, Kara alternately gaped at the gun and then swivelled her eyes towards me. I reached for her hand and gave it a reassuring squeeze. She probably assumed I had some sort of plan and wondered why I wasn't putting it into action. The guy driving the boat kept glancing over his shoulder. He was nervous and I got the impression that no one had bothered to mention guns to him. Still, I couldn't count on him for help. He was probably too concerned about his own skin to try to talk Dave out of doing anything stupid.

Dave was having trouble staying on his feet due to the choppy conditions, and that offered me a glimmer of hope. He grinned, waving an ironic goodbye with the hand not holding the gun. Lining up his shot, he tightened his finger on the trigger at precisely the moment when a big wave hit the boat broadside, drenching us all. The gun discharged harmlessly into the sky, the bullet intended for me hitting nothing more substantial than fresh air.

Dave swore, swayed to one side and fought to regain his balance. He was either grinning or grimacing, it was difficult to tell which, as he shook the water off. Steadying himself by planting his legs more firmly apart on the swaying deck, he lined up his next shot.

A groan distracted him, and probably saved my life. Instead of shooting whilst he had the chance, he risked a glance behind him. Bowling Ball was coming to, pushing himself into a sitting position and clutching his head, blood pouring between his fingers.

"Get over here and help him." Dave motioned to Kara with his gun.

She looked at me for guidance and I nodded. No point in antagonising the bloke further. Besides, since Dave had obviously decided I was his primary target, it would take her out of the direct line of fire, at least temporarily. She climbed onto the bench and struggled across it, heading for the two men. Dave's gun was still trained on me but he no longer appeared to be in such a hurry to pull the trigger. He was more concerned about his mate, who'd always given me the impression of being in charge. Now that he was conscious again, Dave was already deferring to his authority, waiting for instructions.

"What do you expect me to do?" Kara asked, contempt in her voice.

"Get the first aid kit. Stop that bleeding."

She shrugged. "I don't know that I can do much in these conditions."

Do something, anything you like, but not too quickly. I willed her to pick up that thought. During the time they needed Kara's cooperation, they probably wouldn't risk shooting me. That would give the Coastguard a bit more time to respond to the EPIRB. The thugs clearly didn't know I'd activated it, and if the driver had noticed, he wasn't saying anything.

Kara's thoughts obviously weren't in tune with mine today and she had her own ideas on how to handle the situation.

"I don't know anything about first aid," she said, glaring at Bowling Ball's bleeding skull and shuddering. "The sight of blood makes me nauseous."

Oh, Kara! I shot her a look but she didn't seem to get that you should never antagonise someone as close to the edge as Dave—especially when he was holding a gun. I was only a few feet away but it might as well have been miles. The deck between us was blocked with the life raft, and I didn't stand a prayer of getting to him without being shot.

Dave drew back the hand holding the gun and swung it at Kara, connecting with her face with a sharp crack.

She screamed and clutched her cheek, blood pouring from her lip. Gil, squashed behind the inflated life raft close to Kara, reacted with a volley of barks. In one massive bound, hackles raised, a growl rumbling in his throat, he leapt on Dave and sank his molars deep into his ankle.

And left them there.

Dave howled. His finger tightened on the trigger and he let off a shot in my direction. It grazed my shoulder and buried itself in the bench behind me. Pumped full of adrenaline, I barely noticed the pain. Instead my eyes were on Bowling Ball, who'd staggered to his feet in an attempt to reach Kara. The boat rocked sideways, and he fell with a heavy thud. Obviously aware that he was in a life-and-death situation, he immediately pulled himself up again.

"Look out, Kara!"

She swung round just as Bowling Ball's hand brushed her arm. Reacting with lightning speed, she brought up her knee and deposited it in his groin with considerable force. I winced at the ferocity of the attack, applauding her quick thinking. Already debilitated, Bowling Ball fell to the deck, groaning with pain and clutching his family jewels.

Dave had dropped the gun and was trying to kick Gil off. The more he struggled, the deeper Gil sank his teeth into the soft flesh of his lower leg. "Get him off!"

Dave heaved himself up again, hopping about on the leg Gil was attached to, attempting to keep his balance on the heaving deck and strike Gil with his fists. A string of increasingly desperate invectives poured from his lips, lending the lie to his supposed mild manners. I made no attempt to call Gil off, relying on him to do a bit more damage yet. The pain had to be excruciating. I certainly hoped so, anyway. It seemed there was a god after all.

I was astonished by Gil's reaction, but at the same time not altogether surprised. Gil adored Kara and I'd often thought that if threats were directed toward either of us, he'd pick up on the aggression and his protective instincts would take over.

Glad we'd got that one sorted out.

I climbed carefully through the life raft until I reached Dave, picked up the gun and threw it overboard. Bowling Ball was still curled in a foetal position, clutching his scrotum and groaning. I knocked him out with a single blow, buying myself some time whilst I sorted this mess out.

I left Gil in charge of Dave and glanced at *Vagabond*, wondering if the EPP people on board had seen the kerfuffle through binoculars. They wouldn't have heard the shots, not from that distance and with all the noise of the engines. I relaxed. Even if they could see what was going down, they couldn't launch the tender—not in these conditions—and they couldn't get a shot off from the distance they were away.

I wasn't entirely sure I could depend on the driver of the boat to cooperate. He had to be part of the EPP setup, but it was obvious that no one had mentioned guns to him. He'd now slowed almost to a stop and was gaping at the scene in the cockpit, an expression of total bewilderment on his face.

I pulled Kara into my arms. “Are you all right?”

She nodded against my shoulder. “Yes, just a bit shaken up, that’s all.”

“Er, just for future reference, where did you learn to fight dirty like that?”

I sensed her smile. “You don’t want to know.”

She was probably right. I released her and looked at her face. Her lip was split and she’d probably have a nice bruise tomorrow.

“It’s fine,” she said.

“See if you can find a roll of duct tape.” I pointed to the locker beneath the helm position. I was confident there would be one. No boater worthy of the name would put to sea without such a multifunctional tool close at hand. This one proved to be no exception. Kara straightened up, holding the tape triumphantly above her head.

With Gil still restraining Dave, I taped his hands together behind his back. Only then did I tell Gil to release him. I could see that he’d made an excellent job of chewing up his lower calf. Attaboy! I told Dave to sit and taped his bound hands to the guardrail where it wasn’t protected by the canopy. He’d get sea water in his face every time we hit a wave. Petty, I know, but after what he’d put us through I reckoned I was letting him off lightly.

“Here, what about my leg?” Dave asked, staring at the bloody mess above his ankle.

“You’ll live.” I paused for effect. “Provided you don’t get rabies, of course.”

He stared at me, his eyes widening in terror. I didn’t

bother to tell him Gil was fully vaccinated and rabies-free. Let the bastard sweat!

Inhibited by the pain in my shoulder where that bullet had grazed it, to say nothing of my ribs and jaw, I manoeuvred my way awkwardly across to Bowling Ball and searched his pockets. He had a gun too and this time I put it in my pocket, along with his mobile phone. Monk would probably be interested in the origins of that gun and the numbers in the phone. Bowling Ball regained consciousness as I bound his hands and deposited him, swearing profusely and promising dire retribution, next to his mate.

"For the record," I said, standing back with my arms folded, regarding the two men. "I thought you lot were against violence and bad language."

"Fuck you! You're a fucking dead man."

I merely shot them a look and turned to the driver. "Do I need to tie you up as well, mate?"

"No, honestly, I was just asked to bring the boat out." He waved his hands about, clearly scared half out of his life. "I didn't have a clue what they planned to do. I don't want any part of this."

"Okay, just move ahead slowly."

"The same course for Dover?"

"Yeah."

Kara sat and made a huge fuss of Gil, who lapped up the attention.

"Good dog!" I told him, ruffling his ears.

Woof!

"I've always said that you underestimated his intelligence," Kara said, kissing his soggy head.

I found an old dog biscuit in my coat pocket and gave it to Gil. He swallowed it without inflicting further wear on his molars. Licking his lips, he looked at me expectantly, as though to say he'd expected a bit more of a reward for his heroic act.

"Later," I told him, scratching his ears. "Once we get back to the boat you'll be having fillet steak, pal."

"Charlie, you're hurt!" Kara's gaze was fastened on the blood pouring from my shoulder.

"It's just a scratch." My ribs were giving me much more grief.

She insisted upon looking at it, proving she didn't mind the sight of blood in the slightest. Expertly she placed a temporary dressing on the wound to quell the bleeding. Once she'd stopped fussing over me, I retrieved Bowling Ball's phone and dialled the number I'd memorised for Monk. He answered on the first ring.

"What the hell's happening, Charlie?" He sounded panicked and most un-Monk-like. "We lost your signal yesterday and didn't know what to think."

I refrained from pointing out that he was supposed to have us under surveillance. I'd always thought that was bullshit. Briefly I outlined events and he told me he'd be there within twenty minutes. Only then did I allow myself to relax, suddenly exhausted now that the flow of adrenaline had slowed. I took Kara's hand, gave Gil's ears another playful tug and then leaned back and closed my eyes, in pain and totally wiped out.

The arrival of two Coastguard's vessels roused Kara and me from where we'd virtually collapsed in a huddle beneath the canvas canopy. A horde of individuals swarmed over both vessels, boarding them with far greater ease than I'd been able to manage. All the villains were taken into custody on the rescue boats, along with the stowaways. We accepted a ride home on one as well since I was in no condition to skipper a vessel myself.

Julie and Mike were frogmarched ashore when we reached Dover. It would have taken a better person than I'd ever be not to have thrown a smug look her way. She glowered at me but, for once, didn't seem to have anything to say for herself.

Needless to say, word had already broken of the government's success in breaking up an illegal smuggling ring bring suicide bombers into the country. The media swarmed all over the place, but not close enough to get pictures of any of us, even with their long lenses. That was part of my deal with Monk. Kara and I didn't want to be part of the media feeding frenzy, or the government's spin campaign for that matter, which appeared to suit their purposes as much as it did ours. They wanted all the glory for themselves.

It appeared Monk had worked his magic, and we were asked only the most rudimentary questions before being allowed to leave. I was glad about that because I wasn't sure how much I was supposed to tell them.

It was late by the time we got back to the *No Comment*. Monk had wanted us to go through everything with him blow by blow, but one look at the state of us and even he didn't have the front to insist. Instead he arranged for someone to dress my wound properly. This paragon of all things medical assured me that my ribs were merely bruised and that my jaw wasn't broken. Easy for him to say.

"That's good to know," I said, my eyes fixed on Monk.

He accepted my refusal to go to casualty and promised to call on us the following day. That suited me just fine. By then I'd be rested and ready to extract a few answers from him. Having been threatened, coerced, bullied and shot at, all in an effort to further his ambitions, I had a right to know what it had really been about.

Monk arrived shortly after eleven the next morning.

"Well," he said, accepting a mug of coffee from Kara with a nod of thanks and arranging himself in his usual elegant fashion on the seating unit. "I think that went very satisfactorily, all things considered." Never one to show his feelings, he nevertheless looked thoroughly pleased with himself. "How are you both feeling?"

"I'm fine," Kara said, dismissing her split lip with a casual wave.

"And I'll live," I added.

He made no comment on my churlishness and turned his attention to Gil instead. "Well done, Gil!" He reached forward to scratch the big guy's ears.

Gil tilted his head to one side, probably attempting to look humble but not quite pulling it off.

"What's happening to those involved?" I asked.

He shrugged. "Richards is in custody and denying all knowledge of the operation." I nodded, unsurprised. "As I speak, his life is being pulled apart. He's a canny individual but I dare say we'll find something to prove his culpability."

"Good. I wouldn't want Tim to carry the can alone," Kara said.

"Perhaps you'll feel a little less sorry for him if I tell you that he tried to pin it all on you. He claimed to be totally innocent and suggested you and Charlie must have smuggled the illegals on board without his knowledge."

I blew air through my teeth—the only part of me not in pain—not bothering to say what I thought about such a desperate ploy.

"I know," Monk agreed. "That wasn't particularly clever but you know how people can be when they get caught out in a lie. We went through the motions and *discovered* yours and Kara's gear in the fourth cabin, proving that he must have been in the crew quarters, but he still won't go for the deal we're offering him."

"Give up what he knows about the people behind the operation in return for a reduced sentence?" I suggested.

"Yes, something like that, but my guess is that Wayne has promised to see his family right if he keeps his mouth shut. They must have discussed the possibility of being caught before Tim got involved and he trusts Wayne to keep his word."

"That figures." I shifted my weight, trying to find a more comfortable position, wincing as my injured shoulder voiced its objections. "What about Julie and Mike?"

He shook his head. "We have nothing to hold them on."

"But that's ridiculous!" Kara cried indignantly. "There must be something. They kidnapped me, for heaven's sake!" Outrage caused pink blotches to spring up on her face and neck.

"Yes, and they'd love their moment in the spotlight. They'd use it to highlight the rightness of their cause." Monk shook his head emphatically. "Just the sort of publicity the government doesn't want them to have."

"So they walk away?"

"I'm afraid so." But he didn't look too upset about it. "We can't win them all."

"It's so unfair!" Anger and frustration shimmered in her eyes. "Why did we bother?"

I'd asked myself that same question with increasing frequency during my latter years in the force. Even so, now wasn't the time to tell her that I'd told her so.

"But the goons on the Sealine who threatened us with guns?" My eyes bored flat and hard into Monk's profile. Julie and Mike getting away I could live with. I could even understand Monk's reasons for letting them walk. But if those two were to escape justice then I really would lose all faith.

"Oh, don't worry, they're being held."

"Won't they use the opportunity to spout the gospel according to the EPP as well?" I asked.

"No, they'll be charged with the illegal possession of firearms and attempted murder. Since the EPP make a big deal out of their nonviolent proclivities, they'll hang them out to dry and the thugs know it. They'll plead guilty and not make waves, is my guess, which will suit everyone concerned."

"I'm sure it will." I stretched my good arm above my head and fired off the question I'd been holding back.

"What about Dannett?" I asked, making it sound like an afterthought. "Does he walk too?"

Monk almost dropped his mug, just managing to place it aside without spilling more than a few drops of coffee down the front of his pristine shirt. He looked at me, his eyes probing as deep as a verbal question. "What makes you think this has anything to do with him?"

"Always answering questions with more questions, guv?" I shook my head, sending my hair cascading across my brow. I pushed it absently aside, casting him a long, considering glance. "Come on, fair's fair. I asked first."

"I would answer you if I understood the reason for your question." Monk had recovered from his initial surprise and retreated behind his customary wall of reticence.

I slapped my thigh. "So he *is* involved?"

"In what respect?"

This was farcical. Monk was a master at prevarication and I wouldn't get anything out of him unless I gave something in return. Succinctly I told him how I'd traced Dannett to the house in Ramsgate.

"You should have mentioned it, Charlie," he said in a tone of mild rebuke.

I quirked a brow. "Really? Just like you've told *me* everything?"

"I told you what you needed to know to get the job done."

I held on to my temper with difficulty, dismayed at the speed with which Monk had regained the upper hand. "I know Dannett's constituency has been earmarked for that refugee camp, which makes the illegal immigrant issue very pertinent to his election campaign. That's why I was keen to see what was in that house."

Monk sat a little straighter, his eyes boring into my features like lasers. "You got into that house?"

"Wouldn't you have been the tiniest bit curious if you'd been me?"

"How did you get in?"

I shrugged my good shoulder. Like I was going to tell him. Wisely, he didn't push the issue.

"Are you going to share your findings with us?" he asked.

"Uh-uh." I shook a finger at him. "You answer my original question first."

He hesitated for a long time, as though weighing up my request. When he eventually bowed his head I knew I'd get some answers, at last. I'd tell him about the laptop, eventually, but only if he was a little more forthcoming than he'd been to date.

"Dannett wants to be the next Prime Minister."

"We already have a Conservative Prime Minister."

"No, Kara," Monk said. "We have a coalition, led by the Tories. That's very different."

"And a lot of Tories think the current PM gives too much power to his coalition partners," I said, recalling stuff I'd seen in the press.

"Right. Dannett is the leader of a growing number of rebels who want to show more backbone when it comes to handling issues that matter to the electorate."

"Like immigration?"

"Like immigration," Monk agreed, nodding at me. "If they crack that nut, then the Tories will be elected free and clear of the need for coalition partners."

"How do they plan to pull it off?" Kara asked.

"Well, that's where the EPP comes in. Dannett and Peter Elliott come from very similar backgrounds." Monk's measured tone made it sound as if giving up confidential information was akin to having his teeth pulled. It probably was. "They were at Eton together and their political ideals aren't that far apart. It's just that, as a Tory, Dannett can't openly express those views for fear of alienating swathes of the faithful, many of whom come from ethnic minorities."

"But when that immigrants' camp was mooted for Dannett's constituency," I suggested, "he decided that drastic action was necessary? Action that tied in with his determination to show leadership qualities in areas that matter."

"Exactly so." Monk inclined his head, as though acknowledging some sort of quick thinking on my part. God knows why. Making the connection was hardly rocket science. "If you listen to the pundits, the most likely outcome to the election campaign will be another hung parliament, which will help no one, especially not the country. But if Dannett can claim the credit for exposing the suicide bombers' smuggling ring, his personal rating will soar, the Tories would most likely leap ahead in the polls, and Dannett would feel secure enough to launch a leadership bid."

"Yes, I can see that," Kara said, paying close attention to Monk's account. "But why would Elliott agree to help the Tories? What's in it for him?"

Monk smiled thinly. "That's where the bond between two old Etonions comes into play. Dannett contacted Elliott and put a suggestion to him. He knew about the smuggling ring and the government's determination to bring it down amidst favourable publicity thanks to his position on an all-party intelligence committee."

"Surely that sort of thing wouldn't be discussed in open committee?"

Monk waved the suggestion aside. "Secrets have a way of leaking out of Whitehall. A sympathetic civil servant probably fed him the information."

"And so, let me guess," I said, cynicism rendering my voice acerbic. 'Dannett suggested to his old mate Elliott that his organisation intercept *Vagabond* in return for..." I was stumped and retreated into momentary silence, staring off into the distance as I thought it through. "In return for what, guv? What's in it for him?"

"Elliott is standing for election as an M.P. Unsurprisingly, the constituency he's chosen is a marginal one and the incumbent Labour M.P. is unpopular, unlikely to be re-elected. Dannett ensured that a very inexperienced, very dull Tory is standing against him, almost guaranteeing that the charismatic Elliott will be elected."

"And when he is?" There had to be more.

"Elliott knows that grass roots support, or protest votes, won't be enough to get many of his members actually elected to the House and so he's looking for power through the back door. Dannett has promised him a seat on an influential committee he plans to set up after the election to govern all future immigration policies in this country."

I let out a low whistle, although why the gutter tactics of politicians still had the power to surprise I was at a loss to explain. "So he gets to be where the power is and has a hand in the sort of policy-making that most interests him. And Dannett gets what he wants by playing both sides against the middle without dirtying his own hands."

"Well, he would have done if the EPP had managed to bring *Vagabond* in," Monk said, a hint of smugness in his tone. "But thanks to you two that didn't happen."

"If I'd known I was helping to preserve the possibility of a hung parliament, then I'd have thought twice about it." I ran a hand through my hair as I pondered what Monk had chosen to share, pretty sure it wasn't all he knew. "The coalition we have now is bad enough."

"So, Charlie," Monk said, probably impatient to know what else I knew but careful to keep the urgency out of his voice. "It's your turn. What did you find in that house in Ramsgate?"

"Did I say I found anything?" I quirked a brow, treating him to a dose of his own medicine, almost enjoying myself.

He offered me a thin smile, not deceived. "I've never known you to leave a place empty-handed."

"Well, there was one thing." I told him about the laptop and my inability to circumvent the password. "What do you imagine is on it?"

"Well, first of all we need to get our hands on it. You did the right thing, not lifting it. Unfortunately, though, we don't have any reason to issue a warrant so I guess my people will have to get creative, just like you did." Monk looked almost cheerful at the prospect. "I dare say we'll be able to copy the hard drive without anyone knowing. Once we've found what's on the computer, then perhaps we'll be able to move against Dannett."

"Glad to hear it." And I was. What Dannett had tried to do was arrogant and despicable.

"No matter how clever people think they've been, they always give themselves away somehow. It's usually because they can't resist committing something to paper, or in this case, to cyberspace."

"Dannett won't escape punishment then?" Kara said.

"Oh, he's already being punished. He went out on a limb, promising to get the Tories elected to government with himself as their leader and without the encumbrance of a coalition partner." Monk flashed a brief smile. "Well, I think he can kiss goodbye to that ambition now."

Monk stood and reached for my hand. I stood as well and clasped it firmly. "Thank you, Charlie," he said with heartfelt sincerity. Well, why wouldn't he? Kara and I had taken all the risks, coming out on top through sheer luck and because I'd taken Gil with us. We probably hadn't done Monk's career prospects any harm, either. "Your contribution can never be formally acknowledged but I dare say a financial token of H.M. Government's deep appreciation will find its way to both of you sooner rather than later."

"So I should bloody well think."

After he left, Kara and I slumped on the seating unit,

Gil sitting expectantly at our feet. He always seemed to know when it was walk time but I wasn't thinking along those lines just yet. We sat there for some time, the silence unnaturally loud, as I waited for Kara to speak. I already had a fair idea what she was going to say.

"So, all that risk, Charlie, and for what?" She let out a long breath, looking decidedly peeved. "We almost lost our lives but are no nearer to finding Gordon Reed. At the end of the day, that's all I ever wanted to do." She turned to face me, tears spilling from the corners of her eyes and trickling unchecked down her cheeks. "Do you think he's dead?"

"Well, I—"

"Come on, be honest," she said impatiently. "I'd much rather know."

"I honestly don't know, Kara, about Gordon, I mean, I—"

Gil was getting impatient. He was now on his feet, barking and wagging, pointing out in his own inimitable style that he wasn't getting the recognition he deserved for saving our lives. I stroked his back just as his tail bashed against the pile of papers on the side table, sending them crashing to the floor. Kara bent to pick them up, her fingers stilling when she came to the photos of Dannett and his mystery friend taken outside that flat in Ramsgate. I'd forgotten they were there and that I hadn't yet shown them to her.

"Who's that?" she asked, holding one picture up.

"That's Dannett but I don't have a clue who the guy with him is."

"You should have asked Monk," she said, squinting at the picture.

"What, and do all his dirty work for him?" I pulled a face. "I've had enough of meddling in politics to last me a lifetime, thanks very much."

"Yes, but these two men look intimately acquainted, if you ask me."

I nodded. I'd thought that too.

"And one of them is Dannett," she said. "A supposedly upstanding family man."

"Yes, but what's your point?"

"My point is that he's trying to dupe the entire country and ought to be shown up for the sleaze ball that he is."

"Monk will never release what he knows about his connections with the EPP. The powers that be will want to use that for political leverage."

"Yes," she said, grinning mischievously, still studying the picture like it told her something it wasn't bothering to say to me. "But if they knew about his sexual proclivities, they'd have acted on them long before now."

"Why do I get the feeling that I don't like where this conversation is going?" I asked, feigning irritation.

"Come on, Charlie! We nearly got killed, but none of the culprits are being made to pay." She looked at me, her eyes unnaturally bright. "But if we discovered the identity of Dannett's boyfriend, the power would be in our hands."

"No!" I said emphatically, standing up and whistling to Gil. "Leave it, Kara."

"Why? What harm can it—"

"You just said it yourself. We almost got killed. Stalking strangers with ruthless connections like Dannett won't do much to improve our life expectancy."

"Oh, he's no stranger," she said, waving the picture beneath my nose.

I narrowed my eyes at her. "What do you mean?"

"I recognise him. That's Gordon," she said, and promptly burst into tears.

TWENTY

"ARE YOU SURE?"

"What sort of question is that?" Kara's eyes flashed a challenge, like she thought I doubted her—which I did. "Of course I'm sure."

I didn't see how she could be. She was emotional, which was hardly surprising given what she'd been through, and her mind could be playing tricks on her.

"The picture's a bit grainy," I pointed out. "You can't see the guy's features."

She offered up an impatient smile. "True, but I don't need to. I recognise his jacket."

"Kara!"

"What?"

"Hundreds of guys wear green jackets."

"Yes, Sherlock, but not with that distinctive logo on the back."

I studied the picture a bit more closely, unwilling to admit I hadn't given the logo a second thought. "What is it?"

"It was something Gordon and Brett designed when they thought about going into the charter business from themselves. Two dolphins leaping in front of the bow of a boat. See?" She pointed to the photo triumphantly, as though her reasoning was irrefutable. "Not original, but very distinctive, especially since the jackets are green. Most boating people wear dark blue, in case you hadn't noticed."

"Even so, presumably other people besides Gordon and Brett had these jackets?"

"Don't think so. They just had a couple done to see if they looked right. Their company never got off the ground so they didn't place an order for the jackets."

"I didn't know Gordon was gay," I said. "No one's thought to mention it."

"Nor did I, but I suppose it explains a lot."

"What do you mean?"

"Well, my brother was gay, remember."

As it happened, I'd forgotten. Or never knew. Whatever. "So, were Brett and Gordon an item?"

Kara shrugged. "Who knows?" She frowned at the picture. "Who would have thought it of Dannett? I'm surprised he's prepared to risk it." She stared straight through me as she struggled to make sense of it all. "I mean, he's always on telly with his wife and kids, banging on about family values."

I shrugged. "Yeah well, we're talking about a politician here, so double standards shouldn't come as any great surprise."

"Perhaps, but even so, Dannett...gay." She shook her head. "It just doesn't seem feasible." She paced the salon, Gil looking up hopefully every time she passed his leash. "But I still don't understand why Gordon hasn't been in touch, especially if he's been in this country ever since he went missing. He must have known how worried everyone would be. Why the hell didn't he call?"

"I'm sure he had a good reason." I took pity on Gil and reached for his leash. "Come on, let's take the mutt for a walk and think it through in the open air."

"Okay." She followed me from the boat, still clutching the picture of Dannett and his friend, frequently glancing at it as we walked along. I still wasn't prepared to accept that it was Reed, but she'd obviously made up her mind.

"Just in case it's escaped your notice," she said in a sweetly venomous tone. "If you'd shown me this when you first got it we could have avoided being kidnapped. And shot at, and almost killed, and all the rest of it."

She had a point. "Sorry, I intended to mention it but, what with all the excitement, I forgot all about it."

She threw a stick for Gil and sighed. "So, what now?"

"Well, I presume you want to see Gordon, if it is him—"

"It is. I'm sure of it."

"Okay, so you want to see him and get some answers?"

"Go to Ramsgate, you mean. Well, yes, that was my first thought, but shouldn't we tell Peter and Sally? If anyone goes, it ought to be them."

"Think about it. If you didn't know your brother's best friend was gay then the chances are that his family don't either. They certainly didn't mention it."

"True, but—"

"I think we should tackle Gordon, tell him how upset his family is and leave him to decide on the next move."

And if it turns out not to be him, we won't have got their hopes up unnecessarily.

"But what if he refuses to speak to them?"

"If he does, we'll rethink our strategy." I shot her a challenging smile. "I want to know what the hell's been going on, even if you don't."

She chewed thoughtfully at the inside of her lip. "Yes, you're right. We'll go and confront him. Of course we will." Gil returned with the soggy stick and dropped it at our feet, wagging expectantly. This time I bent to pick it up and threw it across the rocky beach. Gil's paws scrabbled for purchase on the slick pebbles as he charged after it. "It's just that, having got over my initial euphoria at discovering he's okay, I'm now furious with him for causing us all so much torment. One phone call would have put us out of our misery."

"Would it have, though?"

"Of course. We just needed to know he was alive."

"And you wouldn't have been the tiniest bit curious about his living arrangements?"

She shook her head.

"Come on, Kara, I know you. It might not be your business, strictly speaking, but you wouldn't have settled for anything other than a full explanation."

"I worry for Sally's sake," she said defensively. "I'm in a good position to know what she's going through." She shook her head. "He's being so bloody selfish."

"It seems that way, but remember who he's with. He must be under a lot of pressure to keep Dannett's secret. If they're as attached to one another as that photo suggests, then I guess Gordon feels he owes his loyalty to Dannett ahead of his family."

She pulled a face at me. "I hate it when you're right."

I took her hand and kissed the top of her head. "Get used to it, baby!"

She swatted my bum with the back of her hand, but finally cracked a smile. "Don't try taking advantage of me, just because I'm feeling low."

"As if!"

WE WENT TO Ramsgate the following afternoon. It was a Saturday and I was pretty sure we'd catch Gordon alone. Weekend afternoons are traditionally spent by ambitious politicians in their constituencies, surrounded by their doting families and local party worthies. How they choose to deploy the wee small hours isn't quite so cut and dried but, in Dannett's case, I was prepared to make an educated guess. I couldn't help wondering if his wife knew about his sexual preferences. Quite often women in such circumstances are the last to cotton on.

We arrived at the block of flats in question. Although I knew that the apartment Gordon occupied was on the top floor, there were three to choose from and no doorman to point us in the right direction. That surprised me because this looked like the upmarket sort of place that ought to have someone on duty to keep out the common herd. There again, perhaps that was what had attracted Dannett in the first place. The last thing he needed was overzealous porters making life difficult for him and leaking his secret to the press. Kara peered at the names on the post boxes in the entrance hall and smiled.

"Flat 12," she said, heading straight for the lift.

"How do you know?"

"Because it says Borg on the box."

"Yeah, and that's significant because..."

"Because it's the name Brett and Gordon gave their charter company that never got off the ground. The one that they had the jackets designed for," she added, when I stared blankly at her.

"Borg? How's that related to the sea?"

She scrunched up her face. "Brett or Gordon."

"Oh." Short of pointing out that they weren't exactly business-minded if that was the best they could come up with, there wasn't much else I could say.

We were as silent as the elevator that whisked us upwards, engrossed in our individual thoughts. I had a bad feeling about this, but it was too late to turn back now.

"Er, Charlie." Kara's hesitant tone dragged my thoughts away from Brett and Gordon's doomed business enterprise. "Before we go in, there're one or two things you ought to know about Brett."

"Brett? Why?"

"Well, he took Jasmine's disappearance hard and I have a feeling that he turned to Gordon for solace."

"And you reckon Brett's death might have made Gordon act the way he is now. Turning his back on his family and living in seclusion down here, I mean."

"Precisely."

I sensed her increasing apprehension as we stepped from the lift and approached the door in question. I took a firm hold of her hand and gave it a reassuring squeeze. She was clearly having second or even third thoughts about the forthcoming reunion so I pressed the doorbell before she could bottle it. I waited a minute or two and, receiving no response, pressed it again.

"He's not in," Kara said, sounding both relieved and disappointed. "We'll have to come back another time."

"He's in," I said, applying my thumb to the bell again and leaving it there.

"How can you be so sure?"

"I heard movements inside just now and saw a shadow pass across the glass panel in the door."

"Oh."

The door eventually opened a few inches but the security chain prevented it from revealing any part of the person who'd done the opening.

"Yes," said a disembodied voice.

Kara gasped. "That's Brett's voice," she said, staring at me, deathly pale, her eyes huge with shock.

"Kara," I said gently, wondering if she'd taken leave of her senses. "Your brother's dead. Come on, you've just been talking about Brett, you're feeling fragile, and—"

But I was talking to myself because Kara had fallen to the floor in a dead faint.

TWENTY-ONE

I CROUCHED NEXT to Kara, anxious to see what I could do to help her. She wasn't the type to faint, which told me just how close to the edge she actually was. At least she didn't seem to have hurt herself when her legs gave out, which was something. The thoughts tumbling through my head centred on my own stupidity in bringing her here when I knew she was feeling emotionally unstable. First off, she'd been convinced that Dannett's lover was Gordon Reed, now she had him pegged as her dead brother.

Brett Webb was definitely dead. His body had been identified by his father. There'd been an inquest, a funeral, the works, but I know Kara still missed him. That was why she was so keen to find Reed. A kind of transference of affection, I guessed.

The person on the other side of the door peered through the gap but no offer of help was forthcoming.

"We'd better get her inside," I said, picking her up, concern for Kara and anger at this guy's disinterest conducting a full scale battle inside me.

"Now's not convenient," he said. "I'm expecting someone."

Barely able to believe my ears, I leaned my good shoulder against the door before he could slam it closed.

"The woman needs help," I said, now convinced that he couldn't be Gordon Reed. If he was, he'd have recognised Kara and, presumably, would feel an instinctive desire to help her.

"Move away from the door or I'll call security."

What security? I applied more pressure to the double-glazed door, still holding the dead weight of Kara in my arms, whilst the inside guy tried to slot it back into its frame from the other side. It was farcical. A stalemate situation set to continue until one of us ran out of strength.

Kara resolved matters by regaining consciousness and struggling out of my arms. I held on to her because she still looked decidedly wobbly, and so pale you'd think she'd seen a ghost.

"Brett." She breathed slowly, gaping at the eyes peering through the gap in the door. "Brett, is it really you?"

I glanced at her, then at the eyes, and slowly the truth dawned. She hadn't imagined things. She really *was* addressing her dead brother.

I removed my shoulder from the door and waited out the deafening silence as brother and sister regarded one another. The next move was his. Kara had tracked him down, albeit by default, and if he didn't want to acknowledge her, there was sod all I could do about it. Well, there was plenty I could do about the scheming, conniving little shit, but he *was* Kara's brother so my first thought was for her feelings. She looked on the verge of tears, upset that he even needed to think about letting her in. Probably more upset still for a whole raft of reasons that must only just be occurring to her. That he was alive and hadn't bothered to inform his family.

I shook my head in disbelief. I thought I'd seen it all during my years in the job, but someone coming back from the dead was a definite first.

After what felt like an eternity the chain rattled in its slide as it fell away from the door. Brett pulled it open in stages to start with, and then in one swift, decisive jerk. He stretched his arms out wide, his brilliant smile revealing a set of perfectly capped, unnaturally white teeth. I wasn't sure how Kara would react, now that she could see all of her brother, looking disgustingly healthy for a dead man. She'd either fly at him or fall into his embrace.

She chose the latter course.

I stood back, taking the opportunity to appraise the man who'd risen, Phoenix-like, from the dead. He wore tight-fitting white jeans, artistically ragged in places, and a tank top that displayed an impressive torso, probably honed from hours in a gym. Well, how else did a dead man in hiding pass the time? Tattoos adorned his biceps. His floppy blond hair was streaked with mauves and reds that argued with various shades of brown. He had a diamond stud in one ear and a watch on his wrist that cost a damned sight more than a delivery skipper could ever earn. Brett Grayson Webb, bless him, was living high on the hog on someone else's money.

And it didn't take a brilliant mind to figure out who that someone had to be.

I waited for them to remember I was there, but it didn't look as though that was going to happen any time soon. Their total absorption in one another was touching. I couldn't begin to imagine the emotions Kara must be feeling. Anyway, it made me feel like an intruder as they clung together, laughing, crying, both talking at once and demanding explanations.

"Shall we go inside?"

Brett glanced at me, looking as though he was going to protest. Presumably it was the forbidding set to my features that made him think better of it. He led us into an ultra-modern open-plan lounge with magnificent views over the harbour. It was all blond wood floors, leather sofas, glass and chrome furniture—as clean and sterile as an operating theatre. Someone had poured a heap of dosh into this place without taking the time to stamp their personality on it.

Kara didn't seem to notice the splendour of her brother's living arrangements. She and Brett were still both talking at once, the sort of verbal shorthand restricted to very close siblings. Not so close though that Brett had felt it necessary to put his sister's mind at rest about his situation.

As though reading my mind, Kara acted in a way that brought the cosy reunion to an aggressive end. Without warning she let fly with her fists, hammering them against Brett's chest, tears streaming down her face.

"You bastard! You've been alive all this time and didn't bother to let us know." Hyperventilating, she pummelled away at him. I could have stopped her, but I reckoned it was less than the little weasel deserved, so I let her do her worst. "Have you any idea what you put us through?"

Brett tried to grab her hands but anger lent her superhuman strength. She continued to batter him with fists clenched as tight as her teeth, her features twisted into an expression of misery and disbelief.

"For God's sake, Kara, let up! Give me a chance to explain."

This ought to be good.

"Why should I? I'll never manage to hurt you as much you hurt us—your family—but I'll give it a damned good shot." She glared at him, still striking out, but her blows gradually became weaker, as though the anger had drained out of her. "How could you, Brett?" she demanded. "Especially after what Jasmine put us through."

"I'm not Brett anymore. I go by the name of Karl Finch nowadays. I have a passport and everything in that name."

I didn't doubt it so refrained from comment and left them in the centre of the lounge, moderately certain now that Kara wouldn't kill the brother she'd thought was dead anyway. I'd taken an instant dislike to the guy and didn't much care if she did get in a few blows that were literally below the belt. But still, before she did any permanent damage, I was curious to know how he'd finished up here.

I went in search of badly needed sustenance and found a bottle of white wine in the fridge. I screwed up my nose, unsurprised that there was nothing stronger to hand. It was just the sort of girly drink I'd expect this arse to favour. Still, needs must. I opened it and poured each of us a glass.

"Let's sit down," I said, handing out the glasses. "Then Brett can explain."

"Who the hell are you, anyway?" Brett shot the question at me, his tone sulky yet belligerent.

"This is Charlie Hunter," Kara said. "You remember him, Brett, surely? He used to be a policeman and was involved when Jasmine went missing."

"A policeman!" Brett's eyes darted between Kara and me, rather like a petrified animal frozen in a car's headlights. "You brought a policeman here?"

"He's not in the force anymore."

"But I still have contacts," I pointed out pleasantly, just so he wasn't left in any doubt.

Kara shot me a look I couldn't interpret. "Anyway, when we came here, we didn't expect to see a dead man." Brett dropped his head and said nothing. "I contacted Charlie when you *died*," she said acerbically, "and he helped me to track Jasmine down."

"Ah, I see."

"Jas is dead," she said flatly. "Not like you. She's really dead. I saw it happen."

"I'm sorry, Kara." Brett tried to take her hand but she snatched it away.

"So we reach the crux of the matter," I said. "Why didn't you let Kara know you were okay?"

"About that," he said, turning toward his sister. "I'm sorry, I wanted to but my hands were tied. It was too dangerous to…"

"Too dangerous to what?" I prompted.

"I can't tell you." He leaned his arms on his knees, dropped his head forward and addressed his comments to the floor. "I got involved in some stuff, in over my head, and was lucky to get away with my life. Someone helped me to get out of it, but I can't betray his trust."

"Then let me tell you what I think." I was holding on to my temper by the merest slither as I glanced at Kara and saw so much hurt and confusion in her eyes. "Monk told you where to find Jasmine."

Brett's head shot up. "You know about him?"

"Monk told you where to find Jasmine," I repeated, not acknowledging the interruption. "You agreed to find out what you could about her husband's operation, but his goons warned you off. They attacked you and left you for dead."

I stopped talking and allowed the silence to lengthen. Most people hated silences and Brett Webb proved to be no exception.

"Something like that," he said.

"But you weren't dead. How did you fake your death?"

"Okay, I'll tell you." He released a long breath and paused significantly, as though deciding exactly how much to tell us. Nothing less than the truth would satisfy me, and I'd know if he was lying. "After I was recruited by Monk and he told me where Jasmine was, I got a message to her and asked her to meet me in a pub in Weymouth, but Jas didn't show. I figured she couldn't get away, so I left. But there were these two guys waiting for me outside. They beat me up pretty bad and warned me away from Jas." He paused and drained the rest of his wine in one swallow. "I think they would have killed me but I was saved by this guy from the pub. He'd been giving me the eye all night and followed me when I left. He waded in with his fists and..." He choked back a sob and his words stalled.

"He took the beating instead of you."

"Yes, they laid into him, seeming to forget about me."

"He helped you but you didn't return the favour," I said, aware of the disgust in my own voice.

"I was already on the ground. I was hurting badly and couldn't move." *Like hell you couldn't.* "We were both down and out when they left us. I was semi-conscious but the guy who helped me was out cold."

I saw where he was going with this. "He was dead?"

Brett nodded. "He'd hit his head pretty badly when he fell. There was blood everywhere." He shuddered, more in repulsion than with empathy, if I was any judge. "And that's when I had the idea. If I could just be dead, disappear, and leave all the shitty baggage of my life behind me, I could start again somewhere else with a clean slate."

"So you put your distinctive green sailing jacket on the dead man, put your ID in his pocket and tipped him into the sea."

Kara gasped. "Tell me you didn't do that, Brett."

"He was dead," he said defensively. "What was I supposed to do? Hang about and explain to the police?"

"Has it occurred to you that he has a family somewhere, wondering what happened to him?"

"I know, but I—"

"How did you know he'd be found?" I asked, in no mood for his pathetic attempts to justify the unjustifiable.

"We were inside the marina basin. The chances of his body being washed out to sea were virtually zero. I was confident he'd be found."

"So you called your father, told him what you'd done and blackmailed him into identifying the body as yours?" I said coldly.

He dropped his head again. "Yeah, pretty much."

"Why did he agree?" Kara asked.

"After what he did to me as a kid, he had no choice. He literally fucked my life up."

"We know," Kara said quietly. "That's why Jasmine left, isn't it?"

"Well, if you know," he said sulkily, "you ought to understand why I did it and be more sympathetic."

Kara might be, but I sure as hell wasn't. "So your life's back on track but Jasmine's dead, thanks to you."

Brett shot to his feet. "That had nothing to do with me."

"Leave it, Charlie," Kara said quietly.

Brett resumed his seat and addressed his next remark to Kara. "How's Mum?"

"She fell to pieces when you *died*."

Brett choked on a sigh but didn't respond.

"But she's okay now that I have Jas's children. She helps with them quite a bit."

"God, I hadn't even thought about her kids."

If you asked me, Brett Webb hadn't thought about anyone except himself for a long time now. Out of deference to Kara's feelings, which appeared to be oscillating wildly between joy at finding her brother alive and anger at the deceptions he'd pulled off, I didn't bother to say so.

"Sooooo," I said, drawing the word out until it was four syllables long. "The thousand-dollar question. Where's Gordon Reed?"

Brett wouldn't look at me. "How would I know?"

"Don't lie to me," I said. "If you don't know, then how come you have his jacket?"

"What do you mean?" Kara asked.

"You recognised it in that photo," I pointed out. "You thought it was Gordon's. He and Brett were the only two to have those jackets, and Brett put his on the corpse he threw into the sea like a piece of trash."

"Gordon's dead," Brett said, so softly that I almost didn't hear him.

"Dead dead, or pretend dead?" I asked.

"I guess I deserved that."

Kara nodded decisively. "No question."

"Care to elaborate?" I asked.

I watched him wrestle with himself, trying to decide how much to tell us. The physical resemblance between brother and sister was startling but Brett's sulky expression as he prevaricated made me realise that it only extended as far as facial features. When it came to backbone and integrity, Kara left her brother standing. Brett was weak and spoiled, never having really got over the way his father abused him.

What I couldn't understand was Monk's willingness to recruit him. If I could gauge his character within a couple of minutes of meeting him, Monk must have had him pegged equally quickly. How could he have imagined that Brett Webb would be a reliable inside man? There again, perhaps from Monk's perspective, his obvious character defects made for a convincing cover. No one in their right mind would suspect him of being engaged in intelligence work.

"We know Gordon was recruited by Monk to infiltrate Ultimate Marine's people-smuggling business," I said, tired of pussyfooting around the main issue. My injured shoulder had just given me a painful reminder that I had this guy's lover to thank for almost getting killed. He looked up at me, his features frozen in an expression of abject shock. "What we don't know is how you came to be shacked up here with Dannett and how you can be so certain that Gordon's dead."

"How…how did you—"

"You're obviously not as careful and clever as you thought you were," I said. "You and Dannett were seen together."

"Really?" Brett's face drained of colour. "God, he'll be furious! That must have been the other night. I was going stir crazy and persuaded him to go out for a few hours." He buried his head in his hands. Again. "He'll blame me."

High time someone did. "How did you meet Dannett?"

"He has a place in France. He's not well known there and can be himself. I saw him in a bar. We became friends. And occasional lovers. But only when I was in France. He couldn't risk being seen with a gay man in this country."

"Seems to me," I said, glancing round the opulent

apartment, "that he's risking a damned sight more than that now, keeping you like this."

"Things are different now. We're in love."

I rolled my eyes but refrained from comment, leaving him to continue with his story.

"He was the first person I rang for help when I *died* in Weymouth. I was in a bad way and don't remember too many of the details. All I know is that he got me out of there. I sailed to France on a yacht owned by someone who owed him a favour. He came over when he knew I was there, got me medical help and then I holed up in his place for quite a while."

"But Gordon knew where you were?"

"Yeah, but he was the only person I trusted."

Kara shot him a look. "I can't believe you just said that."

Brett reached for her hand but she snatched it away. "You were better off out of it," he said.

"Tell that to Jas."

"Were you and Gordon lovers too?" I asked.

"No, we never have been." I must have looked surprised because he got all defensive. "Do you shag every heterosexual woman who crosses your path?" He shrugged. "Just because we shared the same tendencies, it doesn't mean we were romantically involved. We'd been good mates since long before we each discovered our true sexuality. He knew what Dad did to me. I could talk to him about that. About anything."

"And so he told you when Monk asked him to get involved with Ultimate Marine?"

"Not at once. He rang me to say he was in France. I

wasn't supposed to be seen out but I took a chance and met him. That's when he told me what he was doing for Monk. I advised him not to take any risks but didn't know about Andrew's involvement with Ultimate Marine at the time." He shook his head, elbows planted on his knees, addressing his comments to the floor. "Andrew surprised me by coming over unexpectedly. He was waiting when I got home."

"And none too pleased that you'd gone out?" I said.

"No, he wanted to know where I'd been, obviously, and why. He knew about Gordon, was aware he knew where I was, but they'd never met. He was angry because I think he suspected us of being lovers."

"So you told him why Gordon was really there?" I suggested.

"Yes, and that's when he went ballistic. I've never seen him so angry before. Anyway, he told me to warn Gordon off, but I couldn't get hold of him."

"Did Andrew kill him?" Kara asked.

"Of course not! He's no murderer."

I thought about the fate of those aboard *Mistral* and could have given him an argument on that one. Brett sipped his wine, looking surprised when he found his glass was empty. I topped it up, anxious to keep him talking. But he stayed quiet, staring off into the distance as expressions of anger and humiliation chased one another across his pretty-boy face.

"We need to know what happened to Gordon," I said, in the hard tone I'd used with criminals when I'd had enough of their crap. It usually worked then, and did now.

"He was in Calais a month or so ago and got in touch."

"You were still there at the time?"

"Yes, and I told him Andrew wanted him to back off. He wanted to know why, but I couldn't tell him because I didn't know much." I raised a brow. "I didn't! Not then, anyway. But I thought Gordon trusted me and had agreed to leave it."

"But he didn't?" God, this was like extracting water from a dry well.

"Obviously not. He told me Wayne was skippering that trip and Monk thought they wouldn't bring illegals back if he was on board."

"I thought you didn't know about that?"

"Gordon told me what Monk had told him."

"Okay, I'll buy that."

"Gordon was just supposed to see if he could find out anything about what Wayne did when he went ashore, so he followed him."

Kara groaned aloud.

"He phoned me that evening," he said, "in a real panic."

"What about?"

"He'd followed Wayne to a bar in a backstreet." I nodded, assuming it was the one the Calais taxi driver told us he'd taken Wayne to. I didn't seek clarification. It didn't really matter, and I didn't want to interrupt Brett's flow. "He said the bar was dark and crowded with locals so Wayne didn't seem him. Anyway, apparently Wayne met some guy and they talked for ages. Gordon couldn't get near enough to hear what was being said, so he risked taking a picture of them on his mobile and then got out of there."

"Why did he tell you this if you'd asked him not to do it?"

"Isn't it obvious?"

Kara and I looked at one another and shook our heads.

"He changed sides. Instead of reporting to Monk, he reported what he found out to Andrew."

"So who killed him?"

"I don't know, but it can't have been Andrew because Gordon was now working for him. And because he knew Gordon was my mate."

I could see his logic. Unless, of course, Andrew thought they were secret lovers and was jealous. He really must have feelings for Brett if he'd risked so much for him. Anything was possible.

"You must have some idea," I said.

"He said two men approached him when he left the bar. English they were and really polite, apparently, but they scared the shit out of him." Brett launched into a physical description. It wasn't really necessary because I knew who they had to have been. "They asked him why he was taking pictures of Wayne."

"What did he tell them?" Kara asked, frowning.

"He was petrified, but no way was he going to drop himself deeper in it by telling them what he was really doing. So he said he'd been taking a picture of a guy at a table behind Wayne. They realised he was gay, I think, so they might have believed him." He shrugged. "They must have done because they let him go. Then someone else started following him."

"Who?"

"He thought it was the man Wayne had been talking to in the bar."

Wayne's contact in France. The one responsible for smuggling the illegals on board.

"But how do you know he was killed?"

"Because," Brett said, looking pale and drawn, "he was talking to me when the guy found him. I heard his screams. I don't think I'll ever forget them."

"Which is why you came back to England."

"I heard Andrew talking with Peter Elliott."

"Hang on. Who did Elliot think you were?"

"Just an English guy who looks after Andrew's boat."

I suspected that Elliott knew the truth, but let that pass. "I assume you overheard them talking about you."

"Yes, Peter insisted I couldn't be trusted to keep quiet after what had happened to Gordon and that it would be best if I disappeared."

"Just a moment," I said, raising a hand to stop his flow of words. "Why were Dannett and Elliott in France together at that precise time? Surely it was dangerous for them to be seen together."

"You know about their association then?" Brett addressed the question to Kara.

"Yes, but I'm surprised he told you."

"He didn't, not then, but since I've been back in England he's told me everything. We have no secrets from each other."

I turned away from his besotted expression. Still grappling to come to terms with the extent of his selfishness, it was the only way to stop myself from knocking his teeth down his throat.

"I should have mentioned that Peter Elliott occasionally came to Andrew's home in France for weekends, out of the way of the British press. That way they could refine their plans without fear of interruption. Anyway, Andrew told Peter he'd deal with me and Peter believed him." Brett shrugged. "Well, why wouldn't he? They were allies and close friends and trusted one another implicitly. Their political futures are entwined, after all. The only thing Peter doesn't know about Andrew is his secret sexual life. He doesn't even suspect."

"Sure about that, are you?" I raked his body with my eyes.

"I can blend in when I need to," he said peevishly. "Anyway, Andrew put everything on the line to save me. That must tell you something."

It certainly did. Probably more than I wanted to know. Monk had been economical with the truth. Again. If Dannett knew Monk was on to him, why had he risked continuing with the operation?

"How did he get you away then, if Elliott wanted you done away with?" I asked.

"Oh, Andrew arranged everything. He phoned Wayne, pretending to be calling for Gordon. He said Gordon had taken another job and couldn't return to England with him." I nodded. That would explain why Wayne was so annoyed when he left him in the lurch. "When *Mistral* went down, he told Peter I'd taken Gordon's place on board."

"Was Dannett was behind *Mistral*'s sinking?"

"No, of course not!" Brett leapt out of his seat. "No, he wouldn't do anything like that." *Oh wouldn't he!* "He knows nothing about it. As far as he was concerned, the boat would be intercepted by the EPP's people and everyone aboard taken into custody."

"Which would have included you."

"Good job I wasn't on board then."

That's a matter of opinion.

"When she *accidentally* went down, Andrew had the idea of pretending I was on board. Peter Elliott wouldn't doubt Andrew's word, so wouldn't bother to check."

No, it simply didn't ring true. I could see that Brett believed it because Dannett hadn't told him how far he'd gone to protect him. I'd wondered all along about that cigarette boat. Why was such a fast boat hanging about, shadowing *Mistral*? If it was supposed to tow her in when she developed an engine fire then she was the wrong boat for the job. She was built for speed, not tough tow work. Dannett had callously sacrificed all those people just to protect his new lover.

It defied belief.

I stalked about the room, endeavouring to curtail my anger and think it through rationally. Whichever way I came at it, Dannett was guilty of cold-blooded murder. My only problem was that I didn't have a prayer of proving it. Despite all the supposed equality in today's society, any unsubstantiated allegations about such a high-profile man wouldn't see the light of day. It was so fucking frustrating.

"Dannett knew the truth. He knew that if they intercepted the next lot of immigrants, then the government forces would be there to spoil the party."

"How?" Brett looked genuinely confused. "How

could Monk have known that? Gordon had switched sides. He wouldn't have told Monk anything."

Perhaps not, but Dannett wasn't taking any chances, and organised matters to suit his own ends. Ergo, bye-bye *Mistral*. What did a few lives matter, just so long as his lover-boy remained safe and his partner in crime remained satisfied. Incredible!

"How long did you think you could live here before anyone found out about you and Dannett?" Kara asked.

"Well, obviously, until after the election. That's why I couldn't risk anyone seeing me. Andrew made me promise. But once he's Prime Minister and the EPP business has died down, I'll be able to stop hiding."

Kara wrinkled her brow. "But how could you still be with Dannett?"

"We'd have found a way." Brett's jaw jutted with stubborn determination.

"He's a family man, Brett. He has a wife and kids."

"Oh, they're just for show." He dismissed their existence with a casual flap of his hand. "His wife leads her own life and doesn't care what he does. Besides, she's having an affair. She thinks Andrew doesn't know but, in due course, it will find its way into the press and he'll be the injured party. They'll be able to divorce with no damage to his reputation. In fact, he'll have the nation's sympathy. Then the spotlight will be off his private life and we can do as we please."

Kara looked as incredulous as I felt. "I don't understand what you expect to get out of this relationship. Andrew's first love is politics, he's driven by ambition and you'd always come second to that." She glowered at him but her voice softened. "Think about it. You'd never be able to be seen together and would always be looking over your shoulder, worried about being caught out. What sort of life would that be?"

"He's going to give me a job as an aide in his office when he gets elected."

"Give me strength," I muttered.

"Anyway, I don't care about anything as long as I can be with Andrew." He turned to me, scowling. "He's the first person I've met who only cares about me."

"What about me?" Kara asked quietly.

"I didn't mean—" He broke off, pacing the room. "What are you going to do about us?" he asked sullenly.

Bloody good question and, as yet, I didn't have a clue how to answer it.

TWENTY-TWO

As soon as we got out of there, I took Kara to the nearest bar and forced a large brandy on her. She took too large a sip and almost choked on it. She hadn't spoken a word since we left her brother in his palatial prison, whinging that his life would be over if we revealed his secret. Begging us not to say anything. Yeah, like that was gonna happen! He was thinking only of himself and didn't seem to care about the lives he'd ruined. I refrained from telling Kara what I thought of the selfish sod. Right now, she didn't need to hear it so instead I waited for the brandy to do its work and for her to relax a little.

"What will happen to him?" she asked, when she'd consumed half her drink in brooding silence. "He must have committed all sorts of offences."

He had, but I knew Monk could make them all go away, if he felt so inclined. Or if I asked him to. The mere thought of doing so stuck in my craw, but there wasn't much I wouldn't do for Kara's sake. "What do you want to have happen to him?"

"I don't know. He's like a stranger." She shuddered, as though it hurt to think about him. "He was always different and, given what happened to him when he was younger, I suppose I can understand why. But this selfishness?" She shook her head. "What he did to Mum and me, I'm not sure I can ever forgive him for that, and I don't think we'll ever be close again. What's more, I've no idea how to tell Mum that he's still alive. She's found some sort of peace in her life now, helping me with the kids. Besides, I'm not sure she'd like the person Brett has become. I don't see how I could keep it a secret, though. That would be even crueller."

"Yes, she'll have to be told. If Dannett's association with Brett becomes public knowledge—"

"Will that happen?"

"That's up to Monk. And Dannett."

"Do you think Dannett arranged for Gordon to be killed? He seems very possessive, and if he was jealous of Gordon and Brett's closeness..."

"No, probably not. Dannett knew Monk was on to him, thanks to Gordon, but still thought he could pull his little scheme off if he had Gordon on the inside, doing his dirty work."

"Then Wayne's contact *was* responsible?"

"Looks that way. Your brother had no reason to lie about that." Unless he was protecting Dannett, but I couldn't see it. "That bar he followed Wayne to. You wanted to follow him there and I wouldn't play because it was in a backstreet, frequented by locals. We'd have stood out."

"But Brett said it was dark and crowded."

"Even so, I bet Wayne's contact saw Gordon take that picture, followed him, saw him being accosted by the EPP people—"

"And got suspicious."

"It's the only explanation that makes sense."

"Well, at least Brett wasn't responsible for his best friend's death."

I squeezed her hand. "No, that's down to Monk." I bought her another drink, pleased to see a little colour returning to her face. "Talking of whom, shall I call him and see what he really knows?"

She offered me the ghost of a smile. "Like he'll tell us."

I chuckled. "So you're beginning to understand how he operates."

I called Monk, told him where we were and asked him to join us. He didn't ask why and arrived not much more than an hour later. As soon as he sat at our table I went on the offensive.

"How long have you known that Kara's brother is alive?" I asked.

"What!"

It was the first and only time I've ever seen him lost for words. So I told him everything we'd just discovered, amused at how quickly he controlled his reaction. Even so, it was equally apparent that he knew nothing about Dannett's sexual preferences. His eyes gleamed, and I couldn't begin to imagine what was going on inside that incisive brain of his.

"What will you do about it?" Kara asked.

He sighed. "Whatever my masters ask me to. I assume," he added, after a lengthy pause, "that you'd like Brett's name kept out of this?"

Told you so.

"Is that possible?"

"Oh, after everything you and Charlie have done for H.M. Government, I'm sure it can be arranged."

"What about Gordon Reed's murder?"

"What indeed. I tend to agree with your assessment. It can only be down to Wayne's paymasters, and the likelihood of our ever finding his body, much less any evidence..." Monk sighed. "Even so, I shall set enquiries in motion on the other side of the Channel."

We talked it over a bit more, and Monk agreed to inform Gordon's relatives of his death. With nothing more to say, I drove us back to Brighton in Kara's car. She was staying with me for the weekend. It was my father's birthday party, and she was keen to attend. Her kids had been invited but in the end she'd left them with her mother. I understood why. Too much had happened too quickly. She needed some breathing space and normal activities. It was a stretch, describing my dysfunctional family as normal, but still.

We spent that night eating takeout food and making love—not necessarily in that order. I already knew that in times of stress, Kara needed bodily reassurance, and was happy to oblige. We talked a lot as well, and I hope I made her feel better about the whole sorry mess.

She seemed more relaxed the next day but was nervous about meeting my father—goodness knows why—but at least we had Harry with us to break the ice. His constant chatter as we approached Paul's flat, Gil on his leash with a large ribbon round his neck, kept us both from our introspective thoughts. Kara's about her bloody brother, and mine about the wisdom of this happy-family business we were about to endure.

Paul appeared to have regained some of his customary flamboyance. He greeted us at the door, wearing cerise trousers that clashed with the colour of Kara's hair.

"Little brother," he said, clapping me on the shoulder. "I thought you might bottle it."

"Don't think I wasn't tempted."

"I made sure he kept his promise," Kara said, kissing Paul's cheek.

Harry and Gil barged in and went straight up to my father. "Granddad, happy birthday!"

"Thank you, Harry."

But no kiss or bodily contact for my son. I sighed. Some things never changed.

"We got you a present." Harry shoved the package into my father's lap, hopping from foot to foot until he opened the biography of a local composer that Kara had found in a secondhand shop. "Do you like it, Granddad?"

"It's just what I was hoping for."

Sound a little more enthusiastic, why don't you?

"Happy birthday, Dad." I shook his hand and gave Brenda the obligatory peck on the cheek. "This is Kara. Kara, meet my father and his wife, Brenda."

"Nice to meet you both," Kara said, submitting to my father's casual scrutiny and Brenda's far closer examination.

We talked stiltedly for a while but I was relieved when our friends Hal and Gloria joined us. There were about thirty people in attendance, almost all musicians. Paul's apartment easily accommodated them. Professional caterers did their stuff and alcohol loosened tongues. I chatted to old friends, aware of my father's eyes constantly following me about the room. He probably wondered what the hell this was all about. I couldn't help wondering the same thing, especially when Paul and I laughed spontaneously at the same time. That had to be a first.

A nod from Paul told me the hour had arrived. Determined to get this thing over with, I left Kara with my father and sat down at the piano. A deathly hush fell over the gathering, reminding me—if any reminder were necessary—that I was in the presence of some pretty good musicians, including my old teacher. Before nerves got the better of me, Paul and I launched into our jazzed-up rendition of Nat King Cole.

It sounded okay, I guess. No, it was better than okay. I could tell that much from the moist look in my father's eye. He'd received his rare book with indifference. But Paul had been right about this. The two of us giving him a recital really ticked all the boxes. I didn't have to wonder what he was thinking about. My mother was at the forefront of both our minds.

We received prolonged applause, but I declined to remain at the piano, going off in search of a fresh drink and Kara. But it was my father who accosted me.

"Thanks, Charlie," he said, shaking my hand with genuine-seeming affection.

"My pleasure." I said, aware that we'd crossed some sort of boundary in our relationship. "Hope it didn't offend your ears."

He laughed. Actually laughed. "You know better than that."

"Yeah, I guess I still remember a few things."

"I'm glad to see you've overcome your hang-ups."

"I play sometimes now, just for pleasure. Kara got me into it."

"She's nice," he said, watching her help Harry to a large slice of birthday cake, laughing as she licked frosting from her fingers.

"I think so too."

"I'm sorry about that business with *Mistral*."

I blinked back my surprise. "You know about that?"

He shrugged his bony shoulders. "I keep my ear to the ground."

Translation, Paul told him. My involvement didn't make the national press and he lived too far away to read the local papers. "It wasn't an experience I'd care to repeat."

"You were on your way back from France at the time? What took you there, then?"

I hesitated. "I…er, well, it was something Paul mentioned about Graham Sullivan. I went to check it out. I know," I said, holding up my hands to prevent his interruption. "You think I'm obsessed about Mum's death, and you're probably right. But, to be honest, since Kara came into my life, it doesn't seem to matter quite so much."

"I'm glad to hear it." He accepted a fresh glass of fizz from a passing waitress with a nod of thanks. "Why Graham?"

"He came into money just after Mum died. I wondered, that's all. I know he liked her, and that the sentiment wasn't returned." I sighed. "But it wasn't him."

"No, Charlie, but it might have been about him."

My head jerked up. "What do you mean?"

"Well, where did he get that money?"

"He said he inherited it."

My father offered me a tight smile. "That's one interpretation." He paused. "Actually, he was providing commodities to the orchestra."

"By commodities, I take it you mean drugs? He told me that much himself."

"Yes, but did he tell you that it got out of hand?" He paused. "Cocaine, even heroin."

"No," I said, my tone glacial. "I guess he forgot to mention it."

"Well, it's hardly something he'd advertise."

Especially not as he'd set out to invoke my sympathy, and tap me for a loan. "Did Mum know?"

"Yes. She told me about it. Said she suspected Graham was deliberately targeting more vulnerable members of the orchestra and asked me what she should do about it."

"What did you tell her?"

"To keep out of it."

"And did she?"

Dad shook his head. "I've been asking myself the same question ever since. Was that bullet really meant for her? Did she say something that threatened Graham's supplier?"

"You didn't think to tell the police at the time?"

"No. I forgot all about it to begin with. By the time I remembered, it seemed too late. All the proof would be gone."

"So why tell me now?"

"Not because I think there're any clues to follow up." He paused, waving to someone across the room. "More to give you a reason that explains the criminal waste of your mother's life, I suppose."

Could this finally be the break I'd spent all these years looking for? Why had my father taken all this time to tell me about it? Presumably because he knew I *would* follow up on it. I glanced up, caught sight of Kara across the room, and the warmth of her smile took my breath away. What the hell did I think I was doing, chasing twenty-year-old ghosts? Dad was right. I'd

wasted all these years pursuing answers that probably didn't exist. I was now being given another opportunity to live, and this time I wouldn't screw it up.

I felt as though a huge weight had been lifted from my shoulders when I realised it was over at last. I would never know the reason why she'd been killed, and it didn't seem so important any more.

"Rest in peace, Mum," I muttered quietly, crossing the room to slip an arm round Kara's waist.

TWENTY-THREE

TWO WEEKS LATER, Kara and I sat in the cockpit enjoying the morning sunshine and a late breakfast. Harry and Kara's two were playing on the pontoon with Gil.

"Oh look." Kara smiled as she pointed to the front page of one of the Sunday broadsheets. "Andrew Dannett's resigned from politics to spend more time with his family." She wrinkled her nose. "How touching."

I slipped an arm round her waist and pinched a bite from her slice of toast.

"Hey, get your own!"

"Where's the fun in that?"

"Do you really think Dannett deliberately arranged for the survivors of *Mistral* to be killed?" She continued to scan the carefully posed pictures of Dannett and his family. "It hardly seems credible. I mean, what motivated him to go to such extremes?"

"Passion," I said, snaffling the last of her toast whilst her attention was still on the article. "Greed, arrogance, feelings of invincibility...all of the above. You have to bear in mind that he came from a background that was very much *us and them* and was used to getting whatever he wanted as a matter of course. Plus the party faithful treated him like the next messiah, and that probably inflated his ego even more." I shrugged. "He fell for his own hype, in other words. So when he met your brother, he wanted to protect him and thought he could."

"Yes, but his protection came at a heavy price."

"He had to be able to tell Elliott that he'd got rid of Brett, as agreed That's why he kept your brother cocooned in that flat. He decided that he *could* have his cake and eat it too, provided he covered his tracks carefully enough."

"By getting rid of *Mistral*?"

"Yep."

"How could someone in his position go about arranging for someone to commit mass murder at sea? Surely he'd be leaving himself open to blackmail?"

"Nah. Thanks to the internet it's possible to arrange just about anything you want to, and pay for it, without revealing your identity."

"Perhaps, but presumably such services don't come cheap."

"Dannett has family money, remember."

"Okay, but even assuming you're right—"

"I am."

She harrumphed. "And modest too."

"Ah now, I never made that claim," I pointed out, winking at her.

"No, even you don't have that much front." She turned to me, frowning as she continued to piece things together. "But, even if Dannett was able to organise that hit as easily as you suggest, surely his conscience would have had something to say about it."

"People like Dannett square their actions by believing they're for the greater good," I said, not bothering to hide my contempt. "He probably thinks he did the country a service by getting rid of potential suicide bombers who were a threat to national security. And as for the crew, well…they knew what they'd got themselves into so he wouldn't have spent too much time worrying about them."

"And the innocent punters on that trip?"

I shrugged. "Wrong place at the wrong time. If he's thought about them at all, he probably considers they were expendable."

"You don't make him sound very attractive."

"Just telling it the way I see it."

"Well, at least he got his comeuppance, after a fashion."

I made no comment about that as I read the article over Kara's shoulder. I'd left Monk to tidy up the mess he was responsible for causing. He told us that Dannett steadfastly denied all knowledge of the smuggling business, as he did about the cigarette boat. Since no one had been able to track it down, it looked as though he'd got away with it.

But there was no getting around the information on that laptop in the house in Ramsgate that I put Monk onto. His people had got in there and copied the hard drive. It proved to be of a highly inflammatory nature, irrefutably connecting Dannett to the EPP. I had to be content with him kissing goodbye to his political career in return for immunity from prosecution.

Monk tried to persuade me that that would be punishment enough for such an ambitious man. I wasn't quite so sure, and sensed the hand of his political masters manipulating matters behind the scenes. They were willing to let him go quietly, anxious to avoid a messy trial for fear of what skeletons might emerge to embarrass administrations past and present.

Brett was pleased about the way things had turned out. Dannett didn't need to play the part of the dedicated family man anymore, so he and his wife would go their separate ways after a decent interval. And that would leave Dannett and Brett free to pursue their own agenda. It didn't seem right to me, but if Brett was happy to spend his life with such a man, then I reckoned they deserved one another. Brett wouldn't be prosecuted for anything. At Kara's request, that was conditional upon his disappearing.

Before he went, Kara refereed an emotional reunion between her mother and Brett. Astonishingly she didn't blame her son for anything but finally turned on her husband, holding him responsible for all the anguish she'd suffered following Brett's supposed death. She repeated, over and over, that her husband had been in a position to relieve that anguish and couldn't forgive him for keeping silent. She moved out of the family home and employed a top-notch lawyer to extract a fair settlement from her ex-nearest and dearest. Good for her.

Wayne Richards was pleading guilty to dumbed-down charges in return for spilling the beans on his contacts in France. He said he knew they'd actually killed Gordon Reed, but whether they'd ever be tracked down and brought to justice was another matter.

And they say crime doesn't pay.

Monk answered the question that had been plaguing

me. When Gordon didn't return from France they suspected that someone had tipped the EPP the wink about his existence, which would explain why the goons followed him to that bar. Only a few trusted people knew of Monk's operation, so it wasn't difficult to track down the mole. He was a lifelong civil servant whose wife was in the terminal stages of cancer, and who desperately needed money for her continued care. In return for immunity from prosecution he'd supplied disinformation to his contact, saying that Monk had wound up his operation because it had been compromised. That way the EPP thought the benefits outweighed the risks and pushed on with their plans. The date of the election would be declared any minute and this promised to be their best chance to get a toehold in the corridors of Whitehall. Quite simply, it was too good an opportunity to pass up.

This time they'd taken the precaution of placing two of their most trusted people in the shape of Mike and Julie—non-card-carrying members of the EPP and therefore with no tangible links to them if things went wrong—on board *Vagabond.* Their job was to make sure she didn't finish up the same way as *Mistral.*

Everything was tied up with a neat little bow, the government had come out smelling of roses, and the bad guys had escaped scot-free.

British justice at its finest.

"At least Monk provided us with a decent pay day," I reminded her. "I'll take you out for a swanky meal next week sometime, if your mum will have the kids."

"Oh, she will and you're on."

"Perhaps I've inadvertently found a new career for myself," I mused, thinking back over the sleuthing I'd done over the past year or so.

"Charlie, don't you dare! In the three cases you've been involved with, you've almost finished up getting killed each time. Don't push your luck."

"Just saying."

"Well don't! I can't bear it."

"Going soft on me?"

"I still feel bad about lying to Sally and Pete," she said, ignoring my taunt.

"You didn't lie, Monk did, and it's what he does best."

"But to say that Gordon is probably dead and died helping the government—"

"He did."

She sighed. "I know, but it doesn't seem right."

"At least they get some closure. They can grieve and put their lives back together." So could the family of the guy Brett Webb had pushed into the sea, for that matter. They had been tracked down and told that their loved one met with an untimely accident. "Would it help Sally and Pete to know that Gordon had been tortured first?"

"No." Kara let out a long breath. "You're very wise, Mr. Hunter, though it pains me to say so. Perhaps that's one of the things I love about you."

"What are the others then?"

"Hey," she said, shaking her head, her eyes alight with mischief. "That's for me to know and you to find out."

"Damn it, you always say things like that when the kids are with us and I can't do anything about it."

She waggled her brows. "Backing down from challenges now, are we?"

How did she know that? I'd been wanting to tell her for weeks now that I was in love with her, but I was afraid of making that ultimate commitment. I kissed her firmly on the lips instead and something about the enthusiastic nature of her response told me that words were unnecessary.

She already knew how I felt.

* * * * *

Author's Note

In the United Kingdom there are two main political parties, Labour and Conservative (Tories). The third party, Liberal Democrats, only ever taste power in the event that one of the two main parties doesn't win an overall majority, when they're called upon to form a coalition.

The British National Party (BNP) referred to in this novel are an extreme right-wing party that actually did gain support on the back of the immigration issue. During a recent election campaign their leader was invited to guest on *Question Time*, a respected political television show, causing great controversy.

The English Patriotic Party (EPP) is fictional.

About the Author

Wendy Soliman grew up on the Isle of Wight, in southern England. She blames the castles, fabulous old buildings and ancient monuments that surrounded her for her enduring love of history. She started writing stories at an early age and basically never stopped.

Wendy now lives in Andorra, dividing her time between there and the west coast of Florida. She lives with her husband and a rescued dog of indeterminate pedigree. When not writing she enjoys reading other people's books, walking miles with her dog, drinking decent wine and generally making the most out of life.

Visit her website at www.wendysoliman.com for more details about her and her books.

Also by W. Soliman from Carina Press:

Unfinished Business
Risky Business